# QUEEN'S MOVE

## Book Two of The Queens

## NIKITA SLATER

"I need a gangsta
To love me better
Than all the others do
To always forgive me
Ride or die with me
That's just what gangsters do."

Gangsta, Kehlani (Suicide Squad)
https://www.youtube.com/watch?v=LAYgZEMMWxo

---

# PROLOGUE

---

Tony Montana had eyes like the devil, wild, hot, angry. He was absolutely wrecked. High on his own product, high on life and himself. His dark hair was a disheveled mess, the end of his crooked nose ringed in the white powder he hadn't bothered to wipe away. His cheekbones were sharper than ever, emaciated from too much cocaine use and too little food. Not that Vee could cast stones, she was high more often than not herself. But she used so she could disappear. To make her bullshit existence feel a little less awful. And the man in front of her was to blame for at least a decade of that misery.

Had she ever loved him? She tried to remember. Think back to her wedding day, the good days, before the constant fighting and abuse. Nothing came though. If she ever loved him it was long gone now. Just a fleeting softness as she remembered his infectious grin when he was trying to win her over. Something he hadn't shown her in years.

"Get out," Vee said coldly.

She wasn't talking to Tony. No, she was talking to the woman on her knees, beneath his desk, trying to suck off a flaccid dick. Vee knew from experience that cocaine did nothing for Tony in the bedroom anymore, so to speak. Back in the old days, when he still enjoyed life, the drug used to lift him up, make him feel invincible, crave Vee's affection. Back then, sex and drugs were the only thing they had in common. Now it was just one of those. And Vee was about done with all of it.

Nobody moved, Tony's eyes flicked to Vee and then glazed over again, unfocused. He was sprawled back in his chair, head tilted back against the leather. He lifted a ringed hand, waving it toward the door, telling her to go.

She was long past able to feel hurt over his constant rejections and mistreatments. She was pretty much numb these days. Tony never took her seriously anyway. She used to be his doll, his lovely trophy wife, now she was so much less. The hag that spent his money and screamed at him on a semi-regular basis. Not even the beatings could stop her tongue. She still had some pride, as unrecognizable as it was.

She wasn't going to have a single problem taking out the master of all her sufferings. She was following the Bolivian cartel's orders. It was time to bring Miami back under control, and she was going to be the woman to do it.

"I said, get the fuck out," Vee snarled, pacing forward. She lifted the gun she'd been clutching when she sought her husband out in his office and slammed it down on his desk. The whore jumped, banging her head on the edge of the desk as she finally surfaced, peeked over to stare at Vee. "Right fucking now, unless you think this pig is worth dying for. Then, by all means, stay where you are. I'll happily do you next."

When the woman didn't move fast enough Vee pointed the gun at her face. She blinked, crawled quickly out from under the desk and ran shrieking from the office, straight out the French doors and into the huge, immaculate back yard.

Vee wanted to laugh at the topless bitch, but again, hypocritical. Vee'd done similar and worse, selling her looks, prostituting herself for protection. The only difference being she was pretty enough, tough enough and bitchy enough to demand a ring for her effort.

Tony ignored the gun completely. She'd handled them before and he knew better than to think his delicate blond wife was going to be any kind of threat. "Fucking unbelievable," he grumbled, Cuban accent strong in his befuddled state. He sat up a little straighter and finally looking at her. "What the fuck you doin' coming in here like that and scaring off my bitch? Now you need to get over here and finish me off."

Vee laughed coldly. "We both know you aren't even hard. Don't act like you could've gotten off, even with a pretty piece of fluff like her."

His eyes sharpened and his brow lowered. "Maybe if I didn't have such a frigid bitch for a wife I'd bang you once in awhile. Maybe if I did that you'd quit acting like a sullen fucking piece of work, moping around the mansion all day, shopping or whatever the shit you do."

He was definitely not going to make this hard.

"I want a divorce, Tony," she demanded, tapping her gun against the wood.

He laughed, banging his hand on top of the desk. Maybe if he was fast enough, cared enough, he could've reached out and grabbed her weapon. But Tony Montana was too much of a macho man to believe his wife would actually threaten him.

"Even if we could get a divorce, we won't. That ain't how it works in our world and you know it as good as I do. You know too much to ever be released from our marriage. No, Vee, we're stuck together. Until death do us part." He snickered at his own cleverness, no doubt planning her death so he could replace her with the inflated bimbo running across the back yard.

"I was hoping you'd see it that way." Vee smiled for the first time in a long time. "I was thinking a more permanent solution might be necessary anyway."

She braced her legs, lifted the gun and pointed it at him. The shit-eating smirk drifted off his lips as his face twisted into an ugly, hate-filled mask. "Put the fucking gun down, Vee. I'm not going to tell you again."

She shrugged. "You don't need to."

"Don't you fucking dare," he snarled, raising up from his chair and slamming his fists down onto the desk. "I'm going to beat the life out of-"

He didn't get to finish his sentence. Vee shot him once, clean in middle of his forehead, and once more through the heart after he was flung back into his chair. She didn't want to risk him surviving, going comatose and becoming even more annoying than he already was. Better just to make it a clean hit.

She wasn't worried about Tony's protection detail. They were either being eliminated or surrendering to the Bolivian's second-in-command, Alejandro. Vee's only job was to cut off the head of the snake. A symbolic action that would help solidify her leadership as the new Queen of Miami's mafia.

Looking dispassionately at her dead husband's body, she felt strong, she felt powerful... she felt relieved. Her legs folded underneath her and she collapsed to the floor, one hand still clutching the gun while the other gripped the edge of the desk. She folded in on herself, allowing herself this one single moment to just feel. To finally feel.

## CHAPTER ONE

### One year later

Vee woke with a start, gun in hand. She expected to see her dead husband standing over her, ready to exact bloody retribution. Chest heaving, eyes wide in the darkness of her bedroom, she once more struggled to banish his ghost as her dream washed away in the reality of late morning. She shoved white blond hair off her forehead and scrambled for the vibrating phone that had woken her up. She kept it on or near her pillow when she slept. It must have fallen into the folds of her blankets when she'd gotten trapped in the hell of her nightmare.

Luckily the iPhone didn't stop vibrating so she was able to locate it quickly and check the caller ID. Casey Reyes. Vee closed her eyes and put a hand to her forehead. Normally she would love getting a call from this woman, but today was going to be an exception.

Vee swung her legs over the side of the bed and answered, her voice husky, "Hello Casey."

"Vee! My god, are you okay?" Casey asked, her voice higher pitched than usual, concern reverberating through her tone.

Vee's lips pulled into a tight smile. At least one of the Bolivians cared enough to check on her health before they sent a hit squad over the fiasco that was last night. "I'm okay," she answered, looking down at the bandage covering her arm and wincing a little. Now that she was up and moving, the slash wound was definitely making itself known. "Fuckers in this town are savages, Casey. No respect for a lady just trying to do a little business."

There was silence for a moment and then Casey said quietly, "Tell me about it."

Vee sighed and made her way to the washroom for a quick pee. She hoped Casey wouldn't be able to hear, but seriously, if girl was going to wake her up after a night like last night and then demand answers, then she was going to have to deal with a little nature. Vee pulled her panties and satin pyjama pants down and got to business in both senses of the word. "Same old. It's the Mexicans acting up again, taking a swipe at my authority in my town. Bastards simply refuse to settle into the new way of life around here. I'm running this city with an iron fist, yet those guys will not bow down to a woman."

"This is the third time, Vee. The third time they've questioned your authority and the third lost shipment," Casey said, her voice catching with worry. "I know you're tough as nails, but what if they get in a lucky shot? I don't want to lose you, babe."

Vee finished up and washed her hands before making her way to the kitchen. She set the kettle on the stove to boil. A little old-fashioned, but then, she was an old-fashioned girl at heart and coffee was no longer an option.

"I'll be fine," Vee replied, wandering to the window of her condo and gazing at the ocean stretching out as far as she could see. The sight never failed to soothe. "Everyone else is falling into line. It's just some of these Latin guys refuse to see a woman as equal. I can handle the bullshit. I handled last night."

"Were you able to put them down decisively this time?"

Vee squeezed the phone tight and pictured the pig that had slashed her. Her guy had held him down while she put a bullet in his head. Her smile turned feral. "I got a few."

Casey sighed irritably. "But not the cause of all this trouble."

"No," Vee acknowledged and turned back to the stove to pull the hissing kettle off the heat. She poured hot water over the herbs in her tea strainer and enjoyed the simple pleasure of peach berry aroma teasing her senses. "I can't get to him from up here and my hold on the city is too tenuous for me to leave and go hunting."

"I understand," Casey said.

And Vee knew that Casey Reyes did understand. Women in their world, the mafia world, held precarious positions. Though she was a wife, Casey was also a partner and a powerhouse in her own right. Her husband built her up and set her up at his side as his queen. Then Casey had convinced him to set Vee up as their Miami contact and distributer on the East Coast. The catch? Vee's husband had to go.

Not a big deal. He was a useless, waste of space fuck with no good head for business. She'd been running most of his operation in the shadows for years anyway. But convincing Tony's contacts to trust her after she'd done the bloody deed? Now that had taken some work. She was ruthless though, and with an army at her back she'd taken control of the city. The only problem had come in the form of the Mexican cartel.

"But your husband doesn't understand," Vee said, her voice hard. She tapped the tea strainer against the edge of the cup to catch the extra drops and tossed it in the sink.

Casey sighed. "He's sending someone."

Fuck.

Vee's arm throbbed viciously as she thought of the type of guy Reyes would send to her city and she nearly dropped her cup. She rested her elbow on the edge of the counter and counted slowly to ten, taking deep breaths to steady herself. Casey remained silent, giving her time. God bless this girl. They really did understand each other, despite nearly a decade difference in age.

Vee opened her eyes and made her way back to the calming picturesque view, clearly visible from the balcony window. The sparkling ocean, sometimes lazy and drifting, sometimes angry and choppy, always soothed her riotous emotions. The reason she lived here, in a secret location, rather than the mansion she'd shared with her husband. Most still believed she lived there. She preferred it that way. She blew on the tea, took a tentative sip and grimaced. God, how she missed coffee. But she no longer used mind-altering substances of any kind. Not even caffeine.

"Alejandro," she finally said, trying to keep her voice cool and steady.

She didn't want the Bolivian's second-in-command in her city. He was brutal, bossy and Latin to his core. He would come in and get right in her business, tear her operation apart looking for flaws. He would find none. But he would piss her off in the process. She would have to keep her head and allow it if she wanted to stay on Reyes' good side. Then she would have to team up with the big Bolivian and allow his help with getting Mexico in line.

The thought of needing anyone's help made her grit her teeth. It was time's like this that she wished she'd been born a man. She was better at this job than any man she'd ever met, yet because she was a woman she had to constantly fight and claw her way through the vicious underbelly of Miami. And just when she thought she'd landed in a sweet spot, the

goddamn Mexican cartel managed to back her into a corner...
again.

"Not Alejandro," Casey told her.

"Who then?" Vee demanded, surprised.

Casey paused, clearly not wanting to say. Damn, this was bad. If not Alejandro, then who were the Bolivians sending to secure their American investment? She could feel sweat beginning to form in her palms.

"Just tell me," she said tonelessly.

"Sotza."

Vee's heart stopped. Blindly she set her teacup down and reached for the sofa, falling onto it in a heap. Fuck. She was so fucked.

"The Gentleman Butcher," she breathed, not even realizing she spoke the words out loud.

"I wouldn't recommend you call him that to his face, Vee," Casey said drily. "He doesn't have much tolerance for nicknames."

Vee's head spun and she had to put her face on her knees so she wouldn't pass out. She forced her whirling mind to focus. She needed a clear brain for this new development. Life had just become very, very dangerous.

"This is bad, Casey," she finally said.

"I know," the other woman acknowledged. "I tried to talk him out of it."

*Him* being Reyes. They both knew that despite Casey's position at his side, when Reyes made a decision he was immoveable. He clearly didn't like the way the Mexicans kept handing Vee her ass and he was going to make sure it didn't happen again. But sending The Butcher to her city...

"He hasn't stepped foot on this continent since..." she trailed off realizing the effect her words could have on her friend.

"Since my mother died," Casey finished for her. "He's over

it, Vee. He's been over it for a long time and he's ready to stamp territory again. He's quiet but deadly. You need to be so, so careful, hon."

Vee laughed a little hysterically. "Don't I know it! He was cutting a bloody path through everything South of the border when I was still in pigtails. The stories I've heard… they make even my blood run cold and I don't scare easily."

"He's not such a bad guy," Casey said as brightly as she could. "I like him."

"That's because you are your mother's daughter, baby girl," Vee said sarcastically. "I'm just the bitch standing between him and the Miami gateway." She grew serious. "And your husband is sending him after me."

"I'm sorry," Casey whispered.

"I'm about to become deposed, aren't I?" Vee's voice broke a little.

Casey didn't say anything for a moment and then, "Don't get dead, Vee."

She laughed bitterly. "No promises."

# CHAPTER TWO

The Gentleman Butcher.

That was what the locals called him. Not to his face, of course. He found the moniker amusing. If he hadn't then it wouldn't have stuck around for as long as it did. He supposed it suited him. He did get his hands dirty, when the occasion necessitated his special brand of intervention. And he was particular; in some ways quite fastidious. What was the point in wearing a $10,000 suit if it was going to get covered in gore? So, he'd developed a habit of removing his suit jacket and tie, rolling up his sleeves and then torturing his victims brutally, ruthlessly while spraying as little blood as possible. His methods had become well known and earned him the nickname of Gentleman despite his being anything but.

He certainly did not feel the gentleman when it came to a certain woman he was supposed to be meeting with. He glanced impatiently at his watch. She was eight minutes late. He'd already planned on removing her, but the disrespect she was showing would earn her some time in his dungeon first. He'd intended on making it quick in deference to her gender and the aforementioned nickname. But, apparently, she was not going to play nice.

Too bad. She hadn't been doing a terrible job of handling Miami. But South America couldn't lose their foothold to the Mexicans and she didn't have the strength to hold out. Now it was up to Sotza to act decisively and brutally to make sure this gateway to their international trade on the East Coast wasn't compromised due to her poor handling of Mexico. She should have asked for help when she had the chance. She hadn't. Now she would have to go.

Sotza had no interest in taking over Miami for Reyes. He was simply doing the man a favour. And it was time for him to visit this strange and beautiful country again. He'd let it go far too long. Time to take back some territory and re-establish his reputation as The Butcher among the Americans before they forgot who he was.

His gaze flicked to the front door of the club; an establishment Reyes inherited from Hernandez during the Miami takeover. An interesting place to meet. Ladies choice, of course. She wanted to meet in public. Smart but ultimately pointless. He was more than capable of getting to her if and when he wanted. He saw her the moment she stepped foot in the door, flanked by two dark-suited bodyguards.

As she walked into the club, she had to blink away the bright Miami sun before she could take stock of her surroundings. He had the advantage of being able to study her for a moment before she caught sight of him. Stunning was too weak a word to describe the Miami madam. She was utterly breathtaking. She certainly stole his breath. Something no woman had done to him. Ever.

It was an... uncomfortable sensation that had him resisting the urge to lift a palm to his chest and rub. She turned her head, her severely cut shoulder-length white blond hair moving with her. Once her eyes settled on him and his men, she moved through the club with detached ease despite knowing exactly who he was and why he was there. She wasn't stupid, and neither was Casey Reyes. This woman had to have been warned. She should be in another country by now, running as far and as fast as she could get. Yet, here she was, meeting with the man that intended to take her throne. She was an astonishingly brave woman.

The feeling in his chest intensified as she approached his table, leaving him momentarily speechless and unable to stand for a greeting. She narrowed her darkly-tinted lashes, perceiving an insult in his refusal to stand. She remained silent and refused to sit, putting them in a wordless standoff. So, he sat and studied her while he attempted to regain his equilibrium. Her clothes, face, hair, nails and shoes were all very deliberately chosen. She wore a high-waisted white pencil skirt that stopped just above her knee. She paired it with a sleeveless rose-coloured silk blouse that sat high on her neck. Her jewelry was a basic silver chain, diamond studs and a gold band on the middle finger of her right hand. Everything about her was understated, basic, but expensive and elegant.

Except her shoes. She wore sky-high silver stilettoes with solid steel heels that ended in an unusually sharp point. Sotza could feel the blood begin to pound through his body and, without conscious thought, he stood, towering over his prey. Even though she wore five-inch stilettos he was still a good half foot taller than her.

"Elvira Montana," he finally said, keeping his voice low and cool. He gave her his hand. He was a little surprised, given his seeming snub when she first walked up to him, that she took it without hesitation, putting her much smaller hand in his and squeezing. He wanted to hold it longer, experience the texture of her skin, press his thumb against her fine bones and feel the beat of her pulse. But she pulled her hand quickly back.

"Vee," she said in a pleasantly husky voice.

He raised an eyebrow. "Pardon me?"

"Please, call me Vee," she corrected him. "I despise both the names Elvira and Montana. So please, just call me Vee."

He nodded, his gaze sliding over her, down and then up until finally their eyes met. Ice. Cold. Incomparable, diamond-hard blue. Her face was smooth, flawless, giving away none of her thoughts. He wanted her on her knees pleading for her life, a life that belonged to him now, those ice chip eyes turned liquid with fear. Yet... he also wanted her in a bed, naked, eyes on fire, begging for the release only he could give her.

He allowed none of his thoughts to touch his face. He'd learned long ago never to allow the enemy to see an emotion until the time was right; usually seconds before death. Elvira clearly had the same training. Her eyes were dead as the grave. Pride swelled in his chest at the way she handled him, alongside the lust and the desire to stamp ownership all over this woman. At his age, he was neither going to question these urges nor go against what instinct was telling him.

His plans had changed. Elvira Montana was no longer going to become a casualty of the upcoming war. The Butcher was about to steal a queen.

## CHAPTER THREE

### Three weeks later

Sotza was waging war in her city. And he was winning.

Vee paced the floor of her office, steel heels tapping impatiently against the marble as she waited for her second-in-command to make an appearance. The back of her white silk blouse fluttered when she turned sharply, making her way back across the pale hardness of the floor toward the opposite wall. The aura of subdued violence surrounding her was unmistakeable. Like a caged tiger, she was ready to hunt and dismember her prey. Only she had no idea where the fucker was hiding.

After their initial meeting when battle lines had been drawn, they had gone their separate ways and she hadn't seen hide nor hair of the Gentleman Butcher. Though his presence lingered throughout the city as her contacts fell one by one, whether through clever negotiation, or, when that hadn't worked, brutal persuasion. Sotza was making a very clear impression in the Miami underground. There was a new commander in town.

She wanted to gut the man, dance on his spilling entrails and laugh like a loon while she did it. She'd never felt this kind of all-consuming rage before. Not even during the years of humiliating abuse she'd suffered at Tony's hands. And that had really been something. She'd learned cool poise and the ability to conduct herself perfectly in all circumstances while under Tony Montana's regime. She became the ultimate ice queen, never allowing anything to touch her. And now Sotza walks into her city and takes over, makes the entire East Coast hub roll over, without so much as a by-your-leave.

She wanted the man dead more than she'd even wanted Tony dead. And that was saying something considering that by the end Tony had been her least favourite person on the planet.

Vee had even tried to enlist Casey's help, knowing the phone call would prove useless. But desperate time's... Sure enough, Casey apologized and told her that she'd already tried to get Reyes to call off the Venezuelan, but he was firm. Reyes wanted Miami under new leadership. Vee had been given her chance and she'd fucked it up by letting the Mexicans humiliate her.

Casey had ended the call echoing her previous advice. "Don't get dead."

*No promises.*

The Butcher had no mercy. He was certainly showing her city none as he cut a bloody swathe through it while staking his claim. The increased violence was noticed by everyone, not just the underworld. News channels reported on gang wars throughout the area. Soon Sotza would tire of the battles and come knocking on her door to finish the war. Though she was well-armed with a veritable army at her disposal, she knew the man well enough to know it likely wouldn't be enough. He was a ghost. If and when he wanted her dead, she would get dead.

The fingers she had crossed over her arms tightened until her long, coral-tinted nails nearly pierced skin, reminding her that, for the time being, she was still alive. She would make the most of her remaining time. She wouldn't go out like her husband, arrogant on his throne, a weak shadow of his former self. She would die the way she lived, cool and proud to the end, fighting for her place. No regrets.

A loud knock interrupted her grim thoughts. Expecting this particular company, she made her way behind the large, ornate desk and called clearly and sharply, "Come."

Danny Russo, her second-in-command, entered the room, his face expressionless. Stocky and muscular, loyal to the last bone in his body, Danny was the man behind much of her success in Miami. Accompanying him was another of her men and between them a somewhat roughed up, shaken half-Cuban who looked as though he would prefer to be anywhere but in the Montana mansion, facing the wrath of the Montana widow as she stood to confront him, a letter knife held delicately between her fingers.

She nodded toward a guest chair and then sighed a little. She really didn't want to have this demonstration in the house, but, as she was going to allow Luis to leave the mansion alive, she didn't want him seeing anything beyond her spacious office. Perhaps she should have gone down to her dockyards. No, not hers anymore. Sotza's now. But Danny had deemed the docks too much of a risk. She wanted to show Sotza that she still had power in this city, despite his seeming invincibility. Her people had picked up the head of shipping security himself. The man she'd been bribing for years to help bring her shipments in.

"You've disappointed me, Luis," she said, ice dripping from every word. The man shuddered and shook his head, opening his mouth to lie to her. Vee cut him off. "I'm not interested in listening to your snivelling bullshit. I'm having a bad few weeks and the last thing I wanted to hear today was that the dockyard fell without so much as a single spilled drop of blood."

"Please, Mrs. Montana!" Luis blubbered as she rounded the desk toward him. He would have stood, but Danny held him with a hand on his shoulder. "It ain't like that. H-he threatened us. The Butcher, you know? He told us our lives and the lives of our families were as good as dead unless we gave up the shipments and manifests. We didn't have a choice!"

"And you didn't think your lives would be just as dead if you did?" Vee asked sharply. Without waiting for an answer, she gripped the sharp letter opener in both hands and plunged it down into his leg, just above the knee.

Luis screamed and tried to clutch the knife, but Danny held his arms from behind. Vee pulled the knife out, ignoring the drops of blood that splattered across the hem of her shirt. She held the tip against his neck and snapped loudly, "Shut the fuck up so I can speak."

Luis brought himself under control, sweat streaking from his hairline, his wild eyes on hers. Finally, he nodded slightly, though it was clear he was trying not to pass out. She sighed and rolled her eyes. She despised weak men and this one could barely handle a little stabbing. She really should put him out of his misery and try the next dockyard security expert.

"I'm going to do you a favour, Luis," she told him a cool voice. "I'm going to give you another chance to prove your loyalty to me and mine. Only this time you aren't going to fuck it up or I'll be giving you a whole lot more than this little scratch. You understand?"

Luis nodded frantically. "Yes, thank you, Mrs. Montana. You won't regret it."

She was already regretting it. Her fingers twitched with the effort not the plunge the blade through his eyeball. But she needed him alive. He was the only one who knew exactly when and where her shipments were coming in. She needed that cargo to prove her value to the Bolivians if she was going to stand any chance at survival.

"You're going to redirect the ships holding my cargo containers to new pickup locations, yes?" She arched an eyebrow until it met her severely cut bangs. "And then you will only tell my man, Danny here, where those locations are. Are we quite clear?"

He nodded quickly until she was sure there were spots swimming in his vision from blood loss. She'd been careful not to nick an artery, but the letter opener wasn't small. He now had a quarter-sized hole in his leg. "Quite clear, quite clear!"

"Good," she snapped, straightening. She held the hand with the knife low at her side. "Because if we have to have this conversation again, Luis, I can assure you, it won't be under such pleasant circumstances."

Vee watched as his eyes nearly bugged out of his head. She knew what he saw, what he was thinking. The beautiful madam of Miami, standing in all her glory in front of him, wearing a white, now blood-splattered blouse, black pencil skirt and silver stilettos. The almost matronly pearls she wore at her throat oddly out of place, yet also very much a part of her look.

She crossed to the other side of her desk, set the knife down, then coldly dismissed him. "You may leave."

The look she shot Danny told him that their guest didn't need to get back to the dockyards comfortably. She turned her back on the trio and took a few steps to the window while they exited the office. Damn it, now she'd have to get a cleaner in for the floor and chair. She hated doing business indoors.

# CHAPTER FOUR

Something woke her up. Vee knew better than to question her instincts, they were honed to perfection. She took immediate action, rolling across her bed, one hand reaching for her phone and the other for her revolver. She wasted a few precious seconds to shock when both hands came up empty. Someone had searched the bed while she was asleep in it and had taken both items.

Fuck.

Somehow, someone had managed to bypass her bodyguards and her security to make it into her bedroom. She knew exactly who was capable of such a deed. And she was pretty sure if he was finally here, that he'd decided it was her time to die.

"I won't go down easy," she said into the darkness, pleased to note that she managed to keep her voice as coolly steady as always. No point turning into a snivelling coward now. She'd faced worse and kept her shit together. She remained frozen, kneeling on her bed, listening.

His sinister chuckle seemed to echo through the room. She couldn't tell over her own terror and the pounding of her heart where exactly he was standing. She had no gun, no way to defend herself if he attacked. A click startled her, and lamplight filled the room blinding her for a few precious seconds. Still, she moved her head to the side expecting to see his tall shadowed form standing next to the lamp.

"Wouldn't be much fun if you didn't put up a fight," he said from the end of the bed.

How the fuck had he gotten there so fast?

Vee's head swiveled toward his voice and she blinked a few times until she could see him properly. That voice never failed to send shivers skittering down her spine. The clipped British accent told her he'd either gone to boarding school in England or been tutored by a Brit. Not the standard for Spanish speakers below the border unless they came from money.

He stood a few feet from her, his gaze fixed on her. Every dark hair on his head was perfectly in place, silver touching his temples and sideburns. He was dressed impeccably, expensive suit, fitted perfectly to his tall, muscular frame. He'd taken the jacket off though, removed the tie and rolled the sleeves up. Not a good sign when the Gentleman Butcher made himself more comfortable.

She lifted her gaze to meet his. She was shocked by the warmth in his expression. Was he toying with her? Where was his death mask, his impassivity? Who looked so fucking friendly just before they destroyed someone. She expected her executioner's face to reflect something a little closer to death or emotionlessness at the very least. Instead his dark brown eyes almost glowed from beneath lowered eyebrows as they took in her dishevelled appearance. She'd been so tired from trying and failing to bring the dockyard back under her control that she'd stripped out of her clothes and pulled on her satin pyjama top over a pair of panties and fallen into bed.

A few buttons had come undone while she was sleeping and the top now slid down one shoulder.

Damn, she hated being anything less than professional. And her hair must be a complete mess. She hadn't even washed yesterday's makeup from her face. Mascara would be smudged beneath her lids, giving her a raccoon-like appearance. She heaved an annoyed sigh and shoved a hand though her hair, upending her bangs. "Can we please get on with this execution? At least then I'll be able to get a little sleep."

His lips pressed into a flat line and his nostrils flared a little, clearly unamused by her flippancy. *Well score one for the dead girl breathing*, she thought, expecting to feel the sharp edge of his blade at any moment.

"I didn't come here to take your life," he said, the edge to his voice letting her know that she needed to tread carefully lest he change his mind.

"Why are you here then?" She tried to freeze him out with her tone as she pulled at her pyjama top in an attempt to cover more skin. His eyes tracked the movement. She shivered as though he'd actually touched her, then dropped her hand.

"I brought gifts." He bent to retrieve something. She tensed, ready to roll off the bed and flee. Not that she would make it far, but she was certainly going to try if he did anything she deemed even slightly murdery. Instead, he straightened and set two boxes on the bed in front of her kneeling form. One was bigger, about the size of her pillow and the other much smaller, the size of the palm of her hand. "Open the larger one first."

Hands shaking, she reached for the larger box, pulling it toward her. It was a perfectly square, white box wrapped with a red ribbon. It was heavy, heavier than she expected and something inside rustled when she moved it. She glanced up.

Sotza's expression had gone flat, empty, dead. Whatever was in this box was business.

Heart pounding, Vee tensed her body, knowing she wasn't going to like his 'gift' but with no other choice she pulled the ribbon. The bow unravelled under her trembling fingers, falling easily away. Vee stared into Sotza's eyes as she lifted the lid. His eyes lit with feral satisfaction as the smell of death was released from the box. Her nose automatically wrinkled at the foul odor and she forced herself to look down.

She'd known what was in the box before she opened it. If the prick was expecting her to break into hysterics and cower, he was about to be sadly disappointed. She remained perfectly motionless except to tap one long coral-tipped fingernail against the edge of the box as she forced herself to look at the grisly contents. After a long moment, when she thought an appropriate amount of time had passed, she lifted her chin and gave Sotza an impertinent stare, arching her eyebrow.

"Oh dear," she said in her chilliest voice. "It appears I'll have to find a new contact at the dockyard."

She glanced back down at Luis' severed head, nestled in a cocoon of bloody plastic, his sightless cloudy eyes staring at nothing. "Pity," she continued. "I despised his weakness but enjoyed the benefits of having someone on the inside."

Sotza chuckled, amused by her studied indifference as she replaced the lid on her 'gift' and set the package aside. She eyed him wondering if he'd done the deed himself. Then she decided he had. He'd delivered the package personally, a message to let her know that her interference in the city he was systematically taking over would not be tolerated. He'd somehow found out about her meeting with Luis that morning and intercepted the man, perhaps thinking she needed a lesson in understanding that his nickname of Butcher was well deserved in case anyone had doubts.

"Open the other package," he said, his deep voice becoming a caress.

She looked up at him sharply, noting the intimacy. Not something she was expecting and definitely not something she was used to hearing. Men had become her subordinates, not her equal and definitely not her lover or master.

She reached for the box. It was also perfectly square, though much smaller than the other. Shaped exactly like the other box with a tiny pink ribbon wrapped around it. She was relieved that the ribbon wasn't red like the box containing Luis' head. Using the tips of her fingernails she pulled at the edge of the ribbon until it came apart in her hands. She pulled the lid off the box. Inside was another box, a jeweler's box. Was it a severed finger?

Frowning, she glanced up at Sotza who was watching her with a new intensity. The light from her lamp cast his face into angles, caressing his high, sharp cheekbones and sculpted lips. Sotza was an extremely elegant, handsome man, but only in the same way one might consider Lucifer good-looking. He was also the most terrifying, chilling man she'd ever had the misfortune to meet.

"Open it," he demanded, his voice holding an edge of impatience, telling her she had no choice.

Vee had no idea what to expect, but his countenance, his very presence in her bedroom told her that whatever was in this box would alter the course of her life. However short that life may be. She pried open the lid and dropped her gaze. Icy denial rushed through her, crashing into heart-stopping reason. She knew what this was... yet it couldn't be possible.

She pulled the stunning engagement ring from the box and held it up, her eyebrows disappearing into her bangs. She knew enough about jewelry to know that this was top of the line, worth probably close to a half million dollars. A light pink diamond surrounded by smaller diamonds set in a white gold band. Her heart thumped a crazy rhythm as she tried to make sense of what was happening.

Far from murdering her in her bed, Sotza was... proposing to her? No, that wasn't right. The Butcher wasn't the type of man to ask anyone anything. He took what he wanted, just as he was taking Miami. But Vee wasn't free for the taking. She would never marry again, never again be under the control of another human being.

She stared at him in dismay, a frown creasing her forehead, the ring held out in her fingertips like it was poison. "What does this mean?" she asked hoarsely.

"I'm declaring my intentions," he said, the intimacy in his tone unmistakable now, despite the old-world language he used.

"No!" she said immediately. "You can't."

He stepped up to the bed and reached for her. If Vee had the wits left in her head for self-preservation she would have fled. But shock held her rooted to the bed. He took her wrist in a firm hold, his long, warm fingers banding around her, holding her still while he took the ring from her. He flipped her hand over and pushed the ring onto the third finger. It was a perfect fit. Of course.

With a gasp she tried to tug her hand away, but he held her firm, the steel in his hold translating to his face, turning their encounter into something much deadlier. She stopped struggling, holding perfectly still. He dominated her with that single touch, his tall body leaning over hers, folded on the bed. She tried to lean away but he followed her, catching the back of her head with his other hand and forcing her to remain in his grip. She could feel the strength running through his solid body, though he touched her only with his hands.

He leaned until his face hovered over hers and she could see the gold flecks in the dark brown depths of his eyes. She shivered under the sinister onslaught of The Butcher's perusal. His voice vibrated with authority when he spoke. "This ring does not come off. You understand?"

Vee stared back, her blue eyes icy as the arctic. She refused to speak. Refused to acknowledge his edict. His fingers clenched in the back of her hair, catching the fine strands and tugging. He dropped his lips to hers, startling her with a quick, hard kiss. It was just the press of his closed mouth against hers, opened slightly in a gasp of surprise. It shouldn't have been erotic, yet somehow, it sent lightning bolts zinging through her body sparking an awareness she hadn't felt in years. Perhaps never. Her eyes flew open before he pulled away. His gaze met hers and she saw satisfaction burning there.

He spoke barely an inch away from her mouth, his warm breath marking her. "Take that ring off and there will be consequences, Vee."

He released her, allowing her to collapse back onto the bed. She landed palms down on all fours. She knew the position looked sexual, that he could see her underwear; caught the flash of lustful heat in his gaze before he shuttered it. He scooped up the larger of the boxes and headed out the bedroom door. Vee scrambled off the bed and followed him.

She was extremely conscious of her bare legs but wanted to keep eyes on her deadly intruder at all times. He set the box down on her kitchen island and turned back to her, his gaze sweeping her from head to toe in one heated glance. She shivered and crossed her arms. Then uncrossed them, aware that the hem off her nightshirt rode up the edge of her thighs when she did that.

"I'll be in touch," he told her and left through the front door of her condo, resetting her alarm system. Vee gaped after him. Belatedly, she wondered what the hell had happened to her bodyguards? She hoped they weren't dead.

God, what had she done to deserve this? Comeuppance perhaps for murdering her first husband without a shred of remorse. Now she would be forced into the company of the devil himself?

And what the fuck was wrong with Sotza anyway? Who decided they wanted to get married after a single meeting? To the woman he's supposed to dispose of. The whole concept was bizarre and crazy. But she knew enough about the man that he would be determined once he set a course of action. If he wanted Vee to become his wife, he would do everything in his power to make it happen.

And she was going to do anything and everything she could to get herself out of this sham of an engagement and reclaim her city. Perhaps if he imagined himself in love, or something equally ridiculous, she could eventually get close enough to kill him.

Looking down at the ring that adorned her left hand, Vee did the one thing she knew would declare all-out war with the terrifying man who had just staked his claim on her. She slid the ring off her finger and placed it deliberately on the counter, then turned and stomped back to bed. She would deal with Luis, or what was left of him, and the ring and in the morning.

# CHAPTER FIVE

S otza went to ground while Vee spent the next few weeks desperately plotting ways to keep her city safe from him. She sensed him orchestrating her downfall, manoeuvering each player, each hub, playing a chess game with a foregone conclusion. He planned and executed like the ruler of an oppressed kingdom, as though born and bred to destabilize an entire regime without the worry of tarnish to his crown. Which was exactly what he was; born to be king.

Vee knew it was him stamping his presence all over *her* city, even if no one else actually saw The Butcher and lived to tell. Other gangs, cartel guys and wannabe kingpins working within Miami toppled as his men moved, cleaning house. They rarely touched Vee's holdings, except for the dockyard. It was whispered throughout the city, among Vee's rivals, that she and Sotza had set up a partnership. She knew better. The ruthless cartel boss was just saving her for last. Everyone else was the fucking main course. She was to be his dessert.

"We have to take the dockyard back; it's a key gateway between Miami and most foreign markets," Danny explained, a map of the dockyard spread between him and Vee. "The water isn't near as regulated as air and land."

Vee nodded in agreement. She knew all that. "Won't he expect retaliation? He'll know I'm coming for it."

"Maybe," he shrugged. "It's been a few weeks and security seems to have gotten lax. He probably thinks you're giving it up for now and focusing effort on tightening security on your other investments, yeah? Plus, he's concentrating on the Cubans at the moment. I'm telling you, boss, now is the time to strike. Tonight."

She nodded thoughtfully a slight frown creasing her brows. Sotza didn't seem like the type to let security go lax around a key point. He was not a stupid man by any stretch. So, what was he playing at? But, Danny was also correct. They needed to strike while Sotza was looking the opposite way. If they could somehow bring the Venezuelans to their knees she would stand a fighting chance.

"Okay," Vee agreed, nodding sharply. "We go in tonight. But we go in quiet, as little noise as possible. Take them out one at a time if we can, just in case this is some kind of trick to draw us in."

"Vee..." he started to say.

"I'm going," she snapped, cutting him off. "Non-negotiable. I'll meet you in a few hours. Have an entry plan ready for us and several exit plans in case anything happens. Bring as many guys as you think we'll need, but make sure they know how I want this going down. No mistakes, no casualties, you hear me?"

He nodded, his face set in grim lines as he turned away. She sighed and left him to let himself out, going to her room to see what she had for stealthy dockyard takeover wear. Though he balked, Danny understood that she needed to be present for business meetings and such. But he absolutely despised when she insisted on joining the men for combat situations. Too fucking bad, she was the boss. She refused to send her people into places and situations she wouldn't enter into herself. She may not be as combat ready as most of the men on her payroll, but she was fast, and she had a few tricks up her sleeve.

# CHAPTER SIX

Stumbling from her front door into her kitchen, Vee snatched up a clean glass from the sink and twisted the tap for cold water, desperately wishing she had something stronger in her house. The dried blood on her skin smeared across the glass as her hands became wet. She didn't bother to wash it away. What was the point? She had so much blood on her hands, what was a few drops more?

She placed a shaking hand on her forehead, smearing more blood on her face and in her hair, as she drank the entire glass of water. It quenched her thirst and helped to steady her a little. Lowering the glass, she filled it once more, this time drinking with a little more grace and less of the desperation she'd been feeling since she flung herself in her Maserati at the dockyard and drove home.

She hadn't turned on any lights when she came in, preferring the shadows. It was what she did, lived in the dark. At first it had been a reaction to her circumstances, constantly hiding, knowing that enemies could see her if she surrounded herself by light. Then she got used to the dark, treating it like an old friend. So much so, she no longer needed light to forge a path in her home.

Placing her glass on the counter she reached down and unzipped first one boot, then the other, allowing them to fall to the floor. She was usually a tidy person, but she couldn't bring herself to care about where her things landed right at the moment. Not when lives had been lost. When her own life hung precariously in the balance.

She opened her hoodie and allowed it to fall from her shoulders, leaving her dressed in a pair of black skinny jeans, a black spaghetti strap tank and bare feet. She picked up the water and walked to the balcony. Opening the door, she stepped outside into the cool Miami breeze. She shivered but made no attempt to cover her bare arms. She welcomed the chill. Since she stopped using drugs she learned to enjoy simple things, like the sharpness of tactile sensations. Even though some were less pleasant than others she still welcomed them.

Vee took several deep, calming breaths, using the crisp ocean breeze to cleanse her lungs and clear her head. She wished she could go for a swim in the dark pounding surf. Would've except security would follow her down, watch her, wonder what she was thinking. Appearance was everything for a female mob boss, she couldn't afford to appear anything less than completely put together. She hated that she was so rattled. Her usual calm obliterated in the face of an enemy that that was superior in every way. He had more men, more guns, more skill.

She was going to lose this war.

He'd been waiting at the dockyard. Waiting for her counter-attack. They'd been surrounded, had to fight their way out. The only thing that saved them was Sotza's reluctance to let Vee die. Once she realized none of his men were aiming anywhere near her she yelled for her own crew to get behind her. It was a ballsy move. And her guys had been reluctant to hide behind her, the woman they'd sworn to protect.

"I'll fucking shoot you myself if you don't do as I say!" she screamed her frustration until they fell in around her, surrounding the boss as she demanded. The dockyard had fallen eerily silent after that, Sotza's guys refusing to engage as long as a bullet might hit her. Smoke from flares was thick in the air. Sotza's side had thrown them in a bid to confuse and scatter her crew.

"Come out where I can see you, you coward!" she shouted into the dark stillness.

She felt the tension of her guys as footsteps echoed through the yard. The heels of his shoes striking the pavement. He moved where she could see him, but not close enough for her to do the damage she so badly wanted to inflict.

Sotza's sharp eyes took her in, drinking her up with obvious possession gleaming in the dark depths. She felt stripped bare, right there in front of both sides. Then his eyes focused on her face and neck, the blood splattered in her blond hair. "You're hurt," he growled.

What the fuck was his problem? He attacks her, in *her* territory, in *her* dockyard, with the clear intention of taking out as many of her people as possible. But for some reason the idea that's she'd been hurt in the crossfire displeased him.

"Not mine, asshole," she snarled back. "One of my guys."

A hint of relief shadowed his features before he smoothed his expression. "Good," he replied, casually dismissing the death. She shouldn't be surprised. To secure his place in Venezuela more than two decades ago, he'd breathed, slept and ate death. The murder of one person, a pesky adversary, would mean nothing to him. In fact, it baffled her that he seemed to want her alive so bad.

"You're not wearing my ring." His voice was casual, but she could hear the chill. "I warned you about that."

"I'm not fucking marrying you!" Vee shouted, unable to maintain her usual calm in the face of this weird psycho. Maybe this was his plan. Annoy the hell out of her until she died of bafflement. "You can take that ring and stick it up your ass."

He frowned and shook his head. "You need to watch what you say, Vee. I like your elegance, your cool sophistication. It would be a shame for you to turn into a brat. I'd have to reteach you proper decorum after the wedding."

At that point she wanted to shoot him more than she wanted to breathe. If she didn't have the safety of her men to consider she might have done it. Though she kept her gun hand lowered, her finger twitched against the trigger.

"Concede the dockyard and I'll let you and your men go." His countenance became business-like. "Concede the city and I'll think about letting your people live permanently."

Vee didn't know if she could believe him. While he might want her, he wouldn't want men that were loyal to anyone but him. Sotza wasn't known to be merciful. He mowed down all in his path, staked his claim and enjoyed life as though he wasn't a bloody butcher. She could see movement in the shadows all around him. His men were in place, ready to pick them off if anyone made a false move. She had no choice.

"I'll give you the dockyard," she told him. "Let me and my people leave. No more death."

He chuckled. He'd known she wouldn't concede the city. He was going to have to pry Miami out of her cold, dead hands. "Done." He turned and walked away, the smoky shadows swallowing him up almost immediately.

"Let's go," Vee growled at her men.

Danny fell into step beside her as they made their way back to the vehicles. "You need to stop giving a shit about us,

Vee. You won't win any ground trying to protect your people. There has to be sacrifice in war."

"Back off, Danny." She wasn't in the mood for a lecture. Even if he was right. She'd known the truth of his words even as she called her men off, forcing them behind her. She couldn't be their friend, mother, sister, whatever and win this. But the thought of losing any of them was wrenching. She knew most of them personally, knew their families.

As she stood on her balcony, she acknowledged that she'd never felt so alone. What was she protecting her city, her people, from? And why? If she was smart she would run, far and fast. She had the resources to make her way out of the US, to go hide out somewhere in Europe. Switzerland maybe. She could disappear into the mountains, learn to ski.

But Vee had spent most of her life running, hiding from a terrible marriage through the welcoming arms of cocaine. Now that she'd cleaned up and cleared out her house, she wasn't about to give up all of her hard work. She was done running.

She sighed and rubbed her temple, nose wrinkling when she felt blood flaking from her skin. Time for a shower. And after she would have a cup of herbal tea, something calming, and sit for awhile. Remember to breathe, to just be without the weight of a city on her shoulders.

She made it two steps through the back door when a shadow crossed her path, and Sotza, tall and sinister, moved away from the wall where he'd been leaning. Studying her while she was out on the balcony, vulnerable. She swallowed the scream that leapt to her throat and simply stopped, straightening her shoulders. If he was here to hurt her he would've done it. Maybe tossed her off the balcony or slit her throat while her back was turned. He was silent as a cat, managing twice now to sneak up on her.

"Obviously I need to get better locks and more security,"

she drawled, maintaining her cool since he didn't seem in a hurry to break the silence. Apparently her men needed a lesson on how not to let psycho assholes into her home. What the fuck was she paying them for?

"I agree that you need better security. But nothing would have stopped me from checking on you tonight." He stalked forward, his long legs bringing him right into her space. She tried to appear relaxed, uncaring, but her whole being was rigid with fear and anticipation. This man exuded calm, controlled violence. It seeped out of his very being. It scared the living daylights out of her. Yet the kind of power he exuded, to a woman who lived mafia her entire life, was also attractive.

He walked around her, looking down as he leaned so close she caught a sniff of smoke from the flares, spicy cologne and hard, male sweat. A hint of cinnamon, a scent she wasn't expecting, made her mouth water. He stopped behind her, bending his head toward her shoulder. He didn't touch her, but she felt his heat surrounding her, cocooning, capturing and holding her. "A rare jewel should not be left unprotected. When you become mine, I won't allow such lapses in your protection."

She snorted, leaned to the side, away from him, swivelled her head to give him her best scathing look, and said, "I'll never be yours."

His lips were so close to hers that she could feel each breath he took skitter across her face, her lips, her chin, her cheek. It was... exciting. Who was this fuck who could invade her space so easily, could bridge her ice, make her weak? When her husband became violent, she'd learned to turn that facet of herself off, the part that yearned for a man's touch. It was too dangerous to want a man because then it meant she had to give up a part of herself. The part that was too easily betrayed. Her trust. No, better she remain the ice queen.

But without a single touch, this man was obliterating her beliefs.

He didn't smile, but the slight creases around his eyes deepened in amusement. He said, "You belong to me, Vee, whether you admit it, whether you like it." He waited a beat, giving her time to respond. She wouldn't give him the pleasure. She was a mature, experienced woman, not some easily baited youth. He continued, "It's time to relinquish this city into my keeping. Time to accept defeat and move onto the next chapter."

Her breath caught. Neither of them moved. Like a scene frozen, they stood together. He at her back, her face tilted up in defiance to meet his. She wished that she'd kept her heeled boots on, wished she was taller. She needed the advantage of height in this moment. Felt the need to prove her worth in a man's world, in Sotza's world, and keep her carefully cultivated image. Cool, put-together, always in control.

"And what *exactly* is the next chapter?" Ice dripped from each word.

He didn't hesitate. "You will become my wife."

She let out a short bitter laugh. Took a step forward, away from him. Couldn't have him in her space while they talked. It was too disconcerting, fucked with her head. Made her want things she knew she couldn't have. They were enemies. Period. Nothing more. The 'next chapter' could only end one way. Defeat. Her death or his. Most likely hers. But she'd learned positivity in rehab, so she wasn't willing to write herself off yet.

Denial leapt to her lips, but she swallowed it. Why be so predictable? He knew her feelings regarding their upcoming nuptials. "Why do you want to marry me, Sotza?" She used his name for the first time. She took another step away and turned to face him. His eyes held no expression, gave nothing away.

Finally, he responded. "Why not, Vee?" His voice was warm but calculating. "We're both mafia royalty. You know the role and I can take and rule anything I want. Together we can rule several countries, scores of people, control trade in your country and mine."

She should have considered his words. Calmly considered each point as he made it. But in that moment she hated him, truly hated him. Like her late husband, Tony, Sotza didn't want her for herself. Didn't even want her body. Just wanted an alliance. Well, fuck him! Righteous fury ripped through her. "You can go to hell," she said, eyes narrowed, voice seething.

His face grew stony and his eyes narrowed in return. "You don't want to take this path with me, Vee," he said, calm despite the violence infusing his very essence, outlined in every nuance of his body. He seemed to be restraining himself from grabbing her, shaking her, making her see reason. Good, she wanted him on edge, so he understood how she felt every time they clashed.

Then he hit her where it hurt. "Our union is inevitable. Any resistance on your part will be in vain. It will cost more lives."

He'd figured out at the dockyard that she was unwilling to sacrifice her people in this war. Still, in that moment, she didn't care. "Get out." Her voice held icy command, leaving no room for denial.

He nodded, acquiescing. Perhaps he knew she was reaching a breaking point. Thought she might do something stupid if he kept pushing. He moved toward the front door of her condo, his tread silent, his movements imperceptible unless someone was looking right at him.

God, he was good.

He turned, before leaving, his voice quiet but sinister. "Put the ring back on."

Then he was gone. Once he was out, his overbearing presence gone from her space, she felt like she could breathe. Her knees went weak and she collapsed, crouching in the middle of her living room. She dropped her head into her hands and clutched her hair. She felt helpless. She felt aroused. But most of all she felt angry.

Rage ignited within her, racing through her veins, lighting her up with purpose. Sotza was just another man, trying to push her around, trying to dominate her. She took several deep, calming breaths, dropped her arms and stood, mind racing. An entire year of work completely undermined and dismantled in a matter of weeks. Her precious reputation was in tatters now, thanks to the shadowy, predatory Venezuelan. She couldn't wait to get her hands on the man and carve him into little pieces. First, she had to take back her territory, then she would show him what 'Butcher' really meant, mafia style.

## CHAPTER SEVEN

"I need you to get me a meeting with Juan Domingo."

Danny started shaking his head before the name even left Vee's mouth. "Too dangerous. He's had guys all over you since you took over from Tony. That asshole piece of shit cartel just can't handle a woman in charge."

Vee smirked at his heated remark, despite the gravity of the situation. Danny was not just her protection, he was a friend. He'd been her personal bodyguard when she was still married. He'd seen the bruises, the screaming matches, the constant belittling she'd experienced at Tony's hands. He was the first person she turned to after murdering her husband, had comforted her as emotion had driven her to her knees, tears streaming down her face. Not sadness at the passing of her husband, not fear at possible reprisals. No, she'd been elated. Relieved, unbelievably happy and overwhelmed at the thought of having her freedom. Danny had nodded his approval at seeing Tony's body, gathered her in his arms and held her until there were no more tears, as he'd done in the past when Tony had hurt her. Danny stood firmly by her side ever since.

She'd known he wouldn't like her next plan, but kept her voice firm. "I don't have a choice. I need to talk to him, convince him to accept my leadership. Before Sotza gets to him."

"You think Sotza hasn't already talked to Domingo, brought him onside of the Venezuelans?" Danny sat on the edge of Vee's desk and gave her a stern look. He stayed calm, assured and steadfast. He was the perfect second. He didn't do drama and he didn't do reckless, both of which Vee brought to the table in spades these days.

Vee shook her head. "Word on the street has it Domingo's been deep in his Mexican mountain fortress, probably hiding from Reyes. That stupid fuck knows I'm Reyes' contact here in the States. Bet he dove for cover directly after that last aborted strike, thinking the Bolivian might have my back."

"Yeah, Reyes has your back alright. Handed you over to Sotza on a platter. So what makes you think Domingo'll come up for a meeting?" Danny asked skeptically. "Especially if he knows Sotza's in town. My opinion, most of these guys are more afraid of The Butcher than even your boss, Reyes."

"We'll tell him Reyes is going to shut the borders to him and go to war if he doesn't get his ass up here for a meeting. And I don't want an underling. We're going to have a civilized conversation, boss to boss."

Danny snorted. She didn't blame him for thinking her plan wasn't going to work. It was reckless at best, suicidal at worst. Each time she was supposed to meet with the Mexicans, take a shipment, they attacked her, tried to undermine her regime. Damn near killed her on that last confrontation. But she didn't have a choice. Sotza was backing her into a corner. Alienating her contacts, brutally taking over Miami. If she didn't get the Mexicans on her side then she'd soon have nothing left.

Maybe something in her face finally convinced Danny. He nodded and straightened away from the desk. "I'll see to it."

Danny moved away from her, leaving Vee to contemplate how she wanted to play her upcoming confrontation with Juan Domingo. A man that had plagued her time as Miami's queen. A man that was known to kill family members for fun.

---

Vee strode into the warehouse like she owned the place. She didn't. Technically, the Mexicans owned it. Domingo probably had it listed under a shell corporation. It was a place for him to do business whenever he crossed the border. It was big, it was empty, it was easy. It was also eerily silent.

The Mexican cartel were not known for their silence. Especially not when it came to Elvira Montana. They postured, made noise, generally tried to make her feel uncomfortable and undermined at every opportunity. Not all Mexicans, to be sure. She'd done successful business with the some of the cartels further East. But Domingo and his crew were a bunch of pigs. Unfortunately, they were an evil she had no choice but to work with if she wanted to keep trade flowing under her regime.

"We got the right day?" she asked Danny, who was walking beside her, his shoulders tense, his eyes alert. She was half joking and they both knew it. Danny never made mistakes.

"Friday, noon," he confirmed.

"We should've been stopped by now."

Danny pulled his gun and walked faster, moving in front of Vee. Obviously he agreed. They made their way through the warehouse toward the back offices. No one stopped them.

"At least there're no bodies," she pointed out beneath her breath.

Danny shook his head and kept walking. She knew he was thinking what she was thinking. They should've brought more men. But Domingo's instructions had been clear. She could have two outside the building and one at her side. He promised that he would talk, not negotiate, not yet, but he would talk. If she agreed to call Reyes off. Apparently there had been some rumblings out of Bolivia regarding his attack in Miami and Domingo was finally afraid of reprisals.

Her steel-tipped heels tapped against the concrete, echoing through the space as they approached Domingo's office. Danny said a quick prayer, crossed himself, pushed Vee to the side of the door and opened it.

Vee peeked around his shoulder. "Anticlimactic," she said drily, stepping around her second and into the empty office.

Danny followed close behind, turning so their backs weren't to the open door. "We need to get out of here," he mumbled. "Something's not right. We can get hold of Domingo later, when you're safe. Reschedule."

"Well, fuck," Vee sighed as she approached the desk. It was completely empty except for a white box wrapped with a red bow. "Somehow I don't think Domingo will be able to reschedule."

Vee really didn't want to open the box. She was beginning to think she wasn't cut out for this shit. Perhaps she should throw in the towel, empty her accounts and go someplace where she could happily shop for the rest of her life. Get her nails and hair done, both of which were long overdue. And while she suspected it would be a short life, because no way would Sotza let her just disappear forever, she would be happy. For awhile.

Vee untied the ribbon and started to pry the lid off. Danny grabbed her wrist. "Bomb?" he suggested questioningly.

She shook her head and laughed. "No Danny, the

Gentleman Butcher is more subtle than that." She lifted the lid, glanced inside for a few seconds and then replaced it. "He also has the grimmest sense of humour I've ever seen."

# CHAPTER EIGHT

Sotza debated leaving her alone to stew over this new development. Let the fear gather in her heart. She'd think about running. Maybe take that bodyguard she's so fond of. He wouldn't let her though. He'd scoop her up before she even hit the city limits. And then the actual courting could begin.

But Sotza knew her better than that. He was learning everything he could about the delightful woman that was about to become his wife. Every time she made a move he discovered more, filed away the knowledge of her. How she lived, how she worked, the things she liked, what she didn't like. She certainly didn't like receiving heads in boxes.

He hit her contact on his phone. He wasn't at all surprised when she picked up with, "What, you didn't feel like sneaking into my apartment this evening? I thought you enjoyed preying on helpless women in the dark."

She didn't seem the least bit grateful for this latest gift. In fact, seemed to be in a bit of a temper. He pictured her fair complexion flushing with anger and had to shift in his chair, adjust his pants. "I thought you might enjoy an engagement gift."

"I only enjoy my severed heads followed by absurdly expensive jewelry," she snapped sarcastically. "Why'd you kill him?"

"He had his men shoot at you, Vee. You nearly died during your last run-in with him," he explained calmly. "I can't have people shooting at my future wife. Sets a bad precedent."

She didn't speak for a moment, but he could hear her breath coming out in short angry exhales as she tried to compose herself, tried not to scream at him. "I needed him, Sotza. And you murdered him so you could solidify your claim in the US and undermine everything I've been working for."

"I know." He took a thoughtful pause. She really wasn't getting it. Perhaps he needed to reinforce his position, but just a gentle reminder. For now, anyway. "But you don't need him, Vee. You don't need any of your former contacts. Once we're married you'll stand at my side, running things with me. Not against me. And never in danger."

"You. Are. Insane," she bit out.

He laughed. She really was delightful. "Not really, but you'll soon get a chance to know all of my charming characteristics."

"Over my dead body," she snarled.

"Ah, never that, amor," he assured her. "But if you keep up this resistance, this wonderful dance we're doing, the dead bodies will continue to pile up. Why don't we just cut to the end and you agree to quit the fight and become my wife?"

"You know what happened to my last husband, right?" she asked as though talking to a child.

"Of course, a stellar piece of work there. Executing a weak ruler and flawlessly picking up where he left off." He reached for his drink, Red Rose tea with one sugar, and took a quick sip. "You will make an exemplary partner. I'm honestly becoming as impatient as a young bridegroom."

No response for a moment and he wondered what she was thinking. He found her all the more enticing for thinking that she could change his mind. Nothing she said or did would change his mind. They were a match made in heaven. Had been from the moment he set eyes on her, but he became more convinced each time he saw her, talked with her. She was vicious, intelligent and beautiful. He couldn't have asked for a better woman to come into his life. He didn't mind chasing her around a bit, cornering her in her beloved city until she had nowhere to go but into his waiting arms.

"Alright," she finally said. "Nothing I say is going to convince you otherwise. But if you ever do manage to get me to an alter it will be one hundred percent unwilling. And you'll have to sleep with one eye open for the rest of your life."

"I'm sure we'll settle into married life blissfully," he replied, a smile curving his lips.

"And for the record, no woman likes to receive body parts as an engagement gift, asshole." Each word a little grenade lobbed at him. He let her have the last word, mostly because she hung up on him.

Sotza lowered the phone and took a sip of tea, picturing Vee, flushed with anger, stomping around her condo. She was a beautiful woman, but he particularly liked when her cheeks were blushing pink. It complemented her smooth, silky blond hair. He'd never been particularly attracted to any single type of woman. Thought they were all fine. Fucked the ones that attracted him, when he felt like it. Not often. Women got complicated and annoying. And he preferred not to kill them unless it became unavoidable. But Vee, she was different. Her cool beauty called to him, but her fiery temper captured and held his attention. Her intelligence, her determination, her pride, it all sealed the deal.

There was almost nothing he wasn't willing to do to ensure her place at his side. Including cornering and trapping her in her own city. He'd give her one more move, just for fun. After that, it would be time to collect his queen.

# CHAPTER NINE

"We can't find her, Señor."

Sotza looked up from his temporary desk and studied the man standing before him, assessing him. He didn't frown, didn't get angry, didn't react. That was the thing about the Venezuelan boss, what terrorized the people that knew him, or knew of him. He rarely gave warning before he struck. Simply waited until his victim wasn't watching then killed them, no fuss, no mess. The lucky ones would die before they even knew what happened. The unlucky ones got to find out why he was nicknamed the Gentleman Butcher.

Sotza sat back in his chair, his posture straight. "I must say, Mr. Cruz, I am... disappointed."

It'd been five days since he spoke with Vee, five days since he took out her Mexican connection. He had to admit, he'd been hoping for a vicious comeback from his future bride. Her retaliations were a thing of beauty, the dockyard a particular favourite moment of his. She'd been glorious, facing him down, standing at the front of her crew, surrounded by smoke. Wild and furious, unafraid. He wasn't disappointed with her quiet disappearance though. No, he was intrigued. What could she be up to?

Steve Cruz shifted from foot to foot and tried to look anywhere but at his boss. "The thing is, she ain't at her condo, she ain't at her mansion, and none of us that're sitting on both places saw her leave."

"Which draws us to the conclusion…?" Sotza asked patiently.

Cruz frowned, then he understood. "That she must've left another way, or maybe never was at home to begin with."

"She was home, Cruz, as I told you when I asked you and your men to sit on her residences. To watch her movements and report." Sotza mulled over the possibilities. "Perhaps she didn't leave. Perhaps she's still at home."

"No, boss, we checked."

Sotza stiffened, his back ramrod straight against the leather chair. "What exactly do you mean by 'checked'?"

"We knocked on the door." Watching Cruz explain his actions was like watching a train about to derail. His death was going to be fast, surprising and painful. "When she didn't answer we went in to check on her, see if she was there. But everything was silent, cold, you know, like no one'd been home in awhile."

Sotza refrained from pointing out that he'd specifically asked Cruz and his men to remain in the background, never going near Vee or her people. Now it would appear that Vee had gone to ground in a move he hadn't anticipated, and he had no idea where she might be. If she'd fled the city or was waiting him out.

He also didn't ask why Cruz hadn't thought it strange that there was no security stopping them from entering her home. He didn't want to tip Cruz off to the depth of his fury. Not before he was ready to dispose of the man. "And the mansion? I take it you applied similar tactics?"

Cruz nodded eagerly, wanting to prove his diligence. "No one home there either, Señor."

This is what Sotza got for hiring local thugs. He'd overestimated Cruz's intelligence, expected too much. In hindsight, Sotza should've gotten someone smarter, braver and generally a bit more of everything that Cruz wasn't to watch his woman. The moment he'd decided to keep Vee for himself he should've flown Mateo Gutierrez in. Mateo was a jack of all trades. Sometimes Sotza's second, sometimes his enforcer, sometimes security, and sometimes, on rare occasions, he acted in Sotza's stead. Taking meetings Sotza couldn't or wouldn't make, acting decisively in the Venezuelan boss's name. Naturally, when Sotza had left his estate, he'd left his seat of power vulnerable. The only man he trusted to care for things in his stead was Mateo. But now he needed him in Miami.

When Sotza went a few minutes without speaking, Cruz opened his mouth to say something, break the silence, possibly blubber out an excuse for his poor behaviour. Sotza help up a hand, stopping him. Cruz fell silent while Sotza picked up his phone and dialed Mateo.

"Mateo," Sotza said into the phone when his man picked up, his voice marginally warmer.

"Boss," Mateo acknowledged. "How's Florida? You get down to the beach yet, enjoy some sun?"

Sotza shook his head. Mateo liked to think he was funny. He enjoyed the idea of Sotza in a bathing suit, out of his typical outfit of impeccable black suit with its long coat, white collared shirt, vest and tie. "Regrettably, no."

"Too bad," Mateo said, humour in his voice. "With your once-per-decade tolerance toward vacations I thought you might do what the locals do and go to the beach."

Now Sotza did chuckle. The reason Mateo was calling his trip to Miami a 'vacation' was because they both knew how much Sotza enjoyed a good bloodbath. He loved takeovers, the more hostile the better. It'd been years since anyone had dared to disrupt his life enough that he had to reiterate his brutal reputation. This trip had invigorated him, reminded him of why he loved being boss. And Vee was the icing on the cake. The sweet treat he wasn't expecting when he agreed to Reyes' proposal to travel to the States.

"I need you in Miami," Sotza said, sobering and getting down to business. "Come watch my back while I take care of business."

"With pleasure," Mateo said enthusiastically. He was no less bloodthirsty than his boss. He'd been disappointed, though appreciative, when Sotza left him in charge at home. Now he'd get to join the action. "I'll arrange my arrival just past midnight."

Sotza flicked a glance at his watch. It was 7pm. The flight took around three and half hours. This is what he liked about his man. Didn't fuck around when he had his orders. Made snap decisions that were in both his and Sotza's best interests. Mateo wasn't an amateur. Sotza eyed Cruz, who had remained wisely silent throughout the conversation. He wondered if maybe he shouldn't keep the man alive, perhaps find another use for him.

"Excellent," Sotza said to Mateo. "Bring some reinforcements. I'd like to wrap things up here and wouldn't mind some decisive action to keep Miami in line after I leave."

He hung up the phone and stared coolly at Cruz. "Do you have a friend, Mr. Cruz? Someone loyal, maybe educated? Someone that can help me out until I'm done here."

Cruz nodded emphatically, pleased to be able to finally give the terrifying Venezuelan some good news. "Yes, Señor. My cousin Paulo is real book smart and good on the streets too. He likes to help out sometimes, make a little extra cash for college."

"And how do I get in touch with Paulo?" Sotza drawled.

Cruz quickly wrote down the number and stepped back. "Anything else I can do you for, boss?"

"Yes," Sotza said agreeably. "Lock the door, please. This next part isn't for anyone but you."

## CHAPTER TEN

Vee was not happy. And when she wasn't happy she paced. Back and forth, side to side, crosswise. Paced and thought. Tried to think of ways to make herself happier.

"His head in a box would be great," she muttered to herself. "Hell, I'd even take his severed hands in a box. With a ribbon wrapped around. Have to admit, it's a nice touch. Adds an element of gruesome suspense. A decent bath and a hot cup of tea would also be great. But no need to go overboard, the dead Butcher in a box will do just fine."

Danny raised an eyebrow but said nothing. He was used to her nervous, irritable pacing. She tended to think better when she walked, but her life as an East Coast mafia boss had curtailed her ability to take regular walks outdoors. A shame, she loved to go down to the boardwalk and enjoy the fresh salty sea air, the humid heat of the Florida sun seeping through her clothes and warming her skin.

Vee wasn't happy when she wasn't active. She wasn't happy when she wasn't working. And she especially wasn't happy when she'd been driven into hiding, cooped up in a dilapidated industrial apartment on the wrong side of the tracks.

Danny had convinced her to lay low in the city if she wouldn't actually leave it. It was killing her to keep a low profile, sit back while Sotza took out her contacts and replaced them with his own people. She'd warned some of her people that they needed to leave town and lay low, others she hadn't been able to get hold of.

She badly wanted to take action, but she listened to Danny, decided to play things smart. To give Sotza time. He would be distracted by her disappearance if he was indeed as infatuated with her as he professed. It might slow him down, confuse him. Give her time to come up with a plan.

"What if we went to Bertrand for help?" she asked, louder, so Danny knew she was actually talking to him this time. She turned on her heel as she reached the far wall. She was wearing a pair of comfortable running shoes instead of her usual steel-spiked stilettos.

"Not a good idea," Danny said shaking his head. "Bertrand's loyal to no one but himself and his MC. He'll turn you over to Sotza in a heartbeat in he thinks he can profit."

"I'll offer him more," she countered with a frown.

"You had enough trouble with the Mexicans, now you think you can take on the most vicious biker gang on the East Coast? Bertrand doesn't like a woman's authority any more than Domingo had. Only difference is, Bertrand was able to separate business from personal politics when it came to border trade." Danny crossed his arms over his chest and scowled at her. "How do you think you can outmaneuver both a perpetually angry biker and The Butcher at the same time? Bad idea sweetheart."

Danny was right. Calling on the Quebec boys would only land her in even more trouble. Bertrand was one of a kind: big, mean, cold-hearted and indiscriminate about his kills. True to club life, the wild leader rarely recognized any kind of authority. There was a reason she tried never to see him face to face. With a whole MC filled with men similar to him he had a stranglehold on the entire East Coast of Canada.

She sighed and continued pacing. "What about the Italians? Some of them might remember Tony from his heyday, might talk to me, give me a chance."

Danny actually laughed out loud, incredulous. "You've been encroaching on their territory this entire past year. You think they don't know exactly who took over when you killed Tony? They were front of the line for that show. Only reason they haven't come for you is you had more people at your back than them, you had Reyes."

She flinched when he mentioned Reyes. The man that had effectively targeted her for death by sending Sotza to clean up her operations. No one wanted to be on Reyes' bad side.

Danny continued, "If the Italians find out that your hold on Miami is in question, they'll slit your throat faster than you can say spaghetti."

"I have to do something!" She threw her hands up in the air. She turned to glare at her second. He wasn't being even remotely helpful.

"What you have to do is stay low, keep your head down. Don't do something stupid, Vee. Not worth your life."

"I can't do this indefinitely. I hate hiding, it's not my style. I didn't even lay low when Tony was coming after me, screaming at me," she seethed. "If I could take a beating from him and hold my own, then I certainly won't hide from Sotza."

Danny didn't say anything, just watched silently as she continued to pace and mutter, trying to come up with a solution. It didn't matter what he said anyway, she would go her own way. She was reasonable enough to listen to his advice, but she was headstrong and stubborn. She'd follow her own path in the end, do what she thought was the right thing to solve her problem.

Finally she stopped, her distracted gaze on the floor. "Sotza's trying to smoke me out, corner me, kill my business. He expects fury and retaliation." She looked at Danny, her heart beating harder in anticipation. "What if I surprise him, give him the opposite of what he expects?"

Instead of intrigued or even remotely like he would agree to her plan, Danny looked suspiciously disagreeable. "And what exactly is that?" he demanded. A little disrespectfully, she thought. But she'd forgive him since she'd essentially painted a target on his back by going up against the Venezuelan.

"Me," she said with a smile as the plan formed in her mind. "I'm going to give him me."

---

"I must say." Sotza smoothly slid into the booth next to Vee. He shifted until he was sitting so close his thigh was brushing hers. "I wasn't expecting to dine with such a charming companion this evening."

Vee kept her face as neutral as possible and purposefully slid a few inches away from him. She lifted her water glass and took a sip before carefully placing it back on the table. It took effort to make sure her hand didn't shake, that she didn't accidentally spill the water. She was sitting next to one of the most dangerous men in the world, and though she could be pretty vicious herself, she couldn't hold a candle to him. She boldly studied him, allowing the silence to linger. She'd asked for this meeting so that she could finally take back a little control.

Everything about him pissed her off. From his dignified presence to his impeccably tailored clothing. Every time she saw him he was wearing a version of the same suit: dress pants, white collared shirt with a French cuff paired with appeared to be silk knot cufflinks, silk, Jacquard black tie, vest and coat. He stood out against the Miami backdrop, overdressed for the weather, too formal for the laid back party city. Yet the quiet air of deadly menace that he exuded negated his strange formality. He was not a classically handsome man, face too sharp, features too strong. Thick eyebrows, penetrating dark brown eyes, a long, thin nose, high cheekbones, strong clean-shaven jaw. There was a slight curl to his dark, greying hair, which he groomed to include long sideburns. They only emphasized the sharpness of his facial features, giving him a penetrating, hawk-like appearance.

And though she knew better, should be repulsed by how the man operated, her body reacted to his. Every time she saw him. Something about him was intensely attractive. Not any individual thing, but the whole package together. She didn't like to acknowledge it, but his dogged pursuit of her certainly didn't hurt either. It annoyed her that she reacted so strongly to him, made her want to slit his throat at the earliest opportunity, yet Vee had to admit that a marriage proposal from such a powerful, good-looking man was enough to make even her cold, ice-filled heart flutter.

Finally, after an appropriately rude amount of time had passed, she spoke, her voice cool. "Hiding doesn't suit me."

His thin lips stretched into a semi-smile as his eyes dropped down her body. He shifted slightly, signalling a nearby waiter. "No, my dear, hiding does not suit you." He turned to speak to the waiter. "I'll have a bourbon, neat. And champagne for the lady please." Sotza turned back to her, his arm across the back of the booth, pinning her in.

Vee frowned, her gaze following the retreating waiter. "If I'd wanted a drink I would've ordered one for myself."

Sotza ignored her comment. "Why did you invite me here this evening, Vee? Not that I'm not delighted, but your behaviour thus far has indicated you don't particularly enjoy my company."

Vee's jaw was beginning to ache from clenching her teeth together in an attempt to keep a rein on her anger. She struggled not to give away her emotions, to keep her face as immobile as possible while she studied him with what she hoped appeared to be glacial indifference. Still, she couldn't just let the drink thing go. "You're a heavy-handed prick, you know that?"

He dipped his head in acknowledgment and reached for his drink as the waiter arrived back at the table. Sotza drank deeply, seeming to appreciate the smooth liquor as it slid down his throat. He didn't order another though, simply placed his empty glass on the table and continued to study her. His face said indifference, but his eyes and body spoke of heat and lust. It was a confusing combination. He off-balanced her, made her wonder what his true intentions were. As flattering as it was to receive a marriage proposal, she knew she couldn't trust his motives. No one fell in love that quickly.

"I want to negotiate," she said in her firmest voice, ignoring the drink in front of her. She wouldn't touch it. The waiter came by to see if Sotza wanted another drink and while he was there she handed him back the champagne. "I don't drink alcohol, and if my date had done his homework, he'd know that." Sotza gifted her with a small incline of his head as he waved the waiter away. She suspected Sotza already knew her preferences, was fucking with her. He wasn't the type to leave any box unchecked.

"What are we negotiating?" he asked, tapping his fingers against the booth, just behind her head.

She stiffened at how close his hand was to her hair. Her

voice came out sharper than she intended when she spoke. "My home. Your retreat."

He tilted his head slightly, examining her, eyes appearing to pick her apart. Vee hadn't taken much when she'd fled her apartment, but she'd taken enough clothes to prepare for every eventuality, whether it was murder or dining with the Queen of England. Tonight she was wearing a light pink silk sleeveless blouse that complimented her pale complexion, a fitted rose coloured skirt and a long-sleeved black leather jacket that fit her like she was born in it. On her feet she wore her favourite pair of steel-spiked five-inch heels.

"I want you to give me my city back. I want you to take your people, turn around and go back to where you came from," she said, her voice strong and sure though she was quaking on the inside. "No more threats, no more violence."

He picked up her water glass and drank from it, his lips touching the spot hers had touched. A bolt of pure lightening sizzled through her body. "And what exactly will you give me for such a concession?" he asked, replacing her glass on the table.

She gazed at him, eyes narrowed. "I won't retaliate, won't come after you with everything I have."

"It would be suicide," he said, his fingers tapping faster. She twisted around to look at them and then shot him a pointed glare.

"At this point what do I have to lose?" she asked heatedly. "You've taken everything from me. My city, some of my men, my position, my dignity, even my rivals. Why should I sit back and let you take what's left?"

The lines around his mouth tightened giving him a foreboding look. "You could lose your life, Vee."

"And what's that worth?" she snapped.

His hand moved so fast, so independently of the rest of him that she didn't know what was happening until her head was slammed back against the seat and his face was hovering inches away from hers. He'd tangled his fingers in her hair and wrenched her backwards against the booth, using the strength in his long fingers to twist her head slightly to the side so she was facing him.

"That is not an option," he said, his voice colder than anything she'd heard from him yet.

"What?" She tried to focus on what he meant while shafts of pain contrasted with a heightened physical awareness, which ran from her head down the length of her body. What wasn't an option?

"You don't get to die, Elvira." His lips lifted in a slight snarl, giving away some of the emotion he tried so hard to withhold.

"Why?" she demanded, pushing on despite the dangerous aura pulsating from him. It was never a good idea to piss off The Butcher. "I'm nothing to you, expendable. You've made my presence in this city pretty much unnecessary. So why do you care if I die?"

He leaned in, so close that she could feel his breath caressing her. It was warm, crisp and smelled like cinnamon, as though he'd been chewing gum or something right before their meeting. Had he anticipated a kiss? And why the fuck did she care. They were talking about her possible death for Christ sakes.

His dark, velvety brown eyes now held fire. He emphasized each word he spoke with a quiet assurance. "You are rare, Elvira. A jewel among rocks. Your death would be blasphemy."

Her thoughts scattered. His actions were so at odds with his words. His hands hurt and threatened her, but his eyes and voice caressed her, wrapping her in erotic tension. The only thing she could think to say was, "Don't call me Elvira. I hate that name."

He chuckled, the sound dark and delicious, sending a shiver right through her. His eyes dropped, chased her shudder from the top of her throat, past her breasts, which were peaked beneath her jacket, right down to her lap. He loosened his fingers in her hair and stroked them through, smoothing the strands.

"You belong to me, *Vee*. And no one harms the things that belong to me."

"I'm not a thing!" She jerked her head away from him. "I was boss in this city until you came along."

He shrugged and allowed her some space. "Regimes fall, my dear. If you're smart, you'll follow the path of the victor. Take what I offer and be thankful that staying alive is an option. It wouldn't usually be under these circumstances."

"Fuck you," she snapped, out of options for comebacks.

"You want to be careful what you do and say right now." His cool mask slipping back into place. "We're nearing the finish line and it's just about time to stop playing around. As much fun as I've had here with you I need to get back to my home."

"You're psychotic," she hissed. "Has anyone ever told you that?"

"You are acting like a feral cat, Vee, trapped in a corner. You seem to think the only way out is a fight to the death. I can assure you it's not. I won't allow anything to happen to you, even if it means hurting you in the short term to ensure that there is a tomorrow for both of us."

She frowned and pressed her lips together to stop herself from snapping out another clever comeback like the last one. He was right, she was acting like a trapped animal. Every move she made reeked of fear and desperation. She needed to be smarter, think five steps ahead of him. Only who the fuck knew what was going on in his crazy head? "I think we're done here," she finally said, her voice colder than her eyes as she stared through him.

He sighed regretfully and moved away from her, standing up. Before he left he pinned her with a heated stare. "Last move, my queen. I'm coming for you."

# CHAPTER ELEVEN

Last move...

Vee contemplated Sotza's words as she laid on an uncomfortable mattress in the dark, uninviting industrial apartment she was using. She really should just go home, back to her small luxuries. The Venezuelan probably knew exactly where she was hiding out and was laughing at her new circumstances. Well... probably not. He seemed to harbour a weird soft spot for her. Despite her constant defiance, he didn't seem to want her uncomfortable. She shifted onto her back, kicked at the blanket covering her legs and shoved a hand through her hair. She lay like that, hand on her head, staring at nothing.

Whose last move? Hers or his? The thought chilled her to the bone. If it was her last move then she was royally screwed. She had nothing left to negotiate with. Perhaps there were still a few contacts loyal to her, but they would fall. Either by death or switching sides. Most likely death. She couldn't see Sotza allowing anyone to live who would switch loyalties so easily. The man seemed to have a strange set of ethics, but they worked for him. Far more effectively than hers. She was so busy trying to protect the people under her care that she stopped pushing back lest someone else get hurt. She'd sent most of her backup into hiding. Life was looking pretty bleak.

Tears of hopelessness burned behind her eyelids, but she refused to let them fall. Pressed the heel of her hands hard against her eyes to stop them. She stopped crying years ago. She wasn't about to let some asshole mobster break her. Even if he'd broken everything around her.

Perhaps it was time to give up the fight, stop acting out of desperation and start thinking smart. Cut her losses and go. Find a place he'd never think to look. Because as much as she wanted to think he would allow her to leave unscathed, she knew better. A man like that, once he stated his intentions, would always follow through. If she stayed it would be just a matter of time until he scooped her up. If she stayed, more people would die. More of her beautiful city would burn.

Tomorrow, first thing in the morning, she would leave.

***

"She's on the move," Mateo told his boss, watching from a window across the street from Vee's hiding place. "Taking two bodyguards and a suitcase. Could be moving back home. Maybe she's done with this low-class shit."

Mateo cast a scathing eye around the place he'd been calling home since his arrival in Miami. He was not impressed. It was dilapidated, dirty, bug-infested and there was no running water. Just a tiny, uncomfortable cot and the nastiest toilet he'd come across in awhile. He suspected Vee's accommodations were similar and was somewhat impressed that the delicate blond he'd been charged with watching would put up with it.

"Interesting," Sotza replied. "No, I don't think she would go back home. It would be admitting defeat."

"Isn't running away from the city her way of admitting defeat?" Mateo pointed out. He was in a high enough position within The Butcher's organization that he'd been invited to submit his thoughts and opinions. No one else could offer such an observation without the boss taking issue.

Sotza chuckled. "Perhaps. But leaving the city to a destination of her choice is admitting defeat on her terms. Staying would be bowing to me on my terms. The lady is far too feisty for that."

"Sounds complicated," Mateo said, watching as Vee and her bodyguards drove away. "She's left the area. Won't be able to disappear though, I'm tracking all vehicles that've had contact with her."

"I never doubted it," Sotza said, satisfaction clear in his voice. "That's the reason I brought you here. Your ability to track is unparalleled."

Mateo was flattered, the boss didn't hand out compliments. Still, he felt compelled to respond. "You brought me here to babysit a woman?" Mateo had anticipated war, a bloodbath, standing by Sotza's side as a powerful regime fell to be replaced by their own command. He hadn't expected his entire job to be following a woman around. Albeit an attractive, intelligent woman.

Silence on the other end of the phone made him think he was toeing too close to the line. Though he was the right hand to Sotza, they weren't friends. No one befriended the man. He was cold, intelligent and vicious. Cozying up to the Venezuelan was like an ant wanting to make friends with a shoe. Impossible. Because no matter how close one got within the organization, no matter how high up, one just never knew when that shoe was going to drop.

"I brought you here to track and protect my future wife.

The future of my organization. Her life is vitally important." Sotza spoke with cool authority, but the deadly undercurrent told Mateo that any more sleights against Ms. Montana would not pass.

"Understood," Mateo said. And he did. Though Sotza hadn't shown even a fleeting interest in any single woman since Mateo knew the man, he now understood that the dynamic of the Venezuelan cartel had changed. There would soon be a queen at the top, standing next to Sotza.

"Good," Sotza said, putting the brief but tense exchange behind them and getting back to business. "I want your men on that car. It might have a tracker but that doesn't mean she won't slip away. She's wily." Sotza's voice held a modicum of pride and warmth. Another first.

"I'll get them on it right away, she won't be able to go anywhere without us knowing her every move. What do you want me to do?" Now that Elvira was leaving, and he was assured she would be tracked, his presence at the warehouse was unnecessary.

"I have an extremely important and delicate task for you. I need you to find Vee's daughter and bring her to me."

## CHAPTER TWELVE

Raina Duncan studied the fake ID with critical appreciation. She'd just updated it to say she was 22 years old and added a new, more mature picture. The picture was the most important part. It had to match the person holding the ID, but it needed to be just right so as not to draw attention. Hers was perfect. Not too attention-grabbing, nothing suspicious. She'd worn a pink collared blouse and her gold chain. Her blond hair was left to flow in loose waves around her face, spilling across one shoulder. Piercing blue eyes looked back at her from behind a pair of trendy glasses with thick, light pink plastic rims. She'd wanted to look young in the picture, but not too young. She needed to look as though she could be younger than 22 but only thanks to great genetics.

Her eyes moved to the two ID's next to hers, for her friends, Noah and Cass. They looked just as good as hers, she thought, tooting her own horn. She was damn good at making ID's, including, driver's licenses, state identifications and passports. She needed something to supplement her

University tuition. Pennsylvania State University wasn't cheap and her parents couldn't afford to help her out much. They were farm folk; good, honest and hardworking. And though Raina was willing to put a certain amount of hard work in, she wanted to see big payoffs. Which is why she wasn't nearly as good or honest as mom and dad.

Raina assumed she got a good portion of her personality and all of her looks from her birth parents. Both of her parents had dark hair and eyes, ruddy complexions and stocky builds. Raina was the exact opposite, small, slim, blond, blue-eyed. Her temperament was much different too. She was headstrong, stubborn, sneaky and smart.

Too often her parents hadn't known what to do with her. But she loved them and they loved her, unreservedly and unconditionally. They had stood by her side since she was a baby, protecting her through illness and major surgery. Raina had been born with poorly functioning kidneys. The problem had started to make itself known when she was only five years old. She'd had a kidney transplant at thirteen and been relatively healthy ever since, though she had to watch her diet carefully to make sure her one functioning kidney remained that way.

It was Raina's 19th birthday and she was going to celebrate. Well, it wasn't actually her birthday. It'd been her birthday five days ago, but she and her friends wanted to wait until the weekend to celebrate. Take their hot new ID's and hit up a bar, dance and drink until they either got kicked out or moved on to the next party.

A tall, curvy brunette breezed through Raina's door without knocking and tossed herself onto the bed. She bounced, dropped her purse and then sat up with a grin.

"Hey loser, you ready to go yet?" Cass asked happily. Then her eyes crawled over her best friend. "No, you are not. What the F, Raina? You can't go bar hopping in your Uni sweater and sweat pants. Those are really ugly pants, by the way."

Raina giggled at Cass's refusal to say 'fuck.' Like Raina, Cass had grown up in a small farming community. Unlike Raina, Cass took right after her God-fearing parents. She was fun, energetic and generally a good upstanding citizen. It had taken some convincing on Raina's and Noah's parts to convince the third in their Three Musketeers group to come out and party. But once she got on board with the idea, there was no stopping Cass. She loved to dress up, wear makeup and have a good time. Raina was convinced once they got a few drinks in her she would be dancing on tabletops and saying 'fuck' with the best of them.

Cass dug around in Raina's closet while Raina checked her emails and Facebook. "What about this one?" Cass twirled around with a dress in her hands. Raina glanced up briefly, saw it was her short skirted, peek-a-boo sleeved blue dress with a pattern of tiny white flowers scattered across.

"Sure," she replied quickly. She didn't care much about clothes and fashion, though she had some nice outfits thanks to her ill-gotten money and Cass's shopping addiction.

She dressed quickly, ran a brush through her hair and turned to Cass. "I'm ready."

Cass rolled her eyes. "Not even some mascara? I mean you're gorgeous, girl, but it wouldn't hurt to give those pale eyelashes a little zing."

Raina shrugged, grabbed her purse and the ID's and said, "No one can tell if I'm wearing mascara or not under my glasses. Besides as soon as I take my glasses off I can't see what I'm doing and end up smearing it everywhere."

Cass sighed and dug around in her own purse until she came up with some lip gloss. "Put some of this on. It's got that plumping stuff in it. I love it."

Raina accepted the lip gloss and put it on, mostly so Cass

would stop bugging her. "It tingles," she said with a frown handing it back.

"It's working!" Cass explained, grabbing Raina's arm and dragging her out the door. "Makes your lips plumper."

"I like my lips the way they are," Raina complained.

---

Raina had a good night. She was still grinning as she got out of the Uber, hugged Cass and Noah good-bye and headed to her dorm. She'd done exactly as she wanted for her birthday. She ate hot wings in a pub, drank a beer, shot some pool. Then the three of them moved onto a nearby nightclub where they did sour whiskey shots, drank rum and coke and danced until 2am. Raina had a good head on her. She knew when to stop, knew she couldn't push her fragile body past its limits. She stopped at four drinks, but encouraged her friends to imbibe, have a few shots for her. They toasted to her one good kidney.

Raina skipped toward her dormitory, singing the new Cardi B song and two-stepping her way down the walk. She glanced around for security but didn't see anyone. They were probably around the corner checking on the other building. She frowned, weird though, usually there was always a security guard somewhere in the big square leading to the dorms.

She was rounding the corner of Hastings Hall, stepping through the shadows, when someone grabbed her from behind. She opened her mouth to scream but a hand covered her face and yanked her back against a hard chest. She didn't think twice; she started fighting for all she was worth. She slammed an elbow backwards as hard as she could. She wasn't sure what she hit, but her elbow met something solid. The guy 'oomphed' and stumbled back a step. He still had a good grip on her though and she wasn't able to cry out, get some-one's attention.

Raina frantically dug in her purse while her assailant struggled to get a better grip on her wiggling body. She finally found what she was looking for, a can of bear spray. Gripping it hard in one hand she twisted to the side and swung her closed fist down, aiming for his crotch. She missed but got a solid hit on his thigh. He grunted something that sounded like "motherfucker!" and loosened his grip for a second. Just long enough that she was able to slam another elbow into his stomach.

He swung her around to face him, which is exactly what she wanted. But when she was face-to-face with her attacker she froze. He wasn't some college kid out to get his rocks off, he didn't look like some peeping Tom pervert either. No, this man was big and mean-looking, completely outside of anyone she'd ever met. He looked Latino with darkly tanned skin, black hair and blazing dark brown eyes. Before she'd had a good look at him she had been only pissed off that someone would try to grab her, now she was utterly terrified. What did a man like this want with someone like her?

"You need to calm the fuck down, chica," he snarled, his hands hard on her arms. "You're coming with me. Up to you if you do it dignified and nice or knocked out and tied up."

"You expect me to go along with my own assault? Not fucking likely!" Raina raised the can of bear spray and took aim.

Before she could deploy the painful mist into his face, he moved, so fast she couldn't understand what he was doing until her feet were swept out from under her and she was falling backward onto the pavement. She let out a yelp and cringed, knowing she was about to hit the ground hard. But she didn't. Her attacker controlled her fall, coming down on top of her, making sure she had a soft landing. His grip on her wrist was not as soft though. He had her in a crushing hold, her arm over her head.

He landed on top of her, straddling her waist, his legs pinning hers, his hand over her mouth. He lifted her arm and slammed it into the pavement until her hand opened and she lost the bear spray. She was stunned that he bested her. She thought her karate skills should protect her from would-be attackers. She was fit, strong-ish and thought she was pretty fucking good in hand to hand combat. But this guy made her feel like a baby kitten going up against a tiger.

A chill shiver ran through her body as she was forced to lay immobile, staring up at her captor. How many times had he done this? Was she about to become the victim of a serial killer? Another in a long line of women that disappeared, never to be seen alive again?

Hell no, she was not! And with that thought she began fighting again, twisting, struggling until her legs were free then slamming her knees into his back. He might be big, he might be solid, he might be better than her in combat situations, but he wasn't small and wiry, with a deep thirst to hurt those that hurt her. Raina had never been one to take sleights lightly. She had a mouth on her and wasn't afraid to tell people what was what, call a spade a spade. She was the first to participate in rallies, shout her political opinions at the top of her lungs. She was especially passionate about women's rights and freedoms. And she was definitely anti-kidnapping.

She quickly became aware that he wasn't trying to hurt her. In fact, he was actively trying to do the opposite. Make sure she didn't bruise herself too much in the fight. What the fuck kind of a serial killer-rapist was she dealing with? Didn't matter, his 'gently subdue the girl' approach was going to work to her advantage. As soon as she had a hand free she went for his eyes. He moved his head, dropping it against her chest so her nails raked down the side of his neck. She was gratified to hear him grunt in pain.

Then he decided to get serious. He used his legs to pin her flailing limbs, gripped her hands together in one of his and slammed them over her head. He twisted her face to the side, a large hand wrapped around her jaw, and he leaned in until his lips were just over her ear.

"You need to stop fighting me, Raina. Right. Fucking. Now."

His use of her name immobilized her better than anything else he'd done or said. He knew her name. He fucking knew her name! So, this wasn't just some random kidnapping. She was his intended victim. Somehow, that thought made her situation even scarier. Had this been a random attack, a crime of opportunity, then he truly wasn't invested in her. Maybe she could've fought until she escaped and found a security guard. Instead she was being held in the arms of a man who knew her name, knew she would be walking home alone tonight. A man who seemed determined to take her. He was invested in her kidnapping.

Once she quit fighting he eased his grip on her chin.

"Why are you doing this?" she asked, trying to make her voice a hard demand, but it sounded more breathless and frightened.

"I was charged with finding and acquiring you," he said, shifting until they were both sitting. He moved her hands to the front of her body, still clasped in his hard grip. "My boss wants you where he can keep an eye on you, baby."

She stared at him like he was insane. "I'm not going anywhere with you! I have midterms next week."

"I think," he drawled, his dark eyes gleaming under the dim campus lighting, "you'll have to take a pass. In fact, probably best to take the year off. I suspect you won't be back for awhile."

"Like fucking hell!" she snapped and tried to kick out at him. He shoved himself between her legs and yanked her up against his chest, holding her in an unbreakable embrace. She went with her last resort, the death glare.

He opened his mouth to say something, his fingers tightening around her when a voice interrupted them. "Hey! You okay over there?" She twisted around to see, thought it might be one of the security guards, but the man holding her yanked her fully against his chest. He pulled something from his jacket and pressed it against her side. Not into her body, but pointing away, toward the person who was striding toward them.

Then he kissed her. Full on the mouth, lips pressed against hers. She gasped, accidentally breathing in his scent, a mix of spicy cigar and man. She was too shocked to push back or struggle. She lay frozen against him, accepting the strange moment for what it was. Her first kiss. She wasn't like other girls. Hadn't had a chance to grow up normal. Though she loved to do normal stuff like everyone else, her illness had stopped her. As a result she'd become sheltered as a child, overprotected by well-meaning parents.

Before her brain could fully engage and tell her she needed to snap back to reality, the stranger kissing her lifted his lips a fraction of an inch from hers and whispered, his warm breath rushing over her, "If you say anything, I will kill him. Do you understand, Raina?"

She stared at him in dazed fascination. Who was he? Where was he from? And why were some serial killers so damn attractive?

Apparently she didn't answer him quick enough, because he gave her a little shake, tightened his already hard grip on her arms and said, "I have killed before, chica, many times. You want the death of this man on your conscience?"

His words snapped her back to reality, made her realize

the severity of her situation. He'd killed before! The thought made her heart thunder against her ribcage and another surge of adrenaline to rush through her. She shook her head in a quick, no.

"Then you need to follow my lead. I was walking you back to your dormitory when we got carried away. Nothing else, understand?"

She nodded and held her breath as he leaned in to kiss her again. She felt the press of his gun against her as the guard approached. Her eyes filled with tears as she fought the desperate need to cry out for help. But she couldn't. She didn't want to be the cause of anyone getting hurt. Gripping her hair tightly, as though to warn her, the man turned to the guard, his entire demeanor changing from sinister to lovestruck.

"Good evening officer. Was just walking my girl back to her dorm when we started messing around. Sorry to bother you!" His voice took on a flawless American accent, losing his smooth Latin accent. She barely registered what the security guard said in response. Something about moving along. He nodded, his hair brushing her forehead, his grip still painfully tight. "Of course, sir. I'll just see her back to her room safe and sound and be on my way."

The guard said goodnight and moved away. Raina let out a choked sob as she watched her hope of rescue stride quickly away from them and disappear around the side of a dormitory. Her captor eased his grip and maneuvered her face away from his.

His eyes were hot on her face when he spoke. "Now, you want to stop fighting me, baby girl, or do we do this the hard way?"

She thought about her options, thought about the various possibilities involved in her kidnapping. "Fuck you!" she hissed angrily.

He chuckled and ran his thumb down her arm, where he held her. "You are just like your mother, aren't you?"

She knew her eyes were bugging at his words. Not for one second did she think he meant her adoptive mom. No, he was talking about the woman that birthed and abandoned her. The woman Raina had spent years trying to track down. How did he know her mother? Was he going to take her to the woman?

Before Raina could ask these vitally important questions he stabbed something into her neck. "Ouch!" She reached up to touch the spot. "What did you do?"

He stood, pulling her to her feet. She swayed as dark floaties swarmed her vision. He held her tight against him, his arms wrapped around her back. Her brain was becoming fuzzy and she was starting to feel like she was floating. He turned them around and began walking, too swift for her to keep up.

"But seriously dude, what did you give me?" she asked, her voice drifting through the night. She giggled as she realized how odd her voice sounded when it was coming through a tunnel. Slurred and garbled. She doubted he even knew what she tried to say.

She stumbled against him and reached out to grab his leather jacket. He held her against his side, protectively, she thought. Which was a stupid thought. He was kidnapping her, which was hurting her to begin with. Why would he want to protect her? She tripped over a curb as they entered a parking lot and he caught her before she could fall, swinging her legs out from beneath her and holding her in his arms. She reached out to grip his shoulders, hold onto something solid and stop the spinning, but she accidentally clipped him in the jaw.

She thought he might get mad, but when he looked down

at her he was grinning broadly. Both of his heads floating in her vision were smiling.

"You're going to be a handful, aren't you princess?"

She sighed heavily and allowed her eyelids to close, shutting out the weird floaties and his scarily handsome face. "Probably," she whispered before passing out.

# CHAPTER THIRTEEN

Vee shivered under her blanket, curling tighter against herself. It didn't matter what she did, she couldn't seem to get warm. As far as she was concerned Canadians were insane for embracing their frigid cold environment. She saw them, out and about, doing their daily business and playing outdoor winter sports. Packed into fluffy snow outfits like sausages. If she'd had a choice, Canada would probably not have been on her list of places to flee. At least not during the winter months.

But her choices were slim. Cuba would have been her first choice. She'd had good relations there, with Tony's former countrymen. They hadn't blamed her for his death. In fact, they had seen Tony as a weak leader, a man prone to vices, an embarrassment to the underworld. But she stood out in Cuba and the island wasn't big enough for someone like her to get lost indefinitely. She couldn't go to Mexico, at least not quickly. Not without getting in touch with one of her former contacts, someone not connected with Domingo. And she couldn't fly out of the US, not without leaving a paper trail that she had no doubt Sotza could easily follow.

So she'd crossed the border into Canada using a fake passport and was in the process of trying to blend. It wasn't easy laying low in a small town, a few hundred kilometres outside of St. John's, New Brunswick. There was absolutely nothing sexy about layers but she'd quickly learned that they were essential to survival. She stood out in the town, people knowing immediately that she didn't belong. But they greeted her friendly enough. One of the townspeople even suggested she trade in her stiletto boots for something a little hardier. She thought he was making fun of her but then he gave her directions to a store and suggested a few brands. She was pretty sure Canadians were insane, but she liked them. The ones she met so far anyway. Even the guy she rented her little cabin from came out to chop wood for her fireplace and check on her a few times a week.

It'd been two weeks since she left Miami. The only contact she made back home was with Danny. She'd begged him to come with her, or to go somewhere else. To leave the city that was now unsafe for both of them. He'd politely refused, and she'd understood. Danny's whole life was in Florida. He was born and raised there, had a mom and sisters. A sweetheart he'd been dating for awhile. He wasn't prepared to cut and run.

When she talked to him yesterday, Danny had given her a desperate picture of her home town. "Sotza has everyone under his control. He's placed someone new at the top, but everyone knows that Sotza's pulling the strings. He had Grant Shaw taken out. From the condition of the body, I'd say The Butcher did it himself."

"Shaw isn't exactly a loss to the world." Vee had replied of the dead neo-Nazi, though she shuddered at the destruction Sotza was causing.

"No, Shaw was a piece of work, but Steve Cruz will be a loss."

"What happened to Cruz?" Her stomach twisted. Cruz had been a go-with-the-flow sort of guy. A man whose loyalty floated on the breeze, toward whoever paid better and hurt less. Sotza probably picked him up on the streets, put him to work and then got rid of him when he realized Cruz was pretty useless. He'd been an incompetent idiot whenever she had to deal with him, but he hadn't deserved to die.

"You don't want to know," Danny said grimly.

She inhaled sharply. No, she really didn't want to know.

"What about you?" she asked. "I hate that I had to leave you behind. I really wish you'd reconsider coming up here to Canada. Bring your family, bring your girl. Whatever you need. But please, get out of the line of fire."

She didn't think she could stand to lose Danny on top of everything else. He'd been a good friend, her closest associate. A second-in-command, but also a self-appointed bodyguard. If Sotza got to Danny, Vee didn't know what she would do.

"I'm okay," he reiterated for about the $50^{th}$ time since she'd gone into hiding. "Pretty sure The Butcher knows exactly where I am and where to find me. Hasn't stopped by for a chat though. Which is a cause for concern."

Vee frowned. "Why is that? If he's leaving you alone, shouldn't you be happy about it? No one wants a face-to-face with that guy."

"It's not me I'm worried about, boss. If he's not here asking me about your whereabouts then that tells me he probably knows exactly where you are. Or at least how to find you. My guess is it's just a matter of time before he heads up your way."

"No," Vee whispered.

"You need to think about your next move. Get out of there, find someplace else more remote. Someplace that no one knows about... not even me. If he gets to me I'll try to hold out, but we've both seen what he's capable of. He has ways of getting all the information he needs before sending his victims to hell."

Tears stung her eyes. She didn't want to lose the one connection to home she had left. The one friend who would do whatever it took to keep her safe. If, in her bid for freedom, she let Danny go, then she would be truly alone.

She swallowed and said, "I'm not ready for that yet. If he knows where to find me, why hasn't he made a move yet? No, I'm not ready to cut ties yet."

Danny didn't say anything for several long minutes. She could feel his need to argue with her, but all he said was, "Just take care of yourself, boss. Keep your head up, eyes open and weapon close."

"Always," she promised.

"Call me tomorrow night," he said sternly. "Mandatory check ins until you feel ready to go to ground for good."

"Yes, boss," she replied with a small smile.

His voice still held a note of worry. "Goodnight, Vee."

"Goodnight, Danny. Hi to the family."

After she ended the call, Vee stared into the darkness of the room, seeing nothing. It was always pitch black here at night unless she had the fireplace running or turned on a light. She felt bad for worrying Danny. He really was the closest thing to a best friend that she had. Besides Casey. The two women had become close in the past year, but distance kept them from seeing each other more than a few times. Perhaps she would call Danny back in the morning and let him know she was going to disappear. It would ease his mind.

She crammed one of the pillows against her stomach, tucked a hand underneath her head and drifted to sleep feeling a little safer knowing she would set a more permanent escape plan in motion.

Firelight flickered behind her closed lids, warming her chilled body. The crackling of burning wood drifted through her subconscious. She sighed, feeling more content, more comfortable than she had in a long time. As she swam gently toward wakefulness her dream world gradually melted away. She'd been dreaming that she was at lunch with Casey and the rest of their Tuesday crew. She'd hated the entire bunch of hypocritical, cynical bitches, until she got to know Casey and found a woman as damaged as herself. She'd taken the younger woman under her wing, as much as she could at the time. She would miss Casey when it came time to flee for good. But Casey was loyal to her husband, Vee couldn't divulge her whereabouts without the information making its way back to Sotza.

As she slowly became aware it occurred to her that she hadn't started a fire the evening before. She'd wanted to save the last of her wood for an upcoming cold snap. Her eyes flew open and she sat up in the bed, lunging for her gun on the nightstand. She searched for it, squinting at the shadows, nearly knocking over a glass of water in her frantic scramble. It was gone. Of course.

She shifted into the centre of the bed, pressing her back against the headboard. She shoved a handful of hair out of her face and yanked the quilt up her body, covering her breasts and wishing she was wearing something less revealing than the satin spaghetti strap sleep top. Her eyes travelled the room until her gaze landed on the chair that sat a few feet away from the fireplace. It had been turned so it was facing the bed. She couldn't make him out; he was a shadowy figure and a pair of legs.

"Sotza," she said, her voice nearly a whisper. It was like seeing a phantom. A nightmare come to life. Her heart pounded so hard in her chest that it ached. She pressed a hand between her breasts to ease the feeling, the quilt still clutched against her.

"Vee." That one syllable. His accented voice. It was like deep, dark velvet the way he caressed her name. He didn't move, didn't say anything else. Just sat watching her.

She wanted to say something snappy, something brave. But she was vulnerable. Alone in a cabin in the middle of nowhere, nearly naked. And she was desperately frightened. She had faced down bad situations, held her own among the baddest of them and kept her shit together. But Sotza was different. He couldn't be defeated with words, with bullets or with false bravado. He saw through everything and took lives that were in his way as if they were nothing but specks of dust on his well-tailored suit.

"Are you here to kill me?" She hardly dared to breath. She had no way to fight back if he attacked her. Her only weapon was gone and she didn't for a moment think she could match him in physical combat.

He gripped the arms of the chair and stood. She barely had time to blink and he was standing next to her, beside the bed. She flinched, tried to still the shivers that racked her body, hold the terrible fear inside.

"It has never been my intention to kill you," he said quietly.

She swallowed and licked her lips, then turned her head to the side, looking up at him. The firelight caressed his sharp hawk-like features, making the craggy valleys of his face more pronounced. She thought maybe he hadn't shaved in awhile, several days worth of beard growth darkened his jaw.

"Wouldn't it be easier if I was dead? You wouldn't have to look over your shoulder, wouldn't have to worry about me coming back to Miami, taking back what's mine."

His lips curved into a semi-smile at her little jab. "No,

Vee, your death isn't an option. I've told you this, it's time for you to stop being afraid of me, stop running."

She could see the dark gleam of his eyes in the flickering light, fixed on her, never wavering. "What do you want from me, Sotza?" she asked, trying to be brave.

He seemed to realize that she hadn't meant the obvious. That she was brushing aside his standing marriage proposal and looking for a deeper explanation. "I want everything you have, everything that you are. I want everything you never gave your husband or anyone before him."

She shuddered and curled her legs up against her chest. "You have the wrong woman. I'm not anything special and I have nothing to give you."

He chuckled. "I won't waste time trying flatter you, Vee. Not yet. But rest assured, you are everything I want in a woman, in a wife."

She shook her head, her bangs flopping in her eyes. Fuck, she needed a haircut. Shoving the bangs aside she glared at him. "You're wrong. I'll be a terrible wife. I'll fight you every step of the way. I'll make your life miserable until you have no choice but to get rid of me."

He considered her for a moment and then said, "You really don't have much respect for your own life, do you Vee? I'm not sure if your attitude is a turn on or if it's going to get you in trouble."

She stared up at him. She hadn't meant to throw attitude at him. She really wasn't kidding when she said he would eventually want to kill her. Very few people liked Vee in the long term. Not her family, not her dead husband. She'd been completely dispensable until she took Reyes' offer to take over the Miami underworld. She'd been mafia royalty until Sotza showed up and destroyed all of her hard work in a few short weeks, knocking her off her throne so easily.

"It will never work," she said bitterly. "I'll try to either kill you or run away at every opportunity." Maybe she was stupid for verbalizing her thoughts, but Sotza saw right through her, the way he saw through everyone. He had to know that if he forced her into a union it would become all out warfare. She would make Miami look like a tense tea party.

Still, part of her looked forward to making his life miserable. She knew, no matter what she said or did in the next few minutes she would be leaving with him. She just didn't have the tools at her disposal to get away from him. He was obviously able to track her. Hell, Danny was probably right, Sotza probably knew exactly where she was all alone. Had a bead on her, men sitting on her location, watching in case she made a move.

"I'm not going to make this easy for you," she said stiffly, tensing her body, getting ready to fight and run.

"I wouldn't expect this to go any other way." His voice was a smooth caress that flowed over her skin like the satin of her pyjamas. It wasn't fair that such a horror show should be so sexy. "You're a fighter, Vee. The battle just makes the prize that much sweeter."

"Don't sound so pleased," she snapped.

He laughed, this time the sound was full-throated, deep and mesmerizing. She had to remind herself that she was about to try to fight for her life.

"If you force me to fight you, Vee, I will be taking a kiss for my efforts."

She snorted at the old-fashioned, chauvinistic logic. "Try it and I'll bite your tongue off."

"I have no doubt you'll try," he replied easily.

Neither of them made a move as they watched each other in the shadowy room, the crackle of the fire as loud as a gunshot in the silence. Fear overwhelmed her, along with a healthy, if belated, shot of adrenaline. She recognized this moment as the turning point that it was. Her life was about to change. If Sotza took her away with him her life would no longer belong to herself. He'd take away her independence, she'd lose the freedom to make her own decisions. She would be trapped in another mafia marriage. She feared this one would prove more terrifying, more agonizing than the last one she'd endured.

"You won't stop will you?" she asked, her voice barely a whisper.

He didn't answer her question. Instead he said, "It's time to go, Vee."

# CHAPTER FOURTEEN

Sotza lunged for Vee, so fast she barely registered what was happening. One moment he was standing beside her, talking leisurely as though he had all the time in the world. Next moment he was on top of her, crushing her into the mattress, immobilizing her. She tried to fight, she really did, but it was like a huge sack full of bricks had dropped on her. Vee was small and sleight, but she liked to think she knew how to throw her weight around like it meant something. Sotza quickly proved otherwise, pinning her arms against her body and holding her with a ruthless ease.

"Get off me!" she snarled. "You weigh a fucking ton."

"Are you going to stop fighting?" he asked, easing his weight slightly, but not moving off her. She was trapped under his tall, wiry frame with no way out.

"Yes," she hissed, lying, quite literally, to his face. "What's the point in a struggle. We both know you'll win."

He studied her, his face mere inches from hers. The subtle spicy smell of his cologne touched her senses, making her stomach feel like jelly. "I don't believe you, Vee," he said, his voice growing deeper. She was affecting him. Her body under his, her nearness.

Her mouth watered as she studied his firm lips. She had to give herself a quick mental shake. She absolutely could not lust after the psycho killer. "What do I have to gain by fighting you?" she asked, her own voice husky now.

"Everything," he said, his grip on her arms tightening in warning as he lowered his head. "You have everything to gain by fighting and everything to gain by surrendering. You see, my lovely lady, the end will be the same no matter what you do. I take you, I keep you, you belong to me."

She opened her mouth to tell him to fuck off, but like the hawk he resembled, he swooped, taking her lips in a kiss that shook her to her core. This was no subtle touching of mouths, no gentle exploration. This was a claiming. His lips crushed hers, his tongue invading her mouth, stealing everything she refused to give. Sotza was telling her without words that she was done running and that he was dictating her future now.

*Fuck that!* She was not about to become the conquest of yet another mob boss. Another man who would use her for sex and set her up as a trophy.

She snapped her teeth together in an attempt to sink them into his tongue. He anticipated her move though and retreated for a few seconds, long enough to bring his hand up and grip her jaw in a bruising hold, forcing her mouth open. She let out a garbled protest, but he swallowed the sound in another kiss, this one more intense, more brutal than the last. This was not the prelude to a lover's tryst, this was war. He was raping her mouth, telling her exactly how things would stand between them.

Tears formed in her eyes. She struggled for breath whenever he gave her the opportunity, sucking in quick gasps before he once more settled his mouth over hers, punishing her. He didn't explore her body, didn't tear her clothes away, as she halfway expected. He just assaulted her mouth until she stopped struggling. Once she lay unmoving beneath him, the fight stolen from her, he relaxed the brutality of his kisses, softening them. He still held her jaw immobile, open for his use, but some of her fear ebbed as his kisses turned more playful, more passionate. Like he was rewarding her for not fighting him.

He kissed her lips, licked the inside of her mouth, her teeth, everything. Then he finally allowed his grip to relax, his lips trailing heated kisses across her cheek to her ear and down her neck. Heat flooded her, a warm melting sensation in her stomach.

He lifted his head, looked down at her. His thumb caressed her face, sliding from her chin to her stinging lips. There was a flash of surprise in his eyes, quickly replaced by a hardening of resolve. His cool, authoritarian façade dropped for a moment and she saw the man beneath The Butcher, saw his need to possess her and own her in those soulless depths. But it was that fleeting moment of surprise that terrified her. Her heart beat a frightened tattoo against her chest as they studied each other. She wondered if he would decide he didn't want her, didn't want this. That she'd been fine as the ice queen that would stand at his side, but now that he discovered fire between them, he was having second thoughts.

Finally, after minutes had passed, he spoke. "You have everything to gain by coming to me willingly, Vee. I can give you the world."

Her breath caught in her throat and she tensed. Far from being too freaked out to follow through on his grand plans involving her, he now seemed even more determined to have her. For a split second she thought about the possibilities of what he asked, thought about what life could be like at his side, his queen, his wife.

But no, eventually he would hurt her like Tony did. Memories of the subjugation and pain flooded through her, fresh, as though it had all happened yesterday. She'd known every kind of pain there was to know at Tony's hands. She'd discovered a depth of hatred, directed at both her late husband and herself, that she hadn't known existed. And most of it had hit her after his death, after she'd sobered up. The sharp sting of pain was so much more real when there were no substances to mitigate the awful feelings.

She narrowed her eyes at the man who held her down, tried to force her acceptance and dictate her future. "Fuck you," she hissed, reaching up with the hand he was no longer pinning to the bed and taking a handful of his hair. She yanked his head back as hard as she could. He was caught by surprise, his head following the movement of her fist so he didn't lose a bunch of hair in her vicious hold. She reached behind herself, gripping the hilt of the knife she'd strapped in a short leather sheath against the small of her back. She brought the knife between them and placed it against his jugular. She'd been waiting for this moment, waiting for him to get close enough that she could pull her ace. "I'm not going anywhere with you. You'll have to kill me first."

# CHAPTER FIFTEEN

Vee suspected Sotza could easily overpower her, snap her neck before she even knew what was happening. She saw it in his eyes. Saw it, digested it, and still pressed the tip of the knife against his throat. Fuck it. If she was going down, at the very least she was going to spill a few drops of his blood in the process.

He didn't give her a chance. He twisted away from the knife is one fast, fluid motion. Brutally gripped her wrist, lifted himself slightly and flipped her, forcing her stomach to the mattress, her face smashed into the pillow. He yanked the blankets away from her body, uncovering her sleep top, which was shoved halfway up her back exposing the sheath, and her brief silk shorts. He twisted her arm behind her back, pressing the knife between her shoulder blades before coming down on top of her again. He lay across her body, full weight against her. She held her breath, keenly aware that the sharp blade of the knife was pressed between them, not cutting, but oh so close.

Vee whimpered softly. She didn't want to die, not really. She was only 37 years old. Though she'd lived a lifetime in those years, she also felt like she hadn't lived at all. Hadn't travelled, hadn't known true love, didn't get to finish her run as mafia queen. Although, if she died today, she would really only have one regret.

Sotza leaned harder into her, crushing the breath from her chest. He pulled her hair to the side, away from her face, his touch oddly gentle, incongruent with the violence of their exchange. "I would prefer my new bride to come with me undamaged, all of her fingers intact."

Vee grunted and tried to wiggle, but his weight overwhelmed her. She couldn't move an inch. She couldn't even draw in enough breath for a scathing retort. Instead, she was forced to lay beneath him and draw in quick, shallow breaths. Time slowed. Spots began to swarm her vision and she feared she would pass out if he didn't move.

Finally, he eased his weight just enough for her to draw breath. She wanted to swear at him, to keep fighting, even if it was just verbally. But good sense prevailed and she kept her mouth shut.

"Give me the blade, Vee," he said, a hard edge to his voice. His breath tickled her ear and sent a shiver through her.

She nodded slightly, the movement causing his chin to brush her neck. The intimacy was getting to her. Her body was responding to him. She knew if she checked her panties she'd find herself wet. What was it about these violent pricks that turned her on so much? At least her head knew better than to get involved with this one.

"Fine," she muttered. "Move your heavy ass and it's all yours."

He shifted, leaning the top of his body slightly to the side. He still held her arm wrenched up her back, his long fingers wrapped tight around her wrist. She could feel the tensile strength in his hold. Could feel the depth of his control. He could so easily snap her wrist or break her arm. Yet, though his grip was firm, she didn't feel in danger of an injury. It chilled her to the bone that Sotza knew exactly how and where to apply pressure. He would know how to make his victims suffer, draw out the pain while keeping them alive for torture.

"Slowly now," he commanded her.

Vee was both glad and annoyed at the healthy respect he was showing for her ability and willingness to cut him. If he was wary of her then he'd keep a close eye on her and she might never get the opportunity to murder him. She opened her fingers one at a time, releasing the blade. He took it from her. She heard the clatter of it hitting the floor as he tossed it off the side of the bed. He took her wrist and pulled her arm around to her side and then up by her head. She was surprised when he didn't let her go, move away and get on with her kidnapping. Instead he spread his fingers over top of hers and linked their hand. He shifted his body on top of her, took her other hand and did the same thing, bringing it up beside her head and linking their fingers.

That moment, them together, the fire crackling in the background casting warm, flickering shadows across the walls, could have been the most romantic moment of her life. If he wasn't such a fucking psycho. As they lay together, breathing together, the heat of their bodies mingling, all she could think was, *what's next?* Was he going to haul her out of there, take her back to Miami? Or maybe Venezuela?

"We should be together, Vee," he said quietly, speaking in her ear again, his chin resting against the side of her head. "Don't you see how good we'd be? How powerful? You're smart, beautiful and kind. You would complement me in every way."

Vee let out a breathless laugh. "Kind?" she gasped. He was back to crushing her again, although not quite as much as before. "You did see what I did to Luis before you decapitated him, right?"

"So you can hold your own, make tough decisions when needed. We both know, as a leader, you should've killed Luis, made an example of the man. He wavered in his loyalties. I had your back on that one, made sure his loyalty was unquestionable."

"You're a fucking serial killer is what you are!" she hissed. "You kill them if they remain loyal and you kill them if they switch sides. No one stood a chance when you decided to take my city."

"All is fair —"

"I swear to god if you say 'all's fair in love and war' I will find the super human strength to get you off my back and stab the shit out of you."

He chuckled. "And a sense of humour, Vee. You're the whole package." He moved, sliding to her side and sitting up. She tried to roll away from him, but he grabbed hold of her and flipped her onto her back, pinning her arms over her head. She glared at him, the fight reigniting in her eyes. He narrowed his eyes and frowned. "No more, Vee. I really don't want to hurt you."

"I don't understand why you're doing this! If you think I'm the *whole package*," she said scathingly, "then why don't you let me have Miami back? You can set me back up as the queen and then have my back when I need it. We could've done that in the first place, saved all this drama, saved those lives."

"It's too late," he said, his voice a low rumble as his eyes were drawn to her exposed stomach, where her top had ridden up. "Beautiful," he murmured. "Perfect curves, silky skin."

"It's not too late!" she cried out. "What do you want from

me? I'll give it to you. Do you want to fuck? We can do that, just promise you'll let me go."

He gave her a chiding look. "You are worth so much more than just a fuck, Vee. Don't underestimate yourself."

She blew her bangs out of her face, annoyed and frustrated, still a little afraid, although she was about ready to believe he had no intention of killing her. "I'm worth exactly what I say I'm worth," she snarled. "Wouldn't be the first time I traded sex for favours."

He stared down at her, his gaze heated. She didn't know what he was thinking. If he was pissed off, pitying, contemptuous. Finally, he replied, "I really think you believe that."

"Of course I do!" she said, yanking on her wrists, trying to free them from his grip. "I used to fuck Tony for all kinds of things. Jewelry, money, drugs, the right to breathe."

His fingers tightened around her hands. He hadn't liked that. "I meant," he said, his voice taking on a hard edge, "that you believe you aren't worth much."

She frowned. What the fuck was this? A therapy session? Was he trying to raise her sense of self-worth, give the old self-esteem a boost? "You're a strange man," she said drily. "Fine, I'm worth a lot. Like, how about a city? Yeah, I'm probably worth the cost of Miami."

He chuckled and then stopped, looked surprised. When he looked down at her it was with a peculiar expression, soft, determined, caring. It made her heart trip. "Vee, mi amor, you make me laugh. I don't do that enough."

"I'm not trying to be funny, asshole."

"You don't have to try to be anything, Elvira. You just are," he said.

"Don't call me that!" she practically shouted. "And can we please get on with this, whatever it is. My arms are getting sore from being wrenched around and held down so much."

His lips curved up and he released her hands. "Whatever the lady wishes."

Vee snorted and brought her arms down. She shoved herself up the mattress, pressing her back against the headboard. "This lady wants you to die. Immediately, if it's not too inconvenient."

He laughed again and reached for her knife, turning his back on her for a second. She eyed the spot right between his shoulder blades. If she had a second knife that's exactly where it would go.

He turned back to her, gave her tiny pyjamas another heated look and said, "You'll need to get changed. All that bare skin will freeze in this climate. Frankly, I'm a little shocked that you chose Canada as an escape. It's vast, easy to get lost, I'll give you that. But is it worth trying to survive in a frozen wasteland?"

"I happen to love it here," she gritted, ignoring the inner voice that agreed with him completely. The one upside of his kidnapping her is she was pretty sure he was going to take her back south. Still, she wasn't going to give him an inch. "Very fucking beautiful."

She got off the bed cautiously, halfway expecting him to yank her back. He allowed her to stand, following her movements as she paced to the wardrobe and started pulling out clothing. A pair of jeans, a hooded sweater, a pair of panties, bra and socks. When she turned back to him and raised an eyebrow he made no move to leave.

"I'm not changing with you here."

He stood, his tall frame towering next to the bed. "Then you'll be leaving dressed like that. It's going to be a cold trip, but my men will enjoy the view."

Hatred burned in her chest. She wanted to scream at him, lash out and strike him. If she thought she had even a remote chance of landing a blow she might've done it. Instead, she reminded herself that she was a mature adult and that one of these days the tables would be turned. He'd turn his back on her at the wrong time, in the wrong place and she would take extreme pleasure in taking him out.

"I can see your thoughts, my dear." He didn't sound angry though. He sounded like he was anticipating her rage, revelling in the experience.

"You are a twisted man," she growled and yanked on the jeans. She decided against the bra since she had no intention of baring herself in front of him. She was small-chested anyway, didn't need to wear a bra all the time. She pulled the sweater over her head and then sat on the edge of the bed, as far away from him as she could get, to put her socks on.

When she finished and looked up, he was standing in front of her reaching a hand out to her. She ignored it and stood on her own, stepping quickly to the side. He didn't stop her as she left the bedroom.

"Coat and boots," he told her, following her into the main room. "Wear all of your new winter gear. You'll need it for the ride to the airport. We have to drive into St. John's before we can fly out."

"A little midnight cross-country kidnapping," she grumbled as she sat on the bench next to the door to pull her boots on. "Sure, why not, why don't you maim a few people while you're up here? Really make a vacation out of it. Show Canada who The Butcher is and why he has such a devastating reputation."

"Vee," he said her name warningly. "You don't want to cross the line with me."

She stood up and yanked her fluffy winter cherry red parka on. She probably needed a few lessons in the art of blending in, but Vee was never one to follow the pack. When she was ready to go, she stood toe-to-toe with Sotza, glaring up at him. This close, without her signature heels, he towered over her.

"You know what, Sotza?" she snarled, poking him in the chest. "You obliterated the line when you came after me, took my city apart and killed half my town. I don't fucking care about crossing the line with you. In fact, I anticipate it with pleasure."

Instead of responding to her angry tirade, he caught her hand before she could storm out the door. He fished into his pocket and pulled the engagement ring he'd given her back in Miami, brought her hand up between them and pushed it onto her finger. "This doesn't come off again, comprende?"

For once, she didn't argue. His grim expression told her the consequences would be severe.

# CHAPTER SIXTEEN

"You need to eat."

Raina clenched her fist around her fork and glowered at Mateo who was sitting to her left at the head of the table. It'd been nearly a week since her kidnapping. The most she'd gotten out of her captor was his name and that they were waiting for her mother to arrive. She had gleaned a hell of a lot more all by herself, since Mateo's default setting seemed to be silence, even though she taunted him and pushed him at every opportunity.

Raina was pretty sure she'd been taken far south. When she'd woken up she'd found herself on board a private airplane, flying a long way from Pennsylvania. Probably Central or South America given his accent and the easy Spanish that flowed among the house staff when they spoke around her. She figured out that she was staying in the main house or mansion or whatever they called this crazy big house, but there were other buildings on the property. She assumed Mateo lived in one of the other buildings because he didn't stay in the house with her. She wasn't allowed to explore beyond the gardens surrounding the house. And she always had an armed escort to ensure she complied. Near as she could tell Mateo was some kind of temporary babysitter, though given his stature and the fearful respect he received from other staff she assumed he did other, more important things with his time.

After a week of watching routines, inspecting the house and gardens and watching the people within, Raina was fairly certain she could escape. Two things stopped her. She still didn't have a damn clue where she was or how far from civilization she'd been taken. It would majorly suck if she managed to escape only to die in some jungle. The other reason she stayed was because she knew her mother was flying in soon. Though she wanted to be indifferent to her womb donor, she was curious. She had questions to ask and things to say before she was ready to walk away from the woman.

Raina dropped the fork, crossed her arms over her chest and said haughtily, "Eating would imply I condone this kidnapping." She gave him a cold stare. "In case you're in doubt, I really don't."

He stared boldly back at her, his tanned face emotionless. There was a gleam of something in his dark eyes. She thought maybe appreciation, though she hoped for annoyance. "You don't look starved to me, chica."

She glowered. "Are you calling me fat, chico?"

He laughed. "Hardly." His eyes roved over her sleight curves.

Of course, he wasn't calling her fat, she barely weighed 115 lbs. She'd been small all her life. Unhappily she'd given up waiting for her boobs to come in about a year ago.

"I mean you look strong enough to me, Señorita. Like you've been getting into the kitchen perhaps, eating plenty."

"And perhaps I simply don't enjoy enforced mealtimes with the fucker who kidnapped me."

The smile left his face. He lifted his napkin and dabbed it against his lips. "I will have the kitchen locked up at night, staff will be instructed that you are not to be fed unless it is at the table."

She tilted her head, long hair sweeping against the back of the chair. "That's a nasty move, Mateo. Really beneath you, I think."

"Oh, Señorita Raina, you have no idea how low I can sink." The look on his face told her he was more than happy to show her just how mean he could be, should she step too far out of line.

"I would really prefer to eat on my own, in my room. Is my company at the evening meal really worth all this?" she asked.

"Absolutamente." His low voice sent a shiver right down her back.

She gripped the edge of her seat and watched him warily. Raina wasn't a naïve girl. Though she hadn't experienced much of the world in her 19 years, she had eyes, attitude and a good solid brain. She knew how things worked. Yet with Mateo she couldn't figure out what he wanted. One moment she would catch him watching her, intently, maybe lustfully. The next she thought he might want to get his hands on her for another, more violent reason.

He was an intense man. Good-looking in a hard, rugged way. He moved with ease, yet his movements had purpose. As though he thought everything through at lightning speed and then executed. She'd discovered, when he kidnapped her from the campus, just how fast and ruthless he could be. Yet, he hadn't touched her since their arrival. She got this impending sense that he was simply waiting... for something. Probably her mother's arrival, but she couldn't figure out why unless her mother had ordered Raina's abduction. God, she hoped not. She didn't need another reason to hate the woman.

She stared down at the food, convinced that he would indeed starve her into submission. If she was smart she would start eating. Still, Raina had never been one to go the easy way. The way people wanted her to go. In fact, the more she felt pushed into something, the less likely she was to do it.

"You ever seen Beauty and the Beast?" she asked. "The Beast tries to starve Beauty unless she agrees to eat with him."

"Interesting," he said. "And how does this tale end? Did she die of starvation?"

Raina smirked. "No, the manor staff fed her behind his back. They nourished the heroine when the villain refused her basic sustenance."

"The difference," he drawled, "between fairy-tale and reality is that the staff here are human, not clocks and candlesticks. They can bleed, they can hurt and they can die. Very easily, mia chica. These people, they will not help you. They know the consequences of disobeying my orders."

Her mouth went dry and she had to take a quick swallow of water from the crystal goblet in front of her. "So you know the story," she snapped, avoiding eye contact. "Could've just said in the first place."

"But I do enjoy sparring with you, sweet Raina."

Her nostrils flared and she glared hard at the table, still refusing to look up at him. He'd shaken her. She had her suspicions, from the way Mateo spoke, the movements of the staff, the armed guards and they're location, deep in some kind of jungle well south of the US. Mafia. It was the only thing that made sense. The careless way Mateo spoke of torturing the mansion staff. The ease in which he'd kidnapped her. She thought, maybe she'd somehow gotten caught up in the underworld scene. Who exactly was her mother?

"I think your master will not be pleased with my treatment under your care, Mateo." She was making a leap in logic, thinking Mateo wasn't the one who'd had her kidnapped, that maybe he wasn't the head honcho. Though he was strong, smart and capable enough. "Careful, or I might tell him exactly how you're mistreating me."

He dropped his napkin on the table and stood. It took him barely a second and he was right next to her chair, overwhelming her with his size, his scent, his essence. She sat stiffly in her chair, determined not to move. His chin was inches from the top of her head. "No man is my master."

He dropped a kiss on the top of her head, ruffling the fine blond strands. He straightened and strode from the room. She stared after him, for some stupid reason looking forward to their next encounter, the next meal.

She eyed the food in front of her, Atlantic salmon with a dill sauce, sweet peas and herbed rice. It looked delicious, but she'd lost her appetite. She dropped her own napkin on the table and pushed her chair back. It seemed as though she would just have wait until the arrival of her mother. She wasn't getting a damn thing out of Mateo. No matter which way she baited him, the bastard simply wouldn't give.

# CHAPTER SEVENTEEN

"This isn't Miami," Vee observed, watching from the window as Sotza's private jet prepared to land. She felt the gentle thump of the wheels lowering.

"You are correct," Sotza said from beside her, not looking up from his laptop. He'd been on it since shortly after their take-off from St. John's. He'd seated her, ensured her comfort and introduced her to the flight attendant. Though he didn't bother to introduce her to the five or six guys sitting further back on the plane. They in turn didn't look up when Vee was escorted onto the aircraft.

Vee eyed the mountainous rainforest-like land surrounding the small airport. "Pretty sure this isn't Venezuela either. We haven't been in the air long enough."

Sotza closed his laptop and tucked it away into the leather laptop bag. He leaned into her, forcing her to shift away, closer to the window. He glanced past her, out the window and said, "Your knowledge of geography is exemplary, my dear."

She wanted to scratch his eyes out every time he said something in that deep dry voice with his British accent. It was like being mocked, but so subtly she barely noticed. She suspected this was just Sotza though. He appeared gentlemanly and mild-mannered. Until it was time to go to work.

Two could play that game. Vee was nobody's fool. She had a good, smart head and she could be as much of an asshole as him. "Putting my excellent knowledge of geography to good use," she said coolly leaning toward the window again and studying the landscape. "I would say we're probably in Mexico. Maybe somewhere in the Durango region."

He looked somewhat impressed. "Well done my dear, but no, we are currently landing in the state of Sinaloa, though we're very close to the Durango border."

She should have known. "Business," she muttered.

"Indeed," he said, reaching over to fasten her seatbelt as the plane began sharply descending. "We need to refuel somewhere and, since Domingo is no longer an appropriate Mexican contact, I had to find someone else. I will also be discussing business here, with this contact, mitigating some of the damage on the East coast."

Vee rolled her eyes and tried to shove his hands away, but he persisted until she was properly belted in. "It's a little hard for Domingo to do much of anything without his head. Good move there, Sotza."

"You couldn't control the man," Sotza said sternly. "He insulted you at every turn and gave his people orders to attack you. His life could no longer be sanctioned."

"God help anyone that looks at you funny," she muttered, staring hard out the window as the plane landed on the runway with a slight bump. From her vantage point, it looked like there were several vehicles further up the runway, ready to meet the plane. Sotza had clearly organized this meeting ahead of time.

"Are you afraid of me, Vee?" Sotza asked gently.

She turned to give him a scathing look, but it fell away as

she was forced to take in his regal, rugged features. The seriousness of his expression, the hidden depths buried in his enigmatic gaze. She took in a sharp breath and decided to tell him the truth. "Yes, of course I'm afraid of you. Anyone with half a brain would be. You cause a wake of destruction everywhere you go, but you do it in such a way that everything is perfectly organized to your specifications once the dust has settled. It's a terrifying prospect to be your captive."

He reached out and ran his thumb over her lips and down to her chin, pinching it slightly before dropping his hand. "The world can fear me, Vee. In fact, the world should fear me. I will rip it to shreds one piece at a time to get at what I want. And I'll enjoy every moment," he said, a small flicker of savage emotion deep in his dark brown eyes. "But you will never have need to fear me."

She studied him for a moment. "Then let me go."

He unbuckled his seatbelt and stood. She realized the plane had stopped and unbuckled her own belt. He stood in front of her, blocking her path. "Never that, Vee," he said, reaching out a hand to help her up. "Don't ask again."

"Fine, I won't ask again. I'll just leave."

She ignored his hand and slipped quickly past him, pushing herself awkwardly to the side to avoid touching him. He took her arm and swung her around until she was facing him. He allowed his mask to slip, let her see some of the things he shielded from the world, his savagery, his obsessive determination to own everything around him. She shivered and tried to step back but he followed her, pressed her against the side of plane. She was forced to curve herself into the small space.

"My patience isn't endless," he said quietly. "Step carefully, Vee. Leaving me will never be an option, not now and not in our future."

She didn't respond at first. How could she? She certainly

didn't agree with his statement. She'd be leaving him at the very first opportunity. But she also suspected she was dancing close to the edge of his patience. The face he projected to the world was of a man whose calm was eternal. But she was beginning to see the man underneath. He was so much more, so much worse than anyone suspected. She needed to know the worst.

"Or what, Sotza? What will you do to me if I leave?"

His answer was immediate, telling her that he never doubted the course he set his actions on. He was as decisive as he was brutal. "I will find you, kill anyone and everyone that helped you. Then hunt and kill everyone you know until I'm certain there's no one left to help you leave. I will make sure that you are so dependent on me that every thought in your head must first be filtered through me."

She gaped up at him as he allowed his terrifying words to settle in, then pulled her out of the corner and tucked her loosely against his side. Even though she had room for movement, could step away if she wanted, his hand wrapped around her arm was unbreakable. He led her to the exit door, which had been opened by the flight attendant. They left the plane together, side by side, a united front. She suspected this was on purpose as there were several men, Mexicans she thought, standing nearby, eyeing them with speculation.

Sotza leaned into her, bending his head until his lips brushed the top of her ear. "You need to follow my lead. These men cannot for one moment believe that you don't belong to me."

Vee glanced at the AK-47's held by some of the men in the group. A show of force, but the loose way in which they were held, pointed at the ground, told her the cartel didn't see them as a threat. Had they never heard of Sotza before? "I'm not stupid, Sotza. I'm not going to draw any unnecessary attention to our situation. Jumping from your care into a Mexican cartel doesn't seem like a smooth move."

"Not stupid," he agreed. "But sometimes reckless with an alarming disregard for your own safety."

She gritted her teeth but refused to respond. In fact, she thought she had a healthy respect for her own life. It's just that some things were more important. The lives of her friends, the safety of her home town. Perhaps Sotza couldn't identify because he'd never had anything he cared enough about to put ahead of his own health. Then again, the man was indestructible. A legend, practically a phantom in the way he worked. One moment there, attacking with speed and brutal precision, the next, gone, a path of devastation behind him.

Vee turned her attention to the man who had stepped out from the group of Mexicans. He was not quite what she was used to when it came to cartel leaders in this part of the world. He wasn't fat, wasn't dressed any differently from his men. He was tall, built strong, his skin deeply tanned, tattoos covering most of the visible parts of his body. The only thing that stood out on him was his arrogance. It showed in the way he stood, the boldness of his gaze as he watched Vee and Sotza approach.

Vee was somewhat surprised when a grin broke across his face, transforming him from brutal leader to carefree man. He spoke Spanish, directing his comments to Sotza. "My old friend, I am proud to have you in my home."

Sotza released Vee and the two men embraced. The other man kept his hand on Sotza's back. Vee was astonished. She didn't think Sotza liked being touched. As long as she'd known him, she was pretty sure she was the only person he'd touched. Weird. She'd gotten the impression that Sotza wasn't close to their host. Why was he insisting on a united front when he knew this other man? Why not tell him that she was his unwilling prisoner? She was starting to wonder if Sotza had used this meeting as an excuse to keep her in line. Or did he genuinely have business?

"And who is this?" The Mexican asked, turning to Vee. "Muy bonito."

Sotza stepped back toward Vee and wrapped his arm around her waist. He gave the other man a mildly stern look and said simply, "This is my fiancé."

Ignoring Sotza's 'stay away from her' signals, the man took Vee's hand and squeezed it, smiling down at her. She really wished she had her heels on. She didn't trust this man and didn't like being a solid foot shorter than him. Even with heels she wouldn't close the gap, but she would narrow it. There was some power to be had in a snazzy outfit that told men she was both equal and all business.

"You are a lovely woman," he said to her in rapid Spanish, his eyes twinkling. "You should leave Senor Sotza, come spend some time with me. My home is beautiful and I am very rich, easily able to afford a woman of your obvious good tastes." Despite his warm reception, she didn't for one second believe he wouldn't gut her if things went sideways. She wanted to roll her eyes and snort. She was still wearing jeans, a hooded sweatshirt and boots. Good taste, right.

Vee glanced curiously at Sotza to see how he was taking the Mexican's flirtation. He didn't look visibly moved, but she felt a stirring tension about him, a readiness to strike when and if necessary. She didn't get the sense that the Mexican was flirting in any real sense anyway. Almost like he was playing a game, trying to nudge Sotza.

"I am Nicolás Garza, but you may call me Nico," he took her arm and waved them toward the vehicles. Since Sotza maintained his silence, Vee went easily with Nico, Sotza following behind them.

"Vee Montana," she murmured, watching him carefully.

A flicker of recognition passed across his face before he shuttered his response. He looked down at her, more carefully, guarded. He studied her. "Lately of Miami, Florida?" he asked, a new sharpness to his voice.

Before Vee could respond, Sotza reacted, taking Vee's arm from Nico and tugging her back to stand next to him. They stopped at the vehicle. One of Nico's men was holding the door open. Rather than get in, the three stood in tense silence. Out of the corner of her eye she saw the gunmen become more alert as the mood of their leader shifted. Then she noticed Sotza's people had followed them off the airplane and stood at their backs. She barely dared breathe. She'd been in tense situations before, negotiating, renegotiating and having to turn down bad trade deals. But she'd always been in control, able to talk her way out of a situation before it flared into something more. Only the Mexicans had openly challenged her.

"My *fiancé* is late of Miami, si." Sotza stressed the word fiancé as though it held more power than her actual name. She supposed time would tell which was more important to Nico, good relations with The Butcher or getting to the woman that wasn't well loved among his compatriots. "As my wife she will soon become a permanent citizen of Venezuela."

Vee stiffened slightly but kept her mouth shut. He just answered one of her questions, where he was going to take her to live. She'd suspected it was deep in the Venezuelan jungle but hoped he might decide to settle in the US. She should have known better.

Finally, after a nerve-wracking minute of silence, Nico studying Vee from top to bottom, his gaze speculative and cold, Sotza's arm tightening around Vee, Nico nodded at the vehicle and turned, striding around the other side. Vee released the breath she'd been holding and side-eyed the guys with the AK's. They seemed to relax a little. Her palms were sweating as she reached for the door and shifted her body to half face Sotza. She looked up into his grim face.

"What was that?" Vee asked quietly as they slipped into the vehicle.

"He's trying to decide if he wants to fuck you, marry you or kill you. Perhaps all three," he said, climbing into the vehicle after her.

The breath caught in her throat and for a moment she was tempted to climb over her 'fiancé' and run back to the airplane. Then she remembered who she was. She was nobody's bitch. She was a motherfucking mafia queen. She murmured, just before Nico slid in through the other door, taking the seat directly next to Vee, "I don't support any of the above, just so you know. He doesn't look like the marrying kind."

Sotza flashed her a quick smile as Nico waved for his driver to get moving. "Neither was I, but you've worn me down."

# CHAPTER EIGHTEEN

They put her in the same room as Sotza. Of course they did. He requested it, and when Sotza made a request it became a demand. She hadn't said anything as the female servant escorted Vee and two of Sotza's men to the big, lush bedroom. The men stayed outside the room while the servant showed Vee around. A large canopy bed took up a good portion of the suite and there was a washroom off the bedroom with a large whirlpool tub, a shower and a private toilet. Vee didn't know what was going on, how long they were staying, how long she would be forced to stay in Nico's villa, feeling threatened and on edge.

Vee didn't like not knowing things. She had grown fond of ruling her own destiny. Not knowing what was happening or what might become of her made Vee feel stabby. She decided if Sotza touched her, even a little, she would stab the shit out of him. No, if he even looked at her in a way she didn't like she was going to stab him.

That thought made her feel better as the serving woman retreated and Vee was left on her own. The first thing she did was check the door, it was unlocked. Then checked the guards. Yup, still there. As she closed the door and turned back to the room she decided she was grateful for the men on the other side of the door, even if they belonged to Sotza. At the very least they would alert her if danger was approaching.

In that case, she would stab whoever came through the door.

Vee walked toward the bed, noting a suitcase on top. It was purple so she was pretty sure it wasn't Sotza's. She opened it cautiously and then tossed the top back when she realized it was filled with women's clothing. They didn't belong to her as she was forced to leave most of her stuff in Miami and the rest in Canada. She frowned as she lifted a cashmere tank top fringed in delicate lace around the collar. Tossing that aside she began digging in earnest. She came up with several more tops, a few pairs of jeans, some black leggings, a pair of shorts and a pencil skirt. There were also several pairs of lacy panties and two bras that matched the underwear. At the bottom was a pair of four-inch heeled stilettos. The heels were made of sterling silver.

She didn't need to check the tags, she knew everything in the suitcase would fit her. Was purchased for her, the store tags still attached. Her heart did a tiny stutter as she tried to decide what it meant. When did he get her this stuff? At what point had Sotza decided she would need a new wardrobe? Or a partial new wardrobe, she thought, eyeing the contents critically. But what disturbed her the most was the accuracy in style. Everything in the suitcase was something she would definitely wear. The clothes reflected her style – business sexy, no-nonsense, semi-functional. But ultimately the outfit was secondary to the attitude of the woman wearing it. And Vee, well, she had an unlimited supply of attitude. She knew how to own her role, give as good as she got. She snorted and turned away from the suitcase. Except where Sotza was concerned.

Vee wandered idly around the room, restless and annoyed. It bothered her that Sotza and Nico were doing business without her. Though she thought she understood the reason for her exclusion. She wasn't exactly safe in Mexico. Not until they established a new trading partner and tensions with Domingo's cartel eased. The cartels didn't typically work too close together, in fact, they were at war with each other more often than not. She was probably reasonably safe, locked away in Nico's compound.

Vee just hoped she wasn't being excluded because she was a woman. Because Sotza imagined they were about to be married. She would have to gut him in a particularly painful way if he thought she was going to stand down and became the barefoot, pretty arm candy type. She'd tried the trophy wife thing with Tony. It hadn't worked out - mostly for him.

She wandered into the bathroom and took a closer look. It was every woman's dream. Clean, light, sparkly and big. A jetted whirlpool tub took up a good portion of the space with a spotless cubicle rain shower right next to it. The toilet was in its own spacious closet and the vanity had two sinks. The space was awash in white marble. She had to admit, Nico had good taste.

She looked longingly at the tub. It had been an age since she'd been able to just sit and soak away her tensions. She felt hot and sticky from travelling between climates and sitting on an airplane for so many hours. But did she have enough time to bathe and change before Sotza appeared? Vee thought she probably did. Negotiations always took time. The men would talk, smoke and drink. She could afford to take some time to herself. It wasn't like she had anything else to do.

She reached for the hem of her shirt, but stopped, glancing around, toward the ceiling. Would Nico install cameras in his guest suites? Probably, she decided. But she couldn't see them if they were there. Did she care? Not really. Vee wasn't a shy woman. She'd changed in front of men all the time. Swiftly stripping down after a job along with her men. It had been impersonal. She was their boss.

She flung her shirt to the floor and reached for the button on her jeans. When her clothes were off she turned on the water, making it was hot as she thought she could handle. She sifted through the bath accessories and chose a strawberry scented bubble bath, adding a large dose to the streaming water. While the tub filled she went through the basket of women's products on the vanity and opened all the drawers, snooping through everything. After her inspection she decided that if Nico wanted to marry her, she would accept. His taste in décor and women's things were spectacular. Somehow, she didn't think Sotza would be nearly as attuned to a woman's desires. She pictured him in a cold, gothic mansion with dark furnishings and secret passages.

Vee brushed her straight, blond hair with a hairbrush and then piled it on top of her head so it wouldn't get wet. She dropped into the tub with a sigh, grateful that she was able to sit facing the open doorway. She picked up the white loufa and sponged her limbs caressing her skin with careful attention. It felt heavenly to simply sit still and pamper herself. When she finished washing she leaned back until her head rested against the porcelain, closed her eyes and tried to let everything go. Life was beyond her control right at this moment, there was no point in worrying or she would drive herself crazy.

She wished she'd thought to light the candles she found in one of the drawers. The ambience would be so much nicer without the bright overhead lights. She was idly wondering if there was nail polish to be found, she didn't remember seeing any, when Sotza stepped into the bathroom.

"If I'd known I would be coming back to this I would've left Garza earlier."

He was like a cat, she decided. Silent, swift and with no sense of boundaries. Without opening her eyes, she said, "You can leave now."

She hoped when she opened her eyes he would be gone. She knew it was a useless hope, but she hoped nonetheless. Sure enough, when she finally looked, it was to find her persistent would-be lover standing over her, looking down at her wet, naked body with glittering carnality lighting his eyes. It stole her breath. Gone was the cool indifference, haughty indulgence, both replaced by a look of lust. Just pure lust. It made the rough valleys of his face appear even more masculine, more aggressive.

He sat down on the edge of the tub, his eyes sweeping hungrily over her. She was in so much more trouble than she thought. She realized in that moment that she was out of her depth. This wasn't going to be a marriage of convenience, with a little boring sex on the side. He seemed out of control, sheer want overriding his cool façade. It scared her, this scared her.

"I want to get out," she whispered, gripping the edges of the tub as if to stand.

"In a minute," he countered, putting his hand over top of her wet one and holding her in place. "I like seeing you this way."

She tried for flippant, though her heart was still pounding. "You like seeing a naked woman? Well that's refreshingly unusual for your species."

He tilted his head a little, studying her. "I like to see you vulnerable." He paused, then added, "And naked. You are as perfect as I knew you'd be."

"And you're a fucking pervert," she snapped, tugging at her hand. "Let me up." She definitely needed to get herself dried off and into some clothes, maybe even those steel-heeled stilettos. She needed armour.

His gave her a flinty look and released her hand only to lean over and catch her chin in a harder grip. He stared down at her for several long seconds. Her heart beat fast and hard against her ribcage. She knew she was pushing him, the way she talked to him with a complete lack of respect. His gaze said everything she already knew. Any other man in his position would've taken her months ago, beaten and fucked her into submission. His patience wasn't limitless and she was pushing her luck by skating so close to the edge. Sotza played with her, enjoyed the game, enjoyed her fight to a certain extent, but she wouldn't be allowed to resist forever.

He gave her a quick, ruthless kiss. She didn't have time to protest, to push him away. He was already pulling back when she brought her hands up to shove him. She pressed shaking fingers against her stinging lips and glared at him. She longed to blast him with every rancid thought running through her head, but he was right, naked and wet, sitting in a tub, she was vulnerable. What could she do if he decided to shove her under the water and hold her down until she'd learned her lesson?

Vee dropped her eyes to the bathwater and sat stiffly, waiting for him to make the next move. He'd won another round and he hadn't even had to use force. No, The Butcher was showing her without words that she would belong to him, no matter what she said or did. Their violent courtship was his playground, and the bully owned every moment.

He stood and stepped away from the bathtub, his gaze lingering on her body. The bubbles were completely gone, she had nowhere to hide. "We'll be dining with Garza this evening. Dress to kill, Vee," he said, his voice flat, no indication of the small battle they'd just engaged in or the sexual tension igniting the air around them. "Wear the heels."

# CHAPTER NINETEEN

Vee realized what Sotza meant by 'dress to kill' when he handed her a small revolver tucked neatly into a small leather holster. It took her a few seconds to realize the strap was clearly meant to fit around a thigh. Fancy. She wished she'd gotten one for herself ages ago. Weapons that were easily concealed in women's outfits weren't easy to come by.

She raised an eyebrow as she accepted the weapon, pulled it from the holster and checked the chamber. Fully loaded. What the fuck was he thinking? She could shoot him where he stood, casually leaning against the tall bedframe, watching her emotionlessly. "Giving me a gun is either brave or stupid." She felt compelled to inform him. Then, as she tucked it back in its holster she said, "Actually, it's just stupid. I'm a good shot and I will kill you the first opportunity I get where I can do the deed and safely disappear."

The edge of his lip quirked and he nodded. "It's your bloodthirsty attitude that makes me feel safe giving you this small gift." He took the three steps separating them and caught her chin, tilting her head up. She had to look way up, even in heels, she was still half a foot shorter. "Of course, I'm still wary of you with a gun. I have a healthy respect for your abilities in the deadly arts. But Vee, you need to know I will never leave you unprotected. Even if it means arming you myself."

The thought that he wanted to keep her safe was alluring. The knowledge that he trusted her to keep herself safe was intoxicating. And the entire mix of emotions was topped off with a healthy dose of confusion because she wanted to hate the man.

She nodded and stepped away, freeing her chin and stepping around him toward the end of the bed. Glancing over her shoulder, she confirmed that his eyes were all over her as she pulled up the tight knee-length skirt of her red dress, nearly to her panties. She lifted her left leg and placed it on the chest at the end of the bed, her metal heel striking the wood. It took a few moments of fussing with the holster strap to get it on just right. She needed it snug around the upper muscle of her thigh, but she also needed it to lay against her skin without puckering the dress. Her profile had to be completely smooth if anyone glanced down her body. She finished and straightened, tugging her skirt back down and smoothing her hands over her hips and thighs.

Turning to Sotza, she asked, "What do you think? Can you tell it's there?"

His voice was a little rough when he replied, "You look stunning, Vee. Absolutely flawless."

Her cheeks heated and she turned away so he wouldn't see her reaction to his compliment. Vee suspected he didn't often compliment people, but he'd been doing it plenty with her. She hated to admit it, but the difference in the way he treated her compared to how he treated other people warmed her heart a little. She'd feel a tiny bit bad when she finally got the chance to kill him. Miss all those pretty compliments.

"You don't look too bad yourself," she said grudgingly,

looking him over with a critical eye and coming up with nothing to complain about. Sotza was everything she might look for in a man. He was tall and surprisingly strong with long, leanly corded muscles. Regally handsome with an edge of rugged. He knew how to showcase both elements of his character, wearing dark, impeccably tailored suits that contrasted with the brutal man so many unfortunate dead people encountered. It was enough to make even her heart stutter a little; both in trepidation and admiration.

She approached him, trying to match her confidence with his and reached for his tie, straightening it. Though she despised the man and his methods, she knew that they needed to project a united front to the Mexican cartel boss. Sotza watched her, his face void of expression as she smoothed her hand down the navy blue tie, flattening it against his chest, her nails briefly scraping the fabric of his shirt. She felt the rapid beat of his heart under her hand and had a small moment of wonder – he was good, keeping his face impassive while his body responded to her proximity.

They stood for a moment, looking at each other. If it had been a different time, a different place. If they had been two completely different people, Vee would have been head over heels for this man. She would have put every ounce of her feminine wiles to work to capture his attention.

She stepped back, bracing herself for the coming evening. Sotza's eyes hardened and he became all business. It was time to go to work. She straightened her back and stared past him, awaiting his next move. He didn't disappoint, turning at her side and taking her arm in a firm grip. "Let's get this over with," he said, leading her from the room.

Nico looked extremely handsome in his formal suit, cowboy boots with black hair slicked back. His jaw was freshly shaven and he smelled like Dior Homme cologne as he bent over Vee's hand, kissing the skin lightly and then rising to press a quick kiss to her cheek. Vee felt Sotza's tension as the Mexican boss handled her, but he didn't make a move.

Nico turned and introduced his companion, a stunning Latina woman that took even Vee's breath away. Though it was less her looks and more the intense concentration in her eyes that put Vee on edge. Desi was a little taller than Vee's height in heels. She wore a black velvet gown that plunged deep down her chest, the two sides held together by strands of interlocking silver loops. Her long black hair flowed in a shiny fall down her back. Vee realized within seconds of meeting the other woman she was most likely Nico's personal bodyguard, possibly even his second. Desi stood to his side and slightly in front, her hands loose and ready to go for a weapon. She didn't look even remotely pleased or relaxed, as the date of a man like Nico might look.

Though the two were obviously fucking. A woman didn't run her hand down another man's arm with such familiarity unless she knew him intimately. That, coupled with the scathing look she shot Vee from behind Nico's shoulder when he kissed Vee, made her positive Desi would kill if she felt either of her positions threatened. Vee simply raised an eyebrow and treated the other woman with cool indifference. The last thing she needed was the drama only a woman throwing a jealous fit could throw down.

"Please, let us be seated," Nico said waving them into the formal dining room.

Vee looked around appreciatively, noting that Nico had incorporated modern accents to the traditional Mexican décor. The combination was stunning. She was a little surprised by his all-around good taste. She would've pegged the tough Mexican as the type of guy who would prefer to be buried deep in the jungle inside an impenetrable concrete fortress. And while she supposed his home was probably fortified to the max, Nico clearly enjoyed luxurious surroundings. It reminded Vee a little of her old life, with Tony.

She caught Nico's eye and he grinned at her, nodding as he noted her appreciation of his home. "You like, Señora?"

She smiled back, her lips stretching tightly. Though she would play her part, she was wildly aware that this 'pleasant' evening was more than light socializing. A sizing up of all the players, figuring out where they fit and if they could ultimately do business in a trade known for its deadliness.

"You have a lovely home, Nico," she assured him. "What I've seen so far is stunning."

He accepted the compliment, taking her arm and guiding her around the table. As their host pulled a chair out for Vee, Sotza did the same for Desi, seating her across from their host before taking the chair opposite Vee's. His dark eyes lingered on her face as Nico sat next to her.

She wondered what he was thinking. There was a snapping tension in the air around him that made Vee's heart flutter, captured her attention and mesmerized her. She barely noticed Nico at her side, speaking on light topics as she stared back at Sotza. Was the tension a result of Nico being near her, acting his part as their gracious host, or was it something else? Something to do with the negotiations.

Though she gave the façade of basic politeness, Desi seemed to be in a mood. Her dark eyes followed everyone with malevolent suspicion and she barely spoke when someone spoke to her. Vee wished the other woman would stop glaring at her as though she wanted to cut Vee's throat. She really needed to have a chat with the woman about having a sister's back. After all, they were two deadly women, working in a man's world.

Though Desi was magnificent, the epitome of Latina perfection, Vee didn't envy her. She pitied the other woman. Living with a man, sleeping with him, and working for him.

This is why Vee had a clear no fraternizing rule. It wasn't professional and led to complications.

"What a lovely dress, Desi, is it Versace?" Vee asked, trying to draw the other woman into conversation. Perhaps if she attempted to befriend the hostile woman, she could ferret out more about Desi's and Nico's relationship status. It could come in useful.

Desi shot Vee a borderline scathing look and answered, her tone carefully bored, "No te entiendo."

Vee doubted very much that Desi didn't understand. If Desi was Nico's second-in-command then she would definitely know how to speak the language of a major trade partner. But Vee switched easily to Spanish and asked the question again. If anything, Desi's countenance grew colder, angrier as she snapped that, yes, her dress was Versace.

Vee couldn't help herself. She probably should, but the old Vee, the one who dined regularly with high society mavens, simply couldn't resist needling the unpleasant woman when it became clear that Desi wasn't going to accept her attempt at friendliness. She continued in flawless Spanish, "And your shoes? Simply marvelous. Where did you get them? What brand are they?"

"Manolo," Desi snarled, barely concealing her annoyance. She snatched up her wine glass a mere second after the servant poured. "My bracelet is Cartier and my make-up is mostly Armani. That about sums up my wardrobe unless you want to talk about my underwear."

Vee nearly laughed out loud. Wow, it was easy to get under Desi's skin. She really wished the other woman weren't so hostile. She suspected they actually had quite a lot in common, even the quick temper. It would be fun to chat her up, see what it was like inside a Mexican cartel from the viewpoint of a powerful woman.

Nico interrupted their fun though by growling across the

table at Desi, telling her to shut her mouth if she couldn't be polite to his guests. Vee was surprised when, instead of looking contrite, Desi turned her furious gaze toward her lover. She didn't speak, and Vee understood. Desi would push Nico too far if she disrespected him directly. Appearance was everything to a cartel man.

After that, Vee got bored. Desi behaved herself, even when Vee tried to bait her into a response. Nico continued acting the perfect host, politely inquiring about their wedding plans. Sotza played ball but gave non-committal responses. Nico didn't try to flirt with her as he'd done on the airstrip. She wondered why. He'd obviously been playing with them earlier, but was his lack of overt attention to Vee a sign of respect toward Desi? That would imply their relationship was deeper than it appeared on the surface.

Vee was curious about their weird little dinner party. It was steeped in hostility and tension, yet nothing spilled into the polite flow of conversation. What was the point? Was Nico simply being polite, inviting his guests to an evening meal while they stayed with him? Or did this meal have a more sinister undertone? Was their host trying to assess them, assess Sotza's strengths, perhaps even his feelings toward Vee? And for what reason? Would be dare to strike out at them while they were vulnerable on his property? It would be a stupid decision. He must know the strength of the Venezuelan cartel. Retaliation would be swift and predictably brutal.

A quick glance toward Sotza confirmed that he was watching, his eyes never leaving Nico. His gaze was neutral, completely blank. Vee shivered as something stirred in those black depths every time Nico spoke or directed a comment to either one of them. She wondered what stopped Sotza's hand. She knew, if The Butcher chose to make a move, to slaughter everyone in the room, they would all be dead before their soup spoons fell. Vee didn't know if it was their need of a Mexican partner that stalled his hand, or if he was playing another game. Somehow, she didn't think it was the negotiations. He'd cut off Domingo's head with nary a thought to the ripple effects of his loss throughout Mexico. He'd simply done as he wanted and moved forward.

When the meal ended, Nico escorted Vee and Sotza to their room. After assuring him they would join him for breakfast he left. Sotza saw Vee into the room and then stepped out for a few minutes to talk to their security. Vee paced across the lush carpet, then pulled her shoes off and tossed them toward the end of the bed. When Sotza entered the room, Vee turned to him and stopped moving. She waited for him to speak first.

He locked the door and glanced over at Vee. He didn't disappoint her expectations. "You were a beautiful sight tonight, Vee. You worked that room like a pro."

Vee was elated and grinned broadly at the compliment. Maybe she should have brushed it off, but right now she felt awesome stepping back into her old role, one where she ruled a room with ease, but this time it wasn't behind a desk or in a warehouse. "Tell me you saw what I saw?" she demanded.

He nodded seriously and strode toward the bed, sitting on the bench to pull his own shoes off. Vee tried to shrug away her sudden discomfort in the intimacy of a man taking his shoes off in a bedroom they would both sleep in. He'd seen her fully naked, the sound of his shoes hitting the floor shouldn't be causing such a flutter in her stomach. "Desiree is clearly his second-in-command. She's a terrible actress. I would lay money that he told her to act stupid, vapid. Just a beautiful bimbo companion to a rich man."

"Exactly!" Vee said excitedly. "She rose to my bait so easily. Even when she finally locked down her emotions, I could still feel her anger and resentment. If her job was to gather intel, she seriously fucked that up. Which is why you don't fuck around with the boss, messes with priorities."

"Agreed, they shouldn't be mixing business and pleasure. Tell me, Vee, did you learn this lesson from personal experience? From Danny Russo?" When he said the words, he stared at her. His mask dropped for a second and she saw The Butcher. He was demanding to know if she's fucked Danny. Probably assumed she had.

Vee crossed her arms and gripped her biceps. She glared at him. "If you're asking if I fucked Danny, than the answer is it's none of your fucking business."

"Even if it meant his life?"

She let out an annoyed huff and gave him the answer he wanted. "I know better than to fuck the staff."

"Who would you fuck, Vee?" he persisted.

She lifted her chin and snapped, "I think you mean, who did I fuck? Do you want a list, Sotza, because it's a long one? Isn't that what you're really after?"

"Careful," he warned her.

"Or what?" she snapped throwing caution out the window.

He sighed and rubbed a hand over his face, the first visible sign he'd given that he might be tired or affected by her constant resistance. The moment passed quickly and he straightened, giving her a glacial look. "You may have noticed that I'm fairly subtle most of the time."

She frowned. That was true, he wasn't particularly heavy-handed, yet he always seemed to get his way. "Yes?"

"Silent contemplation is how I survive in this business. I observe the people around me, find their weaknesses, and come up with creative punishments."

She shivered. She'd heard of his 'creative punishments,' his meticulous brutality. "You would punish me?" she asked, her voice wavering a little.

He nodded. "If it became necessary. I never say anything I don't mean to follow through on."

They stared at each other, a battle of wills. Vee believed him. He always did what he said he was going to do. He'd told her from the beginning that he was taking Miami, that he was taking her, that he would marry her. Vee was starting to believe it. Believe that she couldn't stop him.

"I would punish you back," she said, unable to allow him the final word.

"I believe you'll try," he agreed. And once more she caught a flash of exhaustion etched into the grooves of his face. He spent months chasing after her, taking Miami from her and setting up his own command. All this while he still had his own cartel back in Venezuela, making sure it ran smooth without his presence. And now this negotiation with the Mexican cartel. He would have to be ten steps ahead of Garza at all times. She decided to back off... for now. She didn't want to find the limit of his patience now. Not here in this dangerous place.

"I'm tired," Vee said, opening the suitcase and digging around until she came up with white silk pyjamas, something she would definitely have bought for herself. She looked pointedly at the bed. "Where are you sleeping?"

He grinned suddenly, a wolfish smile that made her heart stutter. She was becoming accustomed to his gentlemanly demeanor, the cool way he carried himself. The sudden heat in his expression took her breath away. He didn't answer the question she posed, instead he said, "Vee, when I'm ready to share a bed with you, you'll know." Then he turned and left the bedroom, the audible click of the lock a stark reminder of her situation.

She shouldn't be sparring with The Butcher, she should be trying to find a way out of the cage he was building around her.

# CHAPTER TWENTY

The flight from Mexico to Venezuela took about five hours. Sotza was happy to be back. Watching Vee's face as they descended over the mountainous jungle region of his home made this landing special. Her professional mask slipped away as she clutched the window frame and leaned in her seat to better see the breathtaking beauty of Venezuela. He could see a combination of excitement, exhilaration and trepidation in her lovely features. He suspected she'd never travelled this far.

Though Sotza didn't know all the details, he did know that Vee had an isolated childhood. She was born and raised in Miami and rarely strayed beyond the Florida borders. Her mother had been a high-class prostitute that became pregnant by a mobster. The man was already married but agreed to set his mistress and the child up in an apartment. Vee met her father a handful of times over the years before her parents split for good. The mother died of a speedball overdose when Vee was sixteen.

Following in her mother's footsteps Vee'd seduced men in high positions within the underworld, keeping herself in the only lifestyle she knew. A lifestyle that probably made her miserable. Perhaps that was part of the reason she turned to cocaine. She used it, liked it and then couldn't get off it because her life was so awful she had no will to try. After several years warming the bed of Frank Lopez, a close friend of Vee's father, she met her future husband Tony.

Rumour had it that Vee wasn't too impressed with the pushy Cuban when he first approached her. But eventually his persistence won out and she agreed to marry him. Sotza had no idea when the marriage turned sour, but he suspected she had never loved her husband. She had simply been swept up in the turning tide of Miami's underworld when Tony took over Frank's operation. Of course, Vee had taken Tony out, ending their turbulent marriage. The death causing ripples through underworld circles. Reyes had taken her under his wing after Montana's death and guided her. A smart choice, Sotza admitted. Who knew the scene and all the players better than Elvira Montana?

This was the extent of Sotza's knowledge of Vee before he'd landed in Miami. Before he set eyes on her. If this had been everything that made Vee, he wouldn't have hesitated in pulling the trigger, ending her tenacious grip on one of the most lucrative markets. Instead she had shown him that she was so much more than an escort turned gold-digger. That she could hold her own in shark infested waters. And she did it with such grace... mesmerizing him. If he wasn't so infatuated by her he would've talked Reyes into allowing her to keep her position with Sotza at her disposal to help her with the Mexico situation.

But Sotza wanted to keep all that icy fire to himself. Apply it to his own organization. Bring it to his bed and wear it on his arm. Vee was the woman he'd been waiting his whole life for. Now that he had her under his command he was determined to spend a lifetime getting to know her, holding her, grooming her and then setting her free to stand at his side. He would open the cage doors when she was ready to accept his rule.

She turned to him, blue eyes sparkling, lips stretched in a carefree grin. "Is this where you live, your home?" she asked, awe in her voice.

"One of them," he replied, feeling pleasure in being with her, having her home with him. He leaned in and glanced past her shoulder. "The main base of my operations."

"I see," she said, studying the land carefully as the airplane headed toward a private runway a few kilometres from the main house. "It looks fairly isolated up here in the mountains. The dense foresting would help keep you hidden, make it hard for any kind of authority to get in."

Sotza appreciated her critical eye. Despite her lack of travel she still managed to educate herself. "Indeed," he agreed with her assessment. "Extremely difficult. Which is why I picked this location. We're unlikely to be disturbed."

"And are you bordering Columbia or Brazil?" she asked curiously.

"We are closer to the Columbian border, although not close enough to either country to make a significant difference. Which is good since there are so many people leaving the country right now. We're high up and isolated enough that there are no refugee paths anywhere near my land."

"Yes," she said softly. "They're starving."

"That's one of the reasons," he said easily. "Though it isn't lack of food so much as the exorbitant price of the food, lack of proper governance. I work with several of the local organizations to bring aid to some of the major centers, Caracas and surrounding area."

"How very Robin Hood of you," she said, though there was no bite to her words.

"These are my people, Vee. I was born here, grew up

among the locals. And though my mother was English and I was educated in England, my heart has always remained in this country."

"These poor people," she murmured her eyes clouding a little. "I can't imagine what real hunger must feel like."

"And you never will," his voice hardened. "I take care of the things that belong to me."

"So you've said," she snapped, and he almost regretted reminding Vee of her captivity. But he couldn't regret acquiring her, bringing her to Venezuela. "What if I decide to go on hunger strike?"

"I would have you force fed. Not a pretty prospect," he replied. "But you're too intelligent to go on hunger strike. It would weaken you too much to fight back. You tend to think in the long term, attempting to stay two steps ahead of everyone else."

She laughed, the sound brittle. "That kind of thinking doesn't work when I'm being pursued by a man that thinks ten steps ahead."

"You have it wrong, Vee. We think very much alike. The biggest difference between us is you have heart."

"And you don't?" she asked.

"I have what it takes to do what's necessary," he assured her. "I will always take that extra step to ensure success."

"It doesn't bode well for the future of our so-called marriage if you don't have a heart," she said, an edge to her voice. As though she cared about his words and was annoyed that she cared. It pleased him that she wanted to know these things, was willing to enter the conversation.

"I have a heart, Vee," he assured her quietly. "It just hasn't been touched in many years."

"And you think I can touch that block of stone?" she asked incredulously.

He chuckled, unable to resist. She pulled so many

emotions from him. While somewhat disturbing, he'd had a few months now to grow used to the feeling, to embrace it. "Imagine what kind of a position you'll be in if my heart beat only for you. One day, when we've reached that point in our relationship, ask me for the world. See what happens."

She stared at him, lost for words. The plane hit the runway, bouncing a little. Vee had been so involved in their conversation that she hadn't noticed the landing. She jumped in her seat, twisting around to stare back out the window. He leaned toward her once more, curving his hand possessively over her shoulder, unable to resist that small touch as he watched the rainforest fly by.

Sotza was home once more, and he brought a queen who, once tamed, would share his throne.

# CHAPTER TWENTY-ONE

Sotza's words echoed through her brain in a constant loop. *Ask me for the world.* What if she did? Then what. Would he give it to her? Was he implying that if he fell in love with her that he would give her anything she wanted? Would he grant her freedom if that's what she asked for? Vee's head spun with the possibilities. She never once thought to cultivate his attentions.

When Vee was younger, in her late teens and early twenties, she'd been forced to do things she wasn't proud of. She had no skills, no education. The only thing she had was beauty, a sharp mind and extensive knowledge of the Miami criminal world. She'd done what she could to exploit that world, but it had slowly chipped away at the good things inside her until she was certain they no longer existed. Sotza said she had heart, but he was wrong. While his might be a block of frigid ice, her chest cavity was empty, a gaping hole. Nothing beat within. Her heart had died decades ago when she lost her mother, the broken, sad woman who had been Vee's whole world.

But something in what Sotza said... and the way he looked

at her, made her non-existent heart beat a little faster. As though it was interested. As though, maybe, possibly he could revive it. It was an exhilarating and terrifying thought.

They got in a waiting all-terrain vehicle, driven, presumably, by one of Sotza's men. She had noticed they all wore a uniform of black fatigue pants and green shirts. Another sign of his need for order and control. They drove a paved road, through a dense forest for about ten minutes then the car pulled into a massive garage. Sotza helped her from the vehicle.

As they left the garage and followed a neat stone path, Sotza took her elbow, leaned down and said, "I have acquired your daughter, Vee. I need your compliance in some important matters we'll be discussing over the next few weeks and I believe her presence will help sway you to my way of thinking."

Vee stopped walking, stumbling on her high heels when Sotza took another step, accidentally dragging her with him. She jerked her arm away and stared at him in horror. She could feel the blood draining from her face. She felt faint, should probably have allowed him to keep his hold on her arm. But in that moment she didn't want the evil bastard's touch anywhere near her. "You have Raina?" she asked, making sure she'd heard him right.

"Correct. My second-in-command collected her from her University campus almost two weeks ago. It's my understanding that she's settling in nicely, though she does take after you. She also toyed with the idea of a food strike."

It took Vee so long to process his words, to understand what he was saying that it took her a full minute to launch her attack. She threw her fist at his face, uncaring if she broke her fingers. She didn't care about anything except destroying the man who allowed his people to lay hands on her daughter. It felt like her heart was breaking, though she didn't know how that was possible, since she didn't care about him.

Sotza moved swiftly to the side, grabbing her fist and swinging her around so her back was against his chest. She wasn't done trying to kill him. Or scream for all the world to hear. "You motherfucking son-of-a-bitch!" she screeched. "You fucking dared to touch my child? MY CHILD!? I will fucking kill you for this, Sotza, I really will!"

She threw an elbow into his side, enjoying his grunt at the impact. When the arm he had around her waist loosened a little she reached between her thighs, tugging her skirt up, going for her gun. He slid a hand over her hip and grabbed her wrist tightly, yanking it up to her waist. "Calm down, Vee."

"Fuck you!" she yelled. "I won't calm the fuck down, you unbelievable asshole. You, you, evil Butcher."

"If you don't calm down right now I'll be forced to haul you into the house, past all my staff and lock you in the bedroom until you stop screaming."

"I will fucking calm down after I've done cartwheels on your grave, you sick child kidnapping monster!"

"Right," he said grimly, his mouth against the side of her head so she couldn't head butt him. "You are clearly not in the mood for rational thinking."

He swung her around so fast her vision spun and she had no idea what was going on until he picked her up off the ground and tossed her over his shoulder, an arm wrapped firmly around her thighs. She gripped handfuls of his suit jacket and pushed herself up, trying to see as he strode toward what appeared from her limited vantage point to be a mansion.

"You kidnapped my daughter, you motherfucking bastard, of course I'm not in the mood," she yelped.

"I had hoped that you would greet my staff, your daughter

and my second with the respect your new position should command. Instead they'll all get a surprising view of your ass as you enter your new home."

"I'm going to stab you the first chance I get," she replied.

"I believe you'll try," he agreed, striding up the stone staircase to a set of open double doors.

Vee saw a flash of people as he walked past all of them, ignoring hastily spoken greetings in both Spanish and English. She tried shoving her hair back with one hand and bracing herself against his back with the other. It didn't work. As soon as he started ascending a set of interior stairs she was jostled and forced to lay flat against his back, bunches of his coat balled in her fists.

"Is that my mother?" a curious voice reached through the pandemonium following their arrival.

"Raina?" Vee yelled.

She wasn't given a chance to confirm that it was indeed her daughter who spoke because Sotza didn't slow. If anything he sped up when they reached the landing above the main floor, his long legs quickly taking them away from the people below.

"Put me down!" she yelled, now panicked that she wouldn't get to see the daughter she hadn't set eyes on since she was a baby. "Please, Sotza!" The last part came out in a sob.

He ignored her pleas, throwing a door open, going through and kicking it shut behind him. The carpet was a beautiful blur as he walked. Then she was flung through the air, shrieking until her breath was slammed from her lungs as her back met the mattress of a bed. She started to scramble back off the bed, but he dropped on top of her, pinning her down with his body.

She froze as she saw his face. He was furious, completely unhinged. Except for his eyes, those held the lust that he could never quite conceal when he looked at her. And though she felt the rapid beat of his heart against her breasts, his breathing was even though he'd just walked a long way with her over his shoulder. The man wasn't human.

"Welcome home, Vee," he said grimly.

"Fuck you."

She threw her fist into his face, connecting with his chin. It hurt like a motherfucker even though he was so close to her she didn't have a lot of leverage. Still, as his head swung to the side, she decided he got the point.

# CHAPTER TWENTY-TWO

Vee watched her daughter from the window of the bedroom Sotza locked her in. Two days had passed since she'd entered his home over his shoulder, screaming obscenities. Since she'd punched him in the face. Her rage was so great that during those first hours of isolation she would have happily burned the estate to the ground if it had been within her abilities. Since that exchange, her anger had dimmed to seething hatred.

Whenever Sotza came to check on her she simply stood silently staring out the window at the grounds below, always searching for a glimpse of her girl. He would talk to her, in his quiet voice. He didn't say anything particularly important, spoke about his home, what life was like there, spoke a little about Miami. He didn't say a word about Raina. He knew she was starving for information on her daughter. Vee thought maybe he knew that and refused to give up the goods until she started speaking to him again.

Now that they were in his home country he tended to speak Spanish. She had to admit he was smooth. His delivery of both languages flawless. Better than hers. She'd started learning Spanish from some of the men who visited her mother when Vee was a child. Later, she'd finished her education in the language formally, through online classes. Despite her fluent knowledge of Spanish, she still spoke in stilted sentences, never quite comfortable with her second language.

No one entered the bedroom except Sotza, and he only came in during meal times. They spent time together in mostly silence because Vee refused to speak and Sotza wasn't a man to fill silence needlessly. He would sit quietly while she ate, watching her, his face blank, and then taking her tray when she finished. Though she stayed silent throughout these exchanges she longed to scream at him, hurl insults, hit him. The rational part of her brain told her none of these tactics would work. Sotza had proven himself both patient and intelligent. If she wanted to outsmart him then she needed to hold in the tantrum that threatened to erupt whenever she looked at him.

Sotza changed the game when he brought Raina here. Before, maybe she could have accepted her fate, but now, there was more at stake than her life. Not only did she need to escape, she had to take her daughter with her. Raina didn't belong here. Didn't belong anywhere near cartel. She'd been raised by a nice, loving family on an isolated farm. Vee'd made sure of it. It pierced her soul that despite everything she did to hide Raina from the world, the sacrifice she made to ensure the child's safety, the girl had been dragged into Vee's mafia world anyway.

Vee mostly blamed herself, not Sotza. The man was born and raised cartel. He was a ruthless weapon. It was in his DNA to find and exploit any and every weakness when he was hunting. And she'd given him the ultimate weapon to use against her, a child. No, she laid most of the blame at her own feet. She should've done a better job of hiding the girl. She shouldn't have checked up on her so often throughout the years. Maybe she should've sent Raina farther, even overseas, where she might have been out of reach.

No matter what Vee thought, she knew that Sotza would've ferreted out her daughter no matter what Vee did, no matter how hard she tried to bury the secret. It was her own fault for bringing the child into a world where Vee's mobbed up life might one day touch Raina. But when she'd found out she was pregnant at eighteen, the father one of a string of ruthless mobsters, she hadn't been as horrified or upset as she thought she would be if she was ever faced with that situation. She hadn't been happy either. Of course not. At the time, she'd been living in a beautiful rental condo, the prize of her latest mafia conquest. She'd been his petted princess, given jewels, clothes, anything her heart desired.

Vee couldn't quite explain how she felt when she found out she was pregnant but terminating the fetus hadn't been an option for her. She'd thought long and hard about it, had even gone to a clinic to gather information. But in the end, as her baby grew, she knew she wanted to set eyes on it. Just once. Then she'd send it off to a better life.

Her pregnancy had been one of the best and loneliest times of her life. The father abandoned her almost as soon as he found out. Vee anticipated his reaction. She sold a bunch of her jewelry and moved into a smaller, cheaper place. She spent the next several months getting to know her child. Talking to it, reassuring it, singing and reading to it. She almost never went out, ordering her groceries from a super-market that delivered. The last thing she needed was for the Miami mafia scene to catch wind of her pregnancy, to know about the child she produced. So she went through the entire thing alone, no friends, no family, no boyfriends.

And now, in Sotza's home, she discovered that all that sacrifice was for nothing. Her child had never really been safe. If it wasn't this, it would have been something else. The child was a pawn, something to exploit. The ultimate bargaining chip against a heartless woman who would sacrifice her own life in a deadly mafia war. But she would never sacrifice Raina.

Vee touched her fingertips against the window, watching as Raina sat slumped on a bench in Sotza's beautiful garden. From her view it looked like a hedge maze. Raina had obviously figured it out and went into it almost daily, spending time among the flowers and shrubbery. Vee watched from above, a relentless sentinel who could do nothing if something should happen to the girl.

She wondered what Raina thought. Was she cognizant of the danger she was in just by existing? Had anyone told her who her mother is? Was she terrified for her life? Was she angry, like Vee? All these thoughts pounded relentlessly through Vee's brain. And though she was terrified for her daughter, she still craved a glimpse. She wanted to see the woman she had given birth to, this person who looked so much like her it was uncanny.

Vee's throat and chest ached with tears at the way Raina hunched her posture, wrapping her arms around her sleight body and rocking gently on the stone bench, her long, wavy blond hair flowing over one shoulder, glasses sliding down her nose, her gaze fixed on the stone path in front of her. Vee tensed when she saw someone approach the girl. It was a man, younger than Sotza, probably a bit younger than Vee. But even from her vantage point she could tell that he was as tough as they came. He spoke to Raina and her head tipped up sharply, her posture going from sad to angry in a matter of seconds. Like she knew him and didn't like him. Was this the man who'd done Sotza's dirty work, kidnapped Vee's daughter while Sotza was busy going after Vee?

Raina stood and poked her finger in the guy's face, snapping something at him before whirling away. He grabbed her before she could stomp away up the path and back to the house. Vee growled, wanting to storm down there, tear them apart and then tear whoever the man was to little pieces. Then she would go and rip Sotza to shreds for bringing her daughter here, for introducing her to the mafia world and putting her in danger.

"She's beautiful," Sotza's quiet voice came from behind her, startling Vee. She didn't turn around or acknowledge his presence as she continued to watch the scene unfolding below her. She was proud to see her daughter holding her own with the tough guy. "Just like you."

Vee bit her lip, holding back the insults and accusations she so badly wanted to hurl at her tormentor. By bringing Raina to Venezuela he'd ruined everything she ever sacrificed to give the girl a good life. And he ruined any feelings Vee might have been developing for him. Her lips curled a little as she got a clear view of Raina's face when she managed to wrench her arm out of the man's grasp, give him the finger and stomp toward the house. She was definitely her mother's daughter.

She felt rather than heard Sotza step closer behind her. He leaned over her shoulder looking out the window at the scene below. She felt her hair stir as his chin brushed against her, raising goosebumps along Vee's arm. She tried to subtlety shift away but he leaned with her.

His mouth was against her ear when he spoke. "We need to talk, Vee." When she refused to say anything, refused to turn around, he curved long fingers over her shoulders and turned her to face him. "Both of us this time. This won't be a one-sided conversation." His voice was low and quiet. Up close he was so much taller, and without her heels, her eyes landed on the middle of his chest. He was wearing a vest over his buttoned-up shirt, but he'd abandoned his tie and suit jacket taking on a more casual appearance.

Vee couldn't help the shiver that went through her at his

touch. She hated that her body was so aware of his, so at war with her own mind. She pushed past him, not wanting him to see his effect on her. She was wearing a short-sleeved silk shirt and a knee length skirt with slits up both sides. Both items were blue, the shirt a softer shade than the skirt. She wore a large ornamental belt at her waist. She had to hand it to Sotza, either he or one of his people had impeccable taste.

"Then talk," she said coolly, speaking for the first time in two days. Perhaps it was time to negotiate with the crime lord. Speak to him on a reasonable level and see if she could get herself out of the bedroom and planning an escape.

His amused gaze followed her as she paced to the bed and sat on the edge. She realized when he followed her that she'd made a mistake. She should have sat in the chair near the armoire. Sotza didn't sit though, he stood over her, watching her, using his physical presence to intimidate. She'd seen the tactic many times before. Probably would have done it herself if she wasn't closer to five feet than six.

"It's time to set a wedding date," he said. "Next week, I think."

Vee nearly swallowed her tongue. Of course, she knew why she was there. He'd told her many times of his desire to marry her. But she couldn't bring herself to think of it as more than a sick joke. People didn't force other people into marriage. Not in this day and age. Yet, she shouldn't be so surprised. The mafia made their own rules, and often followed a code of conduct that could be called old-fashioned. It was part of the reason she'd sent Raina away as a baby. She hadn't wanted the girl raised in such a world, where she might one day become fodder in the war of men.

"I don't think so," Vee replied.

He bobbed his head a little, as though expecting her answer. "Regardless, you will prepare for a wedding."

Vee had absolutely no doubt Sotza would find a way to

make the marriage happen. She'd had two days to decide how she would play this moment. Knowing it was coming. She gripped the edge of the bed and said, "It'll go easier with my consent."

He raised an eyebrow but didn't look otherwise shocked by her comment. Either he had an incredible poker face or he knew what was coming.

"Send Raina back home and I'll marry you," she said, toughening her tone as she would for any other negotiation.

"No." His answer was instant, the hard edge of his voice telling her he wouldn't negotiate for her daughter.

Still, she had to keep trying. "You don't need her once you have me."

"I already have you. That won't change."

"You don't have my cooperation," she bit out. He didn't say anything so she continued, an edge of desperation entering her voice, though she wished she could remain cool. If she had to beg, for Raina's sake, then she would. "If you keep my daughter out of this I'll do what you want. I'll marry you, fuck you, become the ideal wife, whatever you want." A crease showed between his brows. A sign that he was considering her words? She pushed on. "Having her here is going to be a problem, Sotza. If she's anything like me she'll cause trouble. She won't settle into this life. Please, just send her away. I'll give you anything you ask for."

"No," he said, and before she could argue, he continued, "she's vulnerable, Vee. I proved that she can be tracked, picked up. It's good luck that this didn't happen a year ago when you started flexing muscle in Miami. She could have been grabbed by the Mexican cartel if they'd thought to dig into your past."

He had a point. The mere idea of the cartel getting their hands on her daughter made Vee feel sick. She stood and stepped toward Sotza, imploring. "Then send her somewhere else, send her overseas, somewhere she'll be safe. Just not here. You can help me hide her."

He looked down at her, a fire leaping into his eyes at her proximity. He didn't touch her though. "She won't be safe anywhere. Only here, only under my protection."

Vee slapped him. She couldn't help it. All the rage she'd been bottling up spilled out, exploding. He didn't move when her hand cracked across his cheek. A muscle jumped in his jaw, the only sign that he was affected by her hit. She lifted a finger and shoved it into his face.

"You are the reason she's in danger!" Vee vibrated with anger. "You are the son-of-a-bitch who destroyed my daughter's life. The life that I sacrificed *everything* for. I will never forgive you and I will never settle into any kind of marriage with you."

He waited until she said her piece, until she'd spewed her rage at him. Then he grabbed her, moving before she had time to fling herself away. He gripped her upper arms tightly, lifting her onto her toes and bending until his face was inches from hers. Her heart pounded painfully against her chest. It finally sunk in that she'd struck this unforgiving man twice within a few days. She'd struck the man who held her and Raina's lives in his care. She was an idiot to challenge him.

He didn't address the slap though. He just held her like that, staring down at her, his eyes bottomless, dark pits. She felt the tension in his body. She wanted to recall her words, the slap, everything, just so long as he released her. His touch made her feel again, fear, arousal, confusion.

She was seconds away from breaking down completely and begging him to drop her when he said, "You will be my wife, it's as good as done."

He threw her backwards so hard her feet flew out from underneath her. Vee squeaked in fear, as her legs hit the bed and she collapsed backwards, bouncing on the mattress. By the time she surfaced, eyes wide and mouth open in shock he was striding toward the door. He stopped and turned as he twisted the knob. "I'll send your daughter up when she's ready. I tried to get her to come see you yesterday, but she refused."

His words stabbed her in the heart. His assertion that Raina didn't want to see her was nothing less than she expected, but it still hurt nonetheless. She nodded and remained silent. She was surprised by his kindness in allowing the two women to visit, though somewhat confused. Why did he care?

He watched her face as she felt herself crumble, gave her a moment to absorb them and then said, "If you ever strike me again, I will strike you back."

Vee nodded. She'd used up her free passes. If she pissed him off again, The Butcher would come out to play.

## CHAPTER TWENTY-THREE

"You shouldn't be out here alone."

Raina's head snapped up as Mateo's deep voice interrupted her thoughts. She'd been thinking about her parents, knowing that they would be frantic with worry over her disappearance. She shook off her melancholy and straightened her spine, treating him to the glare she'd perfected just for him. The guy was too fucking hot for his own good. He'd been dressing a little nicer since his boss got back. Today he was wearing a pair of black dress pants with a leather belt, a green collared shirt and boots. He'd left his jacket off, leaving his holster and gun visible. Raina wasn't used to seeing weapons displayed so casually. He wore it like it was part of him. She dropped her eyes from the gun.

"What could possibly happen to me out here?" she asked moodily. "Do you think I might get kidnapped or something? Oh yeah, that already happened. I think I'll take the risk, thank you."

His jaw knotted at her tone of voice. She didn't care. What was he going to do? He was back under Sotza's jurisdiction. And though Mateo wasn't exactly subservient to anyone, his boss included, he still seemed to respect Sotza's rule of law. Raina felt fairly certain that Mateo wasn't allowed to touch her without permission. Though, from their frequent meetings, she definitely got the impression he wanted to touch and maybe do more to her. She just wasn't sure if he wanted to kill her or fuck her. She sort of wished she had a little more life experience so she could figure it out.

"Your bratty mouth isn't going to get you far around here," he grunted.

"And for some reason you think I care?"

He stepped closer to where she was sitting, towering over her, his shadow blocking out the sun. Her heart beat fast and hard and her palms grew damp where she gripped the edge of her seat. Why was she baiting him? It was stupid and she knew it, yet she couldn't seem to stop.

"You should care, Raina," he said softly. She was beginning to recognize that tone. She'd heard Sotza use it, and other men around the property. Usually when they were discussing something less than savory.

"You need to fuck off, okay?" she snapped. "You did your job, you brought me here. I shouldn't have to put up with you any more. Doesn't Sotza have something else to keep you busy? I don't need you following me around, acting like some kind of creepy babysitter. I'm done with you."

His lips flattened and his nostrils flared. "I'm not done with you, Raina. And I'm keeping track of your disrespect. One day you'll pay up."

She jumped to her feet and waved a finger in his face. "You can't touch me!"

"You think not?" He seemed almost amused, despite his anger.

"Yes!" she exclaimed. "Your boss won't let you."

Now he did laugh, a short bark, a chilling sound. "No one leashes me, chica. Definitely not the Señor. I am his second because I earned it, because I'm the best at my job. I am loyal, but I am not some employee. If I asked for your life, he wouldn't hesitate to give it to me. And one day soon, I will be asking."

Raina shivered at the viciousness of his words. He was supremely confident in everything he was saying. And she had no come back. Just a desperate wish to disappear before he decided to make good on his words. She spun away from him and stomped toward the house throwing him the bird over her shoulder. She was grateful when he didn't follow her in.

She sighed heavily as she walked into the dark, sinister interior of Sotza's home. She'd been there for 14 days now. She hated everything about the place. From the overbearing furniture with its English influence, to the bedroom that she spent so much time in alone, to Sotza himself. The past few days he'd insisted that Raina join him for their evening meal. She had been unable to bring herself to refuse. She didn't dare treat him the way she was treating Mateo. There was something about Sotza that was terrifying and completely unapproachable. She'd heard whispers among the staff about his nickname, the Gentleman Butcher. Raina didn't need further explanation to understand that he was a man better left alone.

Though she tried to be respectful with the man who'd had her kidnapped, she'd nearly crossed the line the evening before when they sat down to eat together. He'd explained to Raina that he would be wedding her mother the following week and that Raina would be attending the church ceremony. She'd understood that there could be no argument.

Raina had been spending plenty of time trying to come to terms with her feelings regarding her birth mother. She knew she would have to meet her. And though she'd spent years searching for the woman, Raina didn't feel ready for a face-to-face, thus she'd refused Sotza when he asked if she wanted a visit. No matter how she tried to look at things, she couldn't stop the deep sense of abandonment every time she thought about Elvira Montana. There was always a streak of resentment when she thought of her mother, though she was mature enough to understand that the woman probably had her reasons. And those reasons were gradually coming to light the more time she spent in Venezuela. If Vee's life in the US had been anything like this, then Raina was starting to understand why Vee had given her up.

She was beginning to suspect that these dinners in Sotza's presence were his way of dealing with Raina's resentment toward her mother. He spoke in his quiet voice about Vee and Miami. Just light stuff, throwing out comments about Vee's interests and how much she enjoyed walking on the beach. He would also ask Raina polite questions about her family and life in Pennsylvania. Though the conversations should have been awkward, they never were. The dinners were not something Raina looked forward to. Sotza spoke with such authority that Raina often felt like a child in his presence. She had no choice but to sit and listen, and then respond if he asked her a question.

Until last evening when Raina finally pushed back. Asked some of the burning questions that she desperately wanted answers to.

"How long are you going to keep me here?" she asked during a lull in the conversation.

He lifted his gaze from the table to study her. When he placed his fork gently on his plate and lifted his napkin to his lips, Raina realized she'd asked a more complicated question than she thought. It made her heart ache. Because if there wasn't a simple answer to when she could go home then that meant she probably wouldn't get the answer she wanted.

"Your presence here is permanent," he said, his dark, cold gaze on her face.

Raina's jaw dropped. It took her a moment to find her voice. He waited patiently until she could speak. "Permanent... as in..."

He didn't speak though. She noticed that about Sotza. Once he said his piece, he didn't repeat himself or clarify unless he felt it was necessary. Still, as clear as he'd been, she just couldn't wrap her head around the idea that she would stay there forever.

"But why?" An edge of panic sharpened her voice. "You have my mother, you said you'll marry her. You said yourself she'll cooperate. Once the wedding is over you don't need me for leverage. My parents will be looking for me, they're probably completely freaking out, wondering if I'm dead or something. You can just let me go back home. I promise I won't say anything about you."

"I'm afraid that's impossible," he said smoothly.

"But I'm nothing to you. You needed me to lure her out of hiding, right? Now you have her, what's the point in keeping me?"

He studied her carefully, his features completely blank. "You are misinformed, child. You were never brought here to be used as leverage against your mother."

Her jaw dropped again. She wasn't? It had been her assumption from the beginning, as soon as she found out her kidnapping had to do with her mother. In a way, the knowledge that she could be used against Elvira created a tiny glow within her. Made her feel like maybe she was more than just a castoff to Elvira. She almost felt a little sorry that she'd been so easily captured. Though she resented Elvira, Raina didn't think her birth mother deserved a lifetime of marriage to this man.

"If I'm not here as a bargaining chip then what the fuck am I here for?" Raina demanded.

"You will watch your language and speak with respect," he said his brows lowering over hard, dark eyes. Something about his swift displeasure made Raina cringe inside. He was one scary son-of-a-bitch. "You are here because you belong to Vee. This is your place now."

Raina frowned and shook her head, trying to take his simple words in and decipher their meaning. "But I don't even know her!"

"You can easily get to know your mother, I haven't blocked your access to her. You should meet her, develop a relationship, she is an extraordinary woman."

Raina guessed as much from what little she got from Mateo and Sotza. She was beginning to understand that her mother was some kind of force to be reckoned with. Raina eyed her captor, her sharp mind whirling. "Why do you want her so bad? Is it because she's so extraordinary?"

"Among other things. She's passionate, loyal, determined. All qualities I admire and wish for in a wife. She is also very beautiful."

"But she seems so cold and unapproachable. I've seen her up in that window, watching everything." Raina didn't really know if Elvira was cold, but it helped her to imagine her mother was awful.

"She isn't cold Raina. She's scared. There's a difference."

"I don't get it, what does she have to be scared of? I saw how angry she was that first day you had her here." Raina had secretly admired the way Elvira had screamed and fought Sotza when he'd dragged her in the house.

"She's scared she'll marry me, fall in love and then I'll turn on her, like her late husband. She's scared you'll reject her even though she loves you more than anyone else on the planet." He delivered the words calmly, though they felt like a punch to the gut for Raina.

She picked at an artfully arranged hole in her jeans while she contemplated his statement. What had Elvira's ex-husband done to her? And why did Raina care, she was a stranger. "So what if I reject her? She deserves it."

"And why is that?" He asked, giving her that look of his that sent shivers straight down her spine. "She deserves to have a daughter who hates her? Why? Because she did every-thing in her power to protect you, give you a life filled with love and certainty."

Raina snorted. "Look how well that turned out. I've been kidnapped and now I'm being held captive, probably for the rest of my life, according to you. Yeah, she did awesome."

"You are spoiled, child."

She was angry with his assertion. She was far from spoiled. She'd worked hard her whole life despite never-ending health struggles. She even managed a lucrative forgery setup. She opened her mouth to tell him off, but he stopped her.

"I don't mean you don't have work ethic. I've seen tran-scripts of your grades and heard about your dedication to martial arts. No, I mean you've been spoiled with love. With an adoptive family that loves you and gave you the best world they were capable of. A child that is content, happy, spoiled, is one that has trouble seeing the world beyond their bubble. You lack compassion for the woman who has given you life and did her best to make that life a good one, despite the pain it caused her."

Raina was speechless. Was she spoiled? Did he have a point? She'd been searching for her mother for years. Telling herself that she wanted to confront the woman who aban-doned her. Now it seemed she needed to adjust her worldview.

Sotza stood, placed his hand on her hair for a second as though sympathizing with her confusion. Raina looked up at him when he spoke again. "You were young when your body began to fail, too young to question where the money came from for your medical bills. But now you are grown, and from what I can see, not entirely stupid. Would a mother who abandoned her child, a mother that didn't love her child, spend nineteen years watching over her?"

Raina sat in stunned silence as Sotza walked from the room, leaving her alone with her confused state of mind.

# CHAPTER TWENTY-FOUR

It took another day before Raina worked up the courage to visit her mother. She'd spent that time turning every tiny detail she knew about Elvira over and over in her mind, until she finally came to the conclusion that she needed to just go see the woman. Decide for herself if Elvira was cold and unapproachable or the caring mother Sotza wanted her to believe she was.

She went to his office and told Sotza she was ready. He'd nodded briefly and sent her upstairs with one of his men. The guy had silently unlocked the door and waved her inside. Raina took a steadying breath and stepped through the door. Her eyes went immediately to the petite blond woman staring out the window. Elvira didn't turn around, giving Raina the advantage of being able to study her for a moment. Elvira's hair was shorter and straighter than Raina's, but otherwise they were probably the same height and weight. Even the way Elvira held her body, stiff, shoulders back, head tilted, was familiar.

"What do you want?" Elvira said coldly, her voice husky.

Raina was shocked until she realized her mother probably

thought she was Sotza. "I can leave if you want," she said tentatively.

Elvira spun around so fast she stumbled and had to reach behind herself to grab the windowsill for balance. Raina's heart thumped painfully and she could feel her face heating. She felt ill-prepared for this meeting and part of her wanted to rush out of the room. But she'd come, and she was going to stay, for a little while at least. Dig up the truth of Sotza's words.

Her mother was a stunningly beautiful woman. Raina had never thought of herself as particularly good-looking. But now, staring into features that were so similar, so arrestingly lovely, she began to feel some pride in sharing facial features with such a beautiful woman. Without thought, she lifted a hand to her own face, touching her cheek for a second. Elvira had the same face shape, same wide blue eyes, same bow-shaped mouth with the fuller bottom lip.

"Raina," she said, taking a few steps toward her daughter.

It was clear from the look on her face that she was not the cool, calculating woman Raina had thought she was. Or at least not when it came to her daughter. Her striking blue eyes were filling with tears and she was shaking with emotion, her breaths coming out in quick, uneven gasps.

Raina felt the wetness in her eyes. There were so many things she wanted to know, wanted to ask. She still felt the same old hurt, but it was softened by the love shining bright and clear in Elvira's face.

Before Raina could speak, Elvira took another step forward and said in a shaking voice, "Please, sit down. I'm sure you have a thousand questions for me."

Raina nodded and took a few steps into the room, her eyes darting around. She decided to sit in the chair. She wasn't ready to get too close to her birth mother. Elvira sat down on the end of the bed, facing Raina. She twisted her hands together, her eyes devouring Raina from head to foot. Raina was doing the same thing. She wanted to see and know everything about Elvira Montana. But she couldn't seem to find her voice.

Elvira's gaze softened. "You must be wondering why." Her voice wavered as she struggled with tears. "Why I gave you up, how you ended up here, in this place."

Raina nodded. She wanted to know all those things, but mostly, she wanted Elvira to keep speaking in her lovely husky voice. She wanted to listen to this woman who gave birth to her, memorize everything about her. Then she felt a sharp stab of guilt, pain as she thought of her adoptive parents. People that she loved unreservedly, but that she hadn't really thought of much since arriving, except a gnawing worry over how they must be feeling with Raina missing.

"I was barely a child myself when I found out I was pregnant. Younger than you are now," Elvira said, her eyes darkening. "But if that had been the only complication, I would have kept you in a heartbeat. I would have made my way as a single mother."

"Then why?" Raina asked, swiping at tears.

Elvira seemed to struggle with her words. Finally, she said, her voice hardening, "I belong to the mafia, Raina. My parents were mafia, I'm mafia – it's my whole life. It's not a proper life for anyone, especially a child, a girl. I didn't want that for you and that would've been the outcome if I'd kept you. I had to make a choice, a hard one."

Raina turned the words over, struggling to reconcile the way she felt about this woman for her entire life and the reality. As Elvira spoke, Raina's resentment ebbed. Raina had never imagined what it might be like to become involved in the mafia, had no real understanding of the brutality that must be involved. She'd been too sheltered. Of course, she knew the mafia existed. Had seen documentaries and the news. But that was a life that never touched her. Until now. These last couple of weeks, being here, with hard men who wore guns and used violence to get their point across. She kind of got it.

"I wanted better for you," Elvira continued, her voice stronger now. "I would have done anything to ensure your future was different from mine."

"But why didn't you just come with me, why not just take me and disappear?" Raina asked.

Elvira opened her mouth to answer, then closed it and shook her head. She looked like she was struggling to find the right words. Finally, she said, "It was too dangerous, Raina. You have to understand, once a person is in the mafia, especially deep, like I was... like I am, it becomes impossible to leave. There really isn't any place to just disappear that they won't find you."

Raina didn't like the answer, but she was beginning to understand. She took a deep breath and asked, "Can you tell me more? Tell me what it was like for you?"

Elvira nodded and settled onto the bed, relaxing slightly. "Some parts of it were amazing. I can't find fault with the money, the jewels and clothes. It wasn't worth the bullshit that came with it, men treating me like a commodity, but those other things were always a nice perk."

Raina's lips twitched and she felt herself beginning to smile despite the intense moment. She'd discovered she also enjoyed the freedom money could buy, had found her own little piece of the underworld to achieve that financial freedom. "How did you meet our lovely host?" she asked, beginning to form her own conclusion. She'd definitely guessed at Sotza's shadiness, but now that she knew her mother was mafia, she pretty much figured Sotza would be the same.

Elvira laughed. "It's somewhat complex, but basically, my boss sent him after me when I started having trouble keeping

Miami under control. You see, I'd managed to climb my way up the ladder until I controlled my own little slice of the pie."

Rather than being horrified that her mother was more firmly entrenched in the mafia than she could have imagined, she was curious. And a little bit proud. If what Raina was understanding was true, then her mother, a beautiful and relatively young woman, was the boss of a criminal organization.

"So your boss wanted you to get married to this Sotza guy?" Raina asked.

"No," Elvira said darkly. "My boss wanted me dead. Sotza's the one that decided he wanted something else from me. I think I intrigued him, the female mob boss that refused to give up her city."

The emotions that whirled through Raina surfaced and clashed one at a time. She was shocked, she was horrified. But she was also impressed. Elvira sounded like a force to be reckoned with. Even if she'd ended up the captive of a powerful man, she'd fought valiantly. "That's so medieval," Raina said, both awe and disgust in her voice. "He's forcing you into marriage and the alternate is... what? Death?"

Elvira's lips twitched again, and she said, "That's a little simplistic, but yes, I suppose you have the basics correct. Although, at this point, I suspect there is no alternative to Sotza."

Raina frowned. "But you have to keep fighting him, you'll find a way out. You can't be forced into marriage."

"It wouldn't be the first time." The words were spoken softly but seemed to hold a wealth of emotion.

Raina was beginning to see the depth of her mother's life. And it hadn't been an easy one. "Can you tell me about it?" she asked, standing. She moved shyly toward the bed. Vee moved over, making room for her. Raina sat, making sure to keep a little distance between them.

Vee sighed. "It's really not a pretty story, but if you want to know, I'll tell you. There are things you'll learn about me that you might not want to know."

"I'll risk it," Raina said with a small smile. "I'd like to know."

"Alright," Vee agreed and looked down at her lap, as though gathering the words. "I was well into my 20's when I met Tony. You'd been gone for several years already. Up until that point I'd only experimented with drugs. I drank too much, but it was part of the life. We women went to the clubs, we drank, we danced, we became conquests for the tough guys. I was smarter than others, used my looks to get as much as I could out of the guys. Then I met Tony. He swept me off my feet, and not in a good way. He was an underling to Frank, the man I was living with at the time. He decided he wanted Frank's empire and, after a while of working for him, Tony took over."

"How did he do that?" Raina whispered, terribly afraid she already knew.

Vee looked over at her, a dullness to her eyes now. "Tony murdered Frank and some of his top guys. Then Tony moved in and set his own people up. A classic takeover. And, as in many takeovers, I was a commodity, passed on to the next guy. Maybe I could have disappeared, tried to leave in the confusion. But Tony had a bead on me, and I'd begun to use more. Become dependent on drugs and alcohol to dull all that shit."

"Drugs?" Raina asked, trying to keep the accusation from her voice. She'd always considered drug addicts as weak, unable or unwilling to find the courage to quit. Now that she was listening to her mother's story, Raina was beginning to question her assumptions.

"Cocaine," Vee said succinctly. "Our main product. Tony became addicted too."

The disdain Vee felt for her late husband was clear in her

voice. "He was pretty awful?" Raina asked softly, feeling more than just curiosity now. She was seeing the incredible, painful life of this woman and it hurt.

"Yes," Vee said, her voice low. "I was his property. His pretty ornament. Just something to decorate his arm and his mansion. He didn't love me and he certainly never respected me. Unfortunately, I wasn't the type to fade into the background. I spoke back to him, often. Which resulted in a lot fighting."

Raina's stomach clenched. She took in her petite mother, saw her as she must have been, addicted to cocaine, fighting for her rights in a world that didn't acknowledge the rights of women like her. "He hit you?"

Vee laughed bitterly and inclined her head in a semi-nod. She didn't elaborate though.

Raina supposed she didn't want to get into the worst of it. "What happened to him?" she asked, though she was beginning to suspect she knew. If Tony had killed Frank and taken over his organization, then Vee must've done something to earn her way to the top of Miami's mafia.

"He's dead." Vee was matter-of-fact, though her shoulders were stiff with tension. No doubt, waiting for Raina's judgment. Her tone of voice indicated the subject was closed, that Raina shouldn't push the how of Tony's death. She wasn't entirely sure she wanted to know yet anyway.

"Good." Raina hardened her voice. Maybe her mother was a murderer, had blood on her hands. Had fought her way to the top of a criminal food chain. But life had shaped her this way. She could have given up years ago, stayed on drugs and lived a shadowed life until she was no longer pretty enough to capture the attention of those tough guys. "You're clean now, you don't take drugs?"

Vee looked at her seriously. "I haven't used in over a year. But that's not long, Raina. Any addict will tell you, once an addict always an addict. And a year clean is only a drop in the bucket."

Raina thought about it, turned her mother's words over in her head. They made sense, but she was beginning to know this woman, beginning to see the extraordinary things Sotza saw in her. "You won't go back on drugs," Raina said confidently.

Vee smiled. A real smile that showed her teeth and she reached out to touch Raina, the first time the two women had touched since Raina was a baby. "Thank you."

Raina nodded as Vee's hand fell away from her arm. She missed the touch. She could feel the spot on her arm, almost like it burned, her awareness was so heightened. She turned on the bed, bringing her knee up and said, "You can't do it again. You can't marry another mobster who... who just takes you. As though you're some kind of prize. It isn't right, you earned more, you deserve more."

Vee blinked rapidly and Raina thought she might cry. She took a couple of breaths and finally said, "I appreciate that you think that, Raina. You have no idea how much it means to me. But I don't have a choice. In less than a week Sotza will marry me."

Raina shook her head. "But why? There has to be a way out! We'll find something."

Vee smiled gently, her face smooth and happy as she looked Raina over. As though pride in her daughter was erasing all the sadness of her situation. And Raina knew, though her mother didn't say a word, that as long as Sotza had her, then Vee would do anything he asked. Even though he insisted Raina wasn't a bargaining chip, Vee would never risk it.

"Now it's time for you to tell me about yourself, Raina." Vee's voice had changed from melancholy to eager. "Don't leave out any details. I want to know everything."

# CHAPTER TWENTY-FIVE

The week that Vee and Raina spent getting to know each other was the best that Vee had ever experienced. Raina came to Vee's room every day and spent hours with her, telling her about her life with her adoptive parents, her time at University, her friends, everything. Vee soaked up each new fact like a starving woman. She thought, if this moment ever came, that it would hurt to hear about her daughter's life separate from hers. But instead of jealousy over her missed time, she could only feel gratitude that Raina had grown into such a lovely young woman.

Vee had more difficulty sharing her own life with Raina, after their first conversation. There wasn't much about her past that she was proud of or that was good enough that it wouldn't be a burden for Raina to know. So instead, Vee encouraged her daughter to talk about herself. Once Raina started to set aside the hurt she'd carried with her since child-hood, she was happy to open up to her birth mother. And Vee was more than happy to listen. She loved knowing that, despite Raina's serious health issues, she'd experienced a contented life. For that, Vee felt she owed Diane and Joe Duncan. They'd done exactly as they'd promised, given Raina everything that Vee couldn't.

Raina showed a maturity for her years that Vee was proud of. Raina was intelligent, determined and independent. She was in the process of putting herself through school, paying for it through a part-time job and her forgery set-up. Vee had wanted to pay Raina's way through University, but the girl was sharp and old enough to have questioned where the money came from. So Vee had watched from the shadows, ready to step in if it looked like Raina was struggling. Far from struggling though, the child had used her keen mind and kept her own source of funds flowing. Vee was pretty sure that she should scold the girl for doing something illegal, that as a parent she was supposed to try to steer her child on the straight and narrow, but she couldn't seem to summon any disapproval. She was impressed with Raina for finding a relatively harmless but lucrative method of supplementing her income.

The more time Vee spent with Raina the more her hatred toward Sotza waned. Despite his less than savoury method of procuring her child, he was still responsible for reuniting the two women. He also encouraged them to spend as much time as they wanted together in the week leading up to the wedding.

Though grudgingly, Vee was also grateful for the safe environment that Sotza provided for their reunification. She couldn't have contact with Raina while she was under Tony's thumb and she couldn't risk contact after she became the queen of Miami. At that point she'd had to let the idea of ever seeing Raina again go. She couldn't risk enemies catching wind of her weakness. Especially when she experienced so many problems from the Mexican cartel. But now, under

Sotza's roof, Vee and Raina were safe. Though Vee was still angry at the way things had played out in Miami, she was grateful for this unexpected opportunity.

After their first conversation, Vee and Raina stopped talking about how to get Vee out of her upcoming nuptials. She assured her daughter that she was fine, that she was would make the best of the situation and eventually escape when opportunity presented itself. Instead they spent the days talking about life, preparing for the wedding and making plans. Though wary of her soon-to-be stepfather, Raina had become decidedly bossy when it came to Vee having the best of everything for her wedding. She directed the ordering of Vee's gown and talked to the chef about their reception.

During her incarceration, Sotza's mealtime visits to her room continued. He talked while she listened, but instead of ignoring him, she occasionally contributed to the conversation. She'd been unable to hold back. She wanted... needed to tell someone about Raina. About how smart the girl was, how proud Vee was of her. She also needed to talk through her feelings. Not something she'd ever really done before. But Sotza's persistent, quietly thoughtful presence wore her down until she found herself telling him things she wouldn't normally ever consider divulging. Not even to Casey, whom she considered her best friend.

"And she's funded almost her entire University education with this document forgery set-up she has going. I think her job at the campus library is just a front in case anyone looks deeper into her financial situation. She must be quite good at forging to be doing as well as she is," Vee told him when he stopped in for breakfast that morning. "I mean, part of me thinks I should warn her to stay away from that sort of thing. But she's so smart, I just know she won't get herself in any trouble. What do you think, Sotza?"

He had looked at her, silent for a moment, his dark brown eyes warming a little as he considered her. "I think she's as smart as her mother. She'll figure it out as she goes, and we'll be here for her if she missteps and needs help." Vee felt a tiny glow at the way he said *we*, as though he was as invested in Raina's future as she was. She hadn't known what to say, so she'd stayed silent while he continued. "I also think it's time you started calling me Isaac."

"Why would I do that?" She frowned at him.

His lips curved in genuine amusement. "Because it is my name, cariño."

Her mouth had opened in shock for a moment and then she said the first thing that jumped into her mind. "But I thought your name was just Sotza."

He'd chuckled. "Most people have first and last names, Vee. Sometimes even middle names."

"Do you have a middle name," she asked curiously.

He'd stood and approached her. Vee was too stunned by the knowledge of his first name to think about moving away. So when he touched her, running his hand from her wrist, up her arm to her face and touching her cheek lightly, she just blinked at him, waiting for him to speak. His touch sent tingles through her. It was so light but so evocative. She had the urge to melt into him.

"I suppose you'll have to wait and see if I have a middle name."

"Wait for what?" she whispered, tilting her head up to look at him. She liked the way his face softened just a little whenever they talked like this.

"You'll have to wait for the priest to say our names on our wedding day, joining them together," he said, his voice dropping a little. Her breath caught and fire erupted in her veins as both his fingers and his words touched her. It was probably the most romantic thing anyone had ever said to her, yet it had that tiny bit of his sinister brand.

Sotza dropped his lips to hers, kissing her. It wasn't exactly a chaste kiss nor was it punishing. Instead, his lips coaxed hers. He curved his long fingers along the side of her head burying them in her hair and holding her face still. He pressed his mouth to hers, breathing in as he lowered his head, taking in her scent and groaning a little as it hit him. And though she could feel the passion of his kiss, feel the rigid tension in his body, he held himself back from devouring her. She was helpless against him. She hesitated for just a moment and then pressed herself against him, tilting her face to deepen their kiss.

He brought his other hand up, clutching her head, holding her still for his exploration. Her breathing grew rapidly uneven, mingling with his as he deepened their kiss. The slight roughness of his chin and cheeks against her softer skin sent a thrill through her. Her nipples hardened in response and her lower belly felt as though it was melting. She almost wished he would raise her skirt, touch her where she ached to be touched. Where she hadn't wanted anyone to touch her in so long, couldn't stand the thought. Sotza... Isaac... was showing her how wrong she'd been. He was thawing her out.

He didn't lift her skirt, didn't touch her breasts. Instead, he lifted his head. Held onto hers for a moment longer, looking down into her eyes, powerful emotion blazing in his dark depths. Then he released her, stepping away. He kept a hand on her arm until she was steady and then he picked up her empty breakfast tray and moved to the door.

"Do you know my middle name?" Vee asked, her voice huskier than usual. He paused, the grooves around his mouth deepening as he fought a smile.

"I do," he admitted.

"Well, what is it?" she demanded breathlessly.

He chuckled, the sound vibrating through her aroused body and flooding her with more sensations. "I guess you'll find out on our wedding day."

And for the first time, Vee genuinely laughed in his presence.

# CHAPTER TWENTY-SIX

The bride had mixed feelings on her wedding day. Sotza did not. Every step he took with Vee felt right. Felt like destiny. Which wasn't something he'd ever considered before. He believed that life was what you made it. Every move he made was carefully calculated, the outcome prearranged and optimized. He looked at the world and understood how it worked. He made sure there were no surprises, and when there were, he went to work.

Vee had been a surprise. He hadn't expected the Miami madam to take hold of him, sweep him up in her storm and grip him in a way nothing else had. He'd loved before. And he'd lost. That woman was perfection in every way. Light-hearted, carefree, beautiful. She had been the light to his darkness. When she married someone else he had chosen to love from afar. He could have taken her, could have forced her into his life, as he was doing with Vee. But he hadn't, had thought at the time that he preferred to give the woman he loved anything she wanted, even if what she wanted was another man.

Now he understood that his attachment to Sandra,

Casey Reyes' mother, hadn't been as deep as he thought. His feelings for Sandra had been genuine affection and appreciation, heartbreak when she was killed. What he felt for Vee was soul deep. It gripped his heart, the very fibre of his being, and latched on. He didn't know if it was love. It felt like more than love. It was possessive. Intense. Consuming and obsessive. She occupied all of his thoughts, his decisions now based on her best interests, her comfort, hopefully her future happiness. He used to believe that men obsessed with their wives became weak, but Vee made him strong. She made him wary and protective. He would never let her go.

He watched her step out of the vehicle, Mateo on one side of her and Raina on the other. Three more bodyguards surrounded the group. She was magnificent. Her beautiful, radiant exterior the perfect wrapping for a deep, dark woman. A woman that called to him. She owned him. And he was about to make it legal.

He couldn't wait to bind her to him. He believed if she'd still been married when he met her he would've killed her husband and taken her anyway, quite the same way Reyes had acquired his wife. His sharp eyes followed her as she walked up the steps to meet him at the top. She was breathtakingly elegant in her strapless golden wedding dress. The dress draped in a straight line, hugging her petite curves from top to bottom, the colour setting off her radiant glow. It fit her perfectly.

He held a hand out to her as she approached, her intelligent sapphire gaze steady on his face. He wondered if she would take it or if she would ignore it. If she would balk, refuse to touch him and make a show of her reluctance to marry. Though he enjoyed their dance, he found her unpredictable. Never knew if she would attack or treat him with cold indifference. He lived for the moments she finally warmed, unable to help herself from melting as he stole a kiss.

Vee stepped up to him, so close that the bottom of her dress flared a little around her sandaled feet and brushed his pant leg. Without taking her eyes from his she took his hand, sliding her fingers across his palm and locking them together. She might be a reluctant bride, might still be angry, but she was declaring an alliance. Satisfaction flooded through him as he closed his fingers around her slim hand, trapping her in his hold. Together they turned and entered the church.

Sotza had the church built on his land decades ago, a place for his employees and their families to worship. He didn't go often. Didn't feel he had any right to such a place of goodness. But on his wedding day, he felt the need to attach his bride to his side in the humble building, a place that was stamped by him, a place within his control. He wouldn't allow a single security issue to mess up his wedding day.

Their walk to the alter was short. The pews were already occupied by many of his people. He was a little surprised at how many showed up. The wedding wasn't a mandatory event. Yet the place was filled, some even left standing. He nodded toward Armand, head of his internal security. Sotza didn't think he'd ever seen the man in anything less than his full combat gear. He lived, ate and breathed security. Yet, here he was, at a wedding, wearing a suit, a young woman at his side.

What drew them to the church? Was it curiosity, boredom or true loyalty to their leader? Glancing down at Vee, he remembered the loyalty she'd inspired in her people. The way they flocked to her, tried to protect her, would lay down their lives for her. She was vicious in her own right, but she was also passionate, warm and kind, when the occasion warranted. She was exactly the woman he wanted at his side, inspiring these same feelings in his people. Perhaps they were drawn to the church to see the woman that had finally captured Sotza's attention.

Though a catholic ceremony, Sotza had ensured that the ceremony wouldn't be a long one. He was done waiting for this woman, done watching her every move, his imagination wild with the things he wanted to do with and to her. It was like he'd waited years for Elvira and a moment more was too much. He ran his thumb over her hand, feeling the delicate bone structure beneath. Now his to take care of until one of them left the Earth.

He repeated his vows solemnly, only stopping to throw Vee a small smile when their full names were spoken. She blushed when, instead of a simple 'I do' he repeated the vow, "I, Isaac Rafael Sotza, take Elvira Vivian Montana to be my lawfully wedded wife."

When it was her turn, she lifted her chin and repeated the same vow. Almost. "I, Vee Montana, take Isaac Rafael Sotza to be my lawfully wedded husband."

He wanted to laugh but held it in. She was giving him a gift. By repeating their names the way she had, she'd declared in front of God, his people, everyone, that she was now his partner. His equal. The queen that would stand by his side and rule his kingdom with him.

It was perfect.

She was perfect.

# CHAPTER TWENTY-SEVEN

When the wedding ceremony ended they went up to the main house to enjoy an extravagant and delicious brunch, overseen by Raina. For the first time Vee was able to observe her daughter and Sotza together. It was clear that Sotza indulged the girl, had perhaps even grown fond of her, though it was hard to tell. He kept his emotions carefully contained, his face rarely showing his thoughts, though she detected a modicum of warmth in his gaze as he tracked the girl across the room, watched silently while she bossed his staff.

Vee was surprised when Sotza leaned down to tell her that their car was ready. She looked up at him, frowning in question. "Our honeymoon," he explained.

She hadn't thought there would be any kind of honeymoon. She expected him to treat the marriage as more of a business transaction now that the deed was done. She supposed she shouldn't be surprised though, given the fiery nature of their relationship and Sotza's tendency toward the old-fashioned.

After saying their good-byes, they were driven to the airstrip where a plane was waiting for them. It wasn't the same plane she had arrived in. This one was smaller, built to carry fewer people. Sotza opened the passenger side and lifted her easily up into the craft. He took the pilot seat, leaning across her to belt her in. After making sure she was comfortable he checked the instruments and had a brief conversation with Mateo, who he was leaving in charge while they were away.

It was clear that Sotza was an expert at flying. Vee's eyes followed the movements of his strong, veined hands. She watched the way he scanned the horizon and made adjustments to the instruments. It was sexy. There was something about the ease and careful control he showed while flying that got to her. Tony had been controlling, but he hadn't been able to maintain control. He was addicted to his own product, he was violent, but not in the same way as Sotza. Tony had been an angry man. If something didn't go his way then he would become infuriated, blame everyone except himself. Somehow Vee suspected Sotza was far different. He was definitely violent, but every move he made was calculated, controlled to produce a result.

"Where are we going?" she finally asked. She was eager to know, but hesitant to find out.

Sotza looked over at her, the corners of his eyes crinkling. "I have an island off the coast. We'll spend a few days there. I know you won't want to be away from Raina for long."

He was right. It had been a wrench to leave her daughter behind, even for a few days. Just before they left the mansion Raina had hugged her. It was the first time. Vee had teared up but turned her face away so no one would see her emotion. She'd held her daughter close, pressing her tight, for just a few seconds, before releasing her.

"Will we land right on the island?" Vee asked.

"No, we'll land outside of Caracas, drive to the coast and take a boat out to the island."

Caracas. The capital city of Venezuela. Vee had trouble wrapping her brain around the idea that she was in this place. That she'd travelled so far from her home. As sophisticated as she tried to present herself, she was still just a big fish in a small pond when it came to Miami. Travelling internationally had always been a distant dream, something she'd aspired to as she worked on educating herself through the years, but not something she thought would actually happen.

She pressed her hand against the window, watching eagerly as the city unfolded below them. The sun was just beginning to set, lighting up the valley in an array of colours. "It's so beautiful!" she exclaimed, as she tried to search out individual assets of a city steeped in history.

Sotza spoke to her, raising his voice so she could hear him above the engine. He pointed out cathedrals, downtown Caracas, the industrial district. His knowledge of the capital was vast and his pride in his country came through loud and clear. He stopped talking to her as he prepared to land. She admired the easy way he maneuvered the craft, setting them down lightly on the tarmac. There were so many things to appreciate about the man. It seemed strange that they'd started out as bitter enemies. Well... she'd just been business to him, but she'd hated the very idea of him. The Venezuelan Butcher, in her city, sent to take her down.

Now they were married. Thrown together through circumstance but merged through his dogged determination. It was a difficult thing to resist, his unwavering drive to possess her. In her life time Vee had been coveted, she'd been passed around, she'd been a possession. But no one had wanted her the way Sotza did, saw the things in her that he did.

She raised her arms when he leaned in to unbuckle her, reaching up to brush her hair aside so it wouldn't catch in the belt. She breathed in his scent, looked down at the smooth darkness of his hair while he touched her. He was such a strange contradiction of old world formality and sharp intelligence. He saw her strengths and encouraged them, rather than beat them out of her. Now that she was well and truly caught by the Venezuelan arms dealer, she could allow herself to bask in the exhilarating sensation of his deep regard for her.

He jumped out of the plane first, coming around to her side and opening the door. She waited for him, knowing he would want to assist her. When he reached for her, she turned in her seat and slid out of the plane. His strong hands circling her waist, he lifted her out and set her on the ground in front of him. She twisted around and looked up. He searched her face for a moment and then took her hand, leading her toward the hangar.

"Where's our security?" she asked curiously. It had been so long since she'd gone anywhere by herself that the freedom of being alone, without protection, was both frightening and freeing.

"The only person who knows of our honeymoon plans is Mateo. I didn't want anyone else disturbing us. Of course, there's security on the island itself, but they will be discreet."

Vee felt her face heat and wanted to roll her eyes at herself. She was a thirty-seven-year old woman with a lifetime of experience. But something about this man made her feel shy. She hoped he wouldn't be disappointed. While experienced, she hadn't been called on to do much in the bedroom department. Just entertain the men that expected a fuck. Somehow, she thought faking it wouldn't go over with Sotza. He was too subtle, too nuanced. He would want honesty from her. Could she give it to him?

The short drive to the coast was mostly in silence. Vee was too nervous to speak. Normally she might break silence like this with a biting, snappy comment, but today, she had nothing to say. Sotza had lapsed into his typical quiet. He never seemed to feel the need to fill silence with conversation. He only spoke when he had something to say.

Two men, wearing the standard security uniform of green and black, met them at the docks. Sotza briefly introduced Vee to Juan and John. She had to swallow a laugh at their names as she solemnly shook their hands. Sotza instructed her to go to either of the men if she needed anything. He told his men that they were to listen to Vee without hesitation. She understood. He didn't mean they would help her with meals or household chores. Sotza trusted her to recognize threats and to go to these two men if she had concerns about their safety. She wanted to thank him for acknowledging her ability to assess a situation and call the shots when needed, but she held her tongue. Their whirlwind marriage, preceded by a contentious and bloody engagement, made her question everything. Him, herself, their situation. She wasn't ready to feel gratitude toward Sotza.

The sun had set as the boat docked and Sotza reached for her arm and helped her step out of the boat while his men secured it. She walked off the dock and onto the sand. The hem of her skirt brushed the sand and when she tried to kneel down to unbuckle her sandals, the dress stretched tight across her ass and hips, preventing her.

"Let me," Sotza said, his voice a husky timbre.

She held her breath as he went down on one knee in front of her in the sand. The back of his hands brushed her skin, sending tingles up her leg as his sure fingers worked quickly with the tiny, delicate buckle. In seconds she was free.

"Lift your foot," he said sliding his hand up her bare calf, beneath her dress, holding her so she could step out of the shoe. She braced herself with one hand on his back and lifted her foot, sinking it into the sand. He quickly helped her with the next until she was standing barefoot. The smooth, cool sand embraced her.

Vee grinned, turning away from him and walking toward the water. She inhaled deeply, taking in the ocean scent, so familiar yet also different. She walked from dry sand to wet, holding her skirt around her knees, and sighed as the water rushed over her toes up to her ankles. It was wonderful. Slightly cool, but not uncomfortable.

"You missed it," Sotza said coming up behind her.

She nodded. "It's a powerful thing. Sometimes wonderful, sometimes terrifying. But the one thing it isn't, is judgmental. The ocean is steady, it never leaves. No matter what was happening in my life, I could always go back, like I was going home."

"I understand," he said. "I feel the same about my jungle. It's wild, untamed. Growing up, I became a part of it. When I went to boarding school in England the separation was unbearable. Like a physical disturbance in my soul."

Vee looked up at him. His words were quite poetic for such a practical man. She wondered if anyone else had ever heard The Butcher speak in such a way.

He picked up her shoes for her and ushered her toward an all-terrain vehicle. They sat in the back while his men sat in the front. She wondered where the guards would stay. She hoped not in the house with them. Vee was nervous enough without having men she didn't know or trust hanging around too close. She glanced at Sotza. His head was turned toward her, but she couldn't see his eyes in the dim interior. She could feel the heat of his gaze on her though, knew he was contemplating the night to come.

He helped her out of the vehicle, holding the door open for her. She winced when a rock bit into the bottom of her foot.

"I'm sorry, I should have realized," he said, and before she knew what was happening, her feet were swept right out from under her and she was lifted up against Sotza's chest. She knew he was strong, tougher even than many of the younger men that traipsed around his property. He held her effortlessly and strode toward the house. One of his men tried to get the door for them, but Sotza was too quick. In the blink of an eye he was carrying her across the threshold.

"Smooth," Vee murmured. "If I didn't know any better, I would think that was planned."

Sotza stared down at her. There was no amusement in his eyes, just heat. Like he was finally allowing himself to feel everything he'd been holding back, showing her those emotions. And if she was right, he wanted her desperately, lust blazing clear through his dark, enigmatic gaze.

"Leave," he threw over his shoulder.

His men didn't need further instructions, they closed the door and left Sotza and Vee alone. He didn't put her down. He carried her through the house, which was illuminated with soft lighting. Her heart pounded and she could barely catch her breath. She dug her nails into his shoulder and held on tight as they entered the bedroom.

He carried her to the bed, a huge four poster that dominated the room, and laid her on it. He knelt on the bed beside her, looking down at her, his dark eyes ravenous, his features creased in hunger. He looked like a Spanish conqueror. He was a Spanish conqueror. He took the things he wanted without mercy. He'd earned the nickname Butcher through his ruthless bid to claim territory, his effortless ability to take out the obstacles in his path and his terrifying methods of subduing his enemies.

And she was his prize. His wife.

"Sotza... please," she whispered as he leaned back to remove his jacket.

"Isaac," he corrected her.

"Isaac." His name came out a breathless gasp, a plea.

# CHAPTER TWENTY-EIGHT

Vee was afraid.

She hadn't been afraid like this in a long time. She could handle people shooting at her. Knives, gas canisters, whatever. She'd experienced a lot of bad stuff and caused her fair share too. But this... was different. Being intimate with a man like Sotza, it was too much. Though they'd spent a little time getting to know each other, it wasn't nearly enough. Not enough to give her the courage to go to bed with a man like him.

She summoned up some courage and said in the coolest voice she could manage, "Please excuse me, I need to wash up."

She didn't give him a chance to respond. She pushed past him and slipped off the bed. Gathering her carry-all case she walked toward the washroom.

"Closet." Sotza said as she reached for the knob.

She peeked inside. Yup, it was a closet. She felt dizzy from anxiety and reached automatically for the next door as though it were a lifeline. He didn't say another word as she disappeared into the washroom. She let out the breath she'd been holding, slumping back against the door. She covered her eyes with shaking hands and counted, the way her addictions counsellor had taught her if she felt overwhelmed. Each number was a space in time, a pause to consider, a way of appreciating each moment of life. She whispered the numbers out loud, forcing herself to turn each one over on her tongue and in her mind. Feel the pause and appreciate her ability to have that precious time.

When she reached five, she was able to peek through her fingers and sit down on the edge of a spacious cream-coloured marble tub. At six she fully opened her eyes and looked around, taking in the gorgeous washroom. It was elegant with hints of tropical. Even nicer than Nico Graza's washroom, which she had appreciated during their time in Mexico.

"Eight," she said out loud, pausing to reach under her dress for her gun, which she'd strapped to her thigh. She set it on the counter, focusing on it, absorbing the control it gave her. It was the weapon Sotza had given her. He hadn't taken it back. He wasn't stupid enough to have forgotten about it. He allowed her to keep it for a reason. Either he trusted her not to shoot him, which was insane, or he thought he was impervious to bullets. With his reputation he might very well be bulletproof.

"Twelve." The tightness in her chest eased and she took her first full breath since Sotza carried her into the house.

The door opened. He didn't knock, didn't call her name or warn her. He just walked in and looked down at her, his face as grim as ever. He'd only given her a few seconds to compose herself. She wanted to yell at him, tell him he was a pervert, a kidnapper, that he wasn't fair. But none of it mattered. Life wasn't fair. She'd spent decades proving that theory. Life was what you made it. Sotza had been determined to take her, and he did. Now, it was up to Vee to determine the next move.

Her throat was dry, she had to swallow before she could speak. She gave him the best piercing stare she had in her repertoire. Given the incredible make-up job Mariana, Vee's maid, had done for the wedding, Vee knew that her pointed look was both stunning and confident.

"I need more time," she said as steadily as she could.

"No," he said instantly. He was standing straight and tall, filling the doorway. He'd discarded both his jacket and tie, rolled the cuffs of his shirt up his strong arms. As always, seeing The Butcher relax sent warning sparks of trepidation through her.

"Why?" she asked, standing, glad that her legs were steady enough to hold her. She was so much shorter than him that she needed every inch of height she could summon. "It makes no difference if we fuck now or later. I just... I don't feel like it right now. If you'll please leave, I'd like to get ready for bed."

"More time won't better prepare you, Vee," he said evenly, his dark eyes sharp on her pale face. "We will consummate this marriage tonight."

He stepped toward her. Vee stepped back, hitting the edge of the tub. She slid sideways, reaching for the sink. Reaching for her gun. "Consummation is old-fashioned garbage," she said coldly, closing her fingers around the metal. The solid feel of the weapon in her hand calmed her. "I don't feel like fucking right now, please go away."

"This isn't just fucking, Vee," he said calmly, closing the space between them. She brought the gun between them, still holding it low. She couldn't bring herself to raise it just yet, to actually threaten him. "That's why you're so scared, this is something else. Something you've never experienced."

"What are we doing then, if not fucking?" she tried to sound scathing, but the words were breathless as she battled serious anxiety and the beginnings of arousal.

He moved so close the warmth of his big body touched her, wrapped around her bare arms and penetrated the thin fabric of her dress. She realized she was shaking, her hands, her arms, her legs. Everything was vibrating.

"You're going to give your body to me tonight," he said, leaning down, his face so close to hers she could see the tiny golden flecks in the dark drown. "And you're terrified that if you give up your body, you'll give up everything else. Your emotions, your control, your ability to fight. You've been fighting your whole life, Vee." He reached up, slowly, and took her face in his hands. "Stop fighting me, cariño."

And then, heedless of the gun between them, he wrapped an arm around her back, pulled her against his chest and kissed her. He kissed her with passion and longing, with the fire that'd been missing from every other kiss in her life, except her kisses with this man. She let him kiss her. Take her lips as he'd taken everything else that belonged to her. He wasn't holding back anymore. She could feel the difference. Unlike the other times he'd kissed her, this kiss was more urgent, more desperate. It was a prelude.

One of his hands cupped the side of her head, holding her still, while the fingers of his other hand bit into her ribcage, so hard he was almost hurting her, showing her how near to the surface his savage was. As soon as he lifted his lips from hers, she opened her mouth to gasp for breath. She barely had a second and he was on her again. Vee didn't know if she was participating or holding still for his assault. But as her passion rose to meet his, she didn't care. She hung on tight, clinging to him with her one free hand.

He thrust his tongue into her mouth, taking everything in one sweep. He was commanding, demanding and completely unrepentant as he took her roughly. She was experiencing a new side of the Venezuelan mob boss. Passion mixed with violence. The combination of emotions was intensely heady, it called to her own savage. This was a side of Sotza that people sensed, but rarely experienced, except for those few he killed himself.

Finally, after allowing him control for a few stunned moments, she fought him for dominance, winding her arms around his neck and forcing his head down to hers. Her pulse soared, the blood pounding through her body, heating her from the inside out. Her skin felt on fire, alive and clambering for the man whose touch ignited her. She clutched his shoulders, digging her nails into his satin vest, before moving up to grip his head. She accidentally smacked him in the ear with her gun. Neither cared.

Sotza gripped her waist and lifted her onto the counter, his hands spanning her, holding her in place. Vee tried to open her legs, tried to grip him tighter between her thighs, bring him closer to the place that ached, but her skirt was too tight. She whimpered into his mouth. Understanding her dilemma, he held her in place with one arm and reached between them, reached for her skirt, thrusting it up past her thighs. She vaguely heard a seam rip as the delicate fabric gave way to his rough handling. The sound seemed to spur him on. He slammed his hips between her thighs, pressing his erection tight against her pussy. The leather of her thigh holster bit into her skin, heightening her already soaring arousal.

Vee moaned deep in her throat and tilted her head back, giving him access to her throat. She widened her legs and pulled him harder against her, tilting her hips to meet his, savouring the erotic sensations that flooded through her. Her nails scraped against his skin, her fingers desperate as she reached for the buttons on his vest, yanking at them. When they didn't part for her, he reached impatiently between them and pulled the material apart, damaging the fabric.

Vee didn't care, neither of them cared. She yanked his shirt up, desperately needing to feel his skin beneath her fingers. It felt so good, so right to touch him, to be touched by him. She couldn't believe she hadn't willingly done it before. Emotion flooded her as her seeking fingers finally touched bare skin and tears leapt to her eyes. She slid her hands across his belly and around his side, the cold metal of the gun touching his warm, smooth skin. Everywhere she touched he was hard. Skin stretched taut over muscle and bone. She felt the grooves in his belly from an intense workout regime. She wasn't surprised. The man demanded perfection from his men. He would ask no less of himself. Age didn't matter, nor circumstance or position. He was a born leader.

He lifted his head to look down at her, holding her tight while she dug her hands deep into his sides, anchoring herself against him. The cool mask had dropped, leaving behind lust, want, emotion, intense need. She knew her face reflected all of the same things. They were vulnerable to each other.

His lips crashed over hers and he reached between them. He dug his fingers into her lace panties, wrapping them around the soaked crotch and pulling hard. Vee gasped into his mouth as the fabric tore, marking her flesh as thread parted from the force he was exerting. Her hips stung, the tiny bite of pain only heightening her desire. She was now bare to him, vulnerable to the hand he thrust between her legs.

She was dripping for him, for this inevitable moment. Their months-long dance was going to culminate in this explosive encounter. Every move, every death, every fight, it all led to this, their wedding night.

Vee became aware of the gun in her hand, the metal

heated by her tight grip. She raised it slightly, pulling it from beneath his shirt. Between kisses she glanced down at it. She could end everything now. She could kill him, kill his bodyguards, she could try to take back Miami. She could become Queen again. Find a way to rescue Raina.

"Do it," he snarled against her neck, reading her mind.

"What?" she gasped, and then yelled as his fingers finally found her. Finally touched her aching centre, the part of her that begged him, needed him, wept for him. She could barely think as he slid a finger into her snug passage, burying it deep.

"Pull the fucking trigger, Vee," he snarled. "It's the only way we end this marriage."

She barely had a chance to blink, to breathe, and he was removing his finger, unzipping himself and plunging inside her. She grabbed hold of him, crying out at the suddenness of his invasion. There was no finesse, no warning. One moment he was touching her and the next he was fucking her, his thick, hot cock, driving into her body.

"Oh god!" she yelled as her body fought to accept his length. It had been years since she'd done this, years since she'd been penetrated. She wasn't expecting the pressure, the almost painful, but definitely blissful feeling of being filled.

Instead of allowing her time to adjust he gripped her hips and yanked her off the counter, forcing her further onto his cock. Pain and pleasure slammed through her, leaving her dizzy and breathless. She gripped his shoulders and wrapped her legs around him. He held her tight against his body, his arms around her back and waist, his face buried between her neck and shoulder.

"Heaven," he mumbled against her.

Then he dropped them to the floor, so suddenly, that Vee shrieked and clung even tighter. He lowered her gently the rest of the way, one hand cupping the back of her head before laying her on the floor. He was taking more control thrusting deeper into her. His big body dominated hers, pinning her to the floor in the small space, not allowing her any room for movement. She had a bare second to prepare before he was slamming his hips against hers, knocking her back into the floor.

His powerful thrusts, with his frenzied passion, called to her, released her need for control. She lifted her hips accepting every thrust, feeling the intense build of sensations. She screamed as she came, throwing her arms wide and smashing the gun into the side of the bathtub. She was glad that it didn't go off. A bullet hitting marble would ricochet.

Her orgasm continued to flow through her and she flew higher as he continued to pump into her, gripping her hips in a bruising hold so he could penetrate deeper and deeper. She could feel her wetness spilling, trickling from her as he hit every good thing within her pussy, lighting her up, igniting the blood flowing fast and hard through her veins.

His movements grew uneven, his cock becoming bigger within her. She knew he was close to coming. She reached up, wrapping her arms and legs around him, wanting to be as close as physically possible to the man that had dug some-thing out of her she hadn't thought possible. Perhaps he sensed her need for closeness. He pulled her up against his chest and held her tight, his heart pounding against her ear where he pressed her head against his body.

He grunted her name as he came, his lips against the top of her head. She felt the rush of his seed as it spilled into her body. Intense emotion swamped her and she couldn't hold back the tear that slipped from her closed eyelids.

He didn't release her, as she thought he might when he was finished. Instead, he continued to hold her close, his cock still buried within her, connecting them. Her breath was ragged against his chest, her lips pressed against the skin over his heart.

"Vee," he whispered.

# CHAPTER TWENTY-NINE

Vee dropped the gun, cringing a little as it hit the tiled floor. She hadn't meant to, but her fingers were numb where she'd been holding it so tight. The bang as it hit the floor brought them both out of the moment. Sotza lifted his shoulders and gently set Vee away from him, his penis pulling from her body. She gasped and closed her knees. He picked up the gun, gave it a quick look over before placing it back on the counter.

"Loaded," he observed blandly.

Vee had to bite her tongue not to laugh out loud. The most inappropriate responses running through her head. Did he mean, loaded like she wanted to be, so she could deal with the awkward aftermath of whatever the hell that encounter was? Or maybe he meant, loaded like his incredible magical cock.

Instead she bit back the grin that threatened and replied, "Of course, my weapons are always ready to fire."

He studied her for a moment, his lip lifting in a semi-smile, as though he was reading her mind. He glanced around the tight space where they'd managed to consummate their marriage. "My apologies, this is not exactly what I had in mind."

"Roses and lingerie?" Vee asked, pulling herself up against the side of the tub and trying to cover her naked front with the tatters of her golden gown.

"And non-alcoholic champagne, of course," he replied, helping her up.

Vee peeked past him, into the bedroom. "I don't see any of that stuff."

Sotza nodded gravely and stood, tucking himself back into his pants. This was the most undone she'd seen him. The tails of his shirt were out, his belt was unbuckled, the buttons of his vest were all missing. Yet, he looked incredible. Just as good, if not better, then when he was fully suited and in control. This version of Sotza looked like a pirate, or a conqueror. Like a man that got down and dirty in the trenches and came out on top no matter what.

"I suppose I'll have to interrogate the staff, find out who messed up on the flowers," he said thoughtfully.

Vee laughed. "Rumour has it, few survive your brand of interrogation. You won't have anyone left if you start picking on the staff."

He pretended to think over her words. "True," he agreed. "What does the lady of the house think we should do, if not torture?"

Vee opened her mouth, but it took a moment for her to absorb what he said. *Lady of the house*. She was. She was the lady of several houses, a lot of land, people, an entire organization. The thought was mind-boggling. She'd gone from her small slice of the East coast to standing at the side of a man that ruled an entire country.

"She thinks," Vee said, her voice a little wispy as she fought her confused emotions, "that we should serve ourselves if we want something. We're adults. We don't need servants for every little thing."

Sotza studied her seriously. He nodded slowly and stood, taking her hand in his and pulling her up against his side. "I knew you would make a wise queen."

They changed out of their wedding outfits and put on casual clothing. Vee wore an oversized white sleeping shirt that buttoned up the front. She added a pair of shorts for modesty and wandered out to the kitchen while Sotza changed and unpacked their suitcases. She'd noticed that about him. He was always tidy. Didn't like to leave stuff just lying around, and he didn't rely on staff to do things for him, despite what their banter implied.

Vee liked to consider herself tidy too, but she suspected her brand of tidy fell more on the side of neurotic. When she'd gone clean, she had started to pour her energies into other things, like controlling every aspect of her environment. Everything had a place and she needed those places to always be the same. It helped her cope, having everything arranged perfectly. Especially when her job had been so chaotic. Being able to go home to a comfortable, well-organized space soothed her.

She opened the fridge door, took stock of their supplies and called down the hall toward the bedroom, "Isaac, do you like eggs? We can make omelets and toast..." Her voice trailed off as she glanced over her shoulder and saw him standing in the doorway.

He was wearing a pair of jeans, zipped but not buttoned, the belt unbuckled and hanging. His feet were bare, his chest was bare, every part of him was naked except the jeans. He wasn't wearing underwear, she could tell from how low the jeans sat on his hips, a trail of hair going from his belly right down into the denim and thickening before disappearing from view.

He held a T-shirt loosely by his side, as though he intended to put it on but was interrupted when she called him. His tousled hair and the shadow of whiskers across his chin added countless points toward his overall appeal at that moment.

"I like eggs," he said steadily, his gaze devouring her as she stared in open-mouthed awe at his chest, stomach and arms. Though strong, he was a little on the lean side, so she hadn't expected to find such incredible musculature beneath his suits. Slabs of hard muscles corded his entire torso, rippling beneath his tanned skin as he moved. Instead of putting his shirt on, he dropped it and moved toward her, his steps smooth and slow, but relentless. Even if she wanted to run, there was nowhere for her to go. She was trapped between a fridge and a counter.

Every step he took sent arrows of heat rushing through her body, from her peaked nipples right down to her pussy. She didn't have to check to know she wet and waiting for him. The melting warmth flooding through her system and pooling low in her belly told her that she was slick with need. He stopped in front of her and reached past her. Vee held her breath, expecting him to grab her the way he had earlier, in the washroom. Instead, he closed the fridge door. He remained where he was though, leaning into her, his breath rushing past her ear, stirring her hair.

"I want to taste you," he said, his voice deep and seductive. His beautiful accent washed over her like warm honey. Even when he was working and said the most horrific things, she could still listen to him all day long and never get tired of that voice.

She nearly moaned out loud as blatant images flashed through her brain. He dropped his hands down her body, lifted her nightshirt a little and hooked his fingers into the waistband of her shorts. Her breaths became uneven as her mind flew. Was he going to...? He slid her shorts and panties down her legs in one long, seductive movement, his knuckles caressing her skin. When he reached the floor, he took the back of her ankle in a gentle grip and lifted her foot, the way he'd done on the beach when he took her shoes off.

When her shorts were off he stood again. Looking down at her, dark eyes smoldering with lust. Her heart thumped in anticipation. He wanted to have sex again? So soon? He took her by the waist and lifted her off her feet. Vee gasped and gripped his shoulders, the bare skin warm and hard beneath her fingertips, the muscles moving as he stepped back toward the counter and set her on top of it. He burrowed close to her, pulling her hips to the edge of the counter and pressing his denim covered cock into her uncovered pussy. The zipper scraped against her bare, sensitive folds. She gasped loudly and rocked her hips against him.

She was surprised by the sharp rise in passion as warmth sizzled through her from top to bottom. It was like, after that first taste of heaven, she was so much more aware of him. Her nipples hardened beneath the thin fabric of the shirt. He leaned in to kiss her. She thought he would kiss her mouth, but he didn't. He lowered his head to the curve of her neck and explored it with his lips, dipping into each nook and licking her skin, sending even more heat through her body. His mouth should be outlawed, the things it did to her.

He pushed her until her back hit the upper cabinets, then wrapped his arm around her waist and dragged her hips almost over the edge, balancing her ass on the counter while he held her up. He maneuvered her with such casual ease, such strength, that it made her head spin. A tiny part of her feared this kind of strength, the things he could do to her if he was ever really angry. She'd seen him angry before, but it was always carefully controlled. She wondered what wild out-of-control anger would look like. In her experience, all men were capable of it, they just needed to be pushed. But for now, she wanted to enjoy the way his lips moved across her skin, the way his hands gripped her possessively.

He gripped her thigh, wrapping his long fingers around her. He pushed her leg, opening her up, but apparently not enough for his satisfaction, as he moved his hand down to her knee, gripped it and lifted. He guided her foot up onto the counter, then trailed his hand over her leg, pausing to tickle the super sensitive skin of her inner thigh, before moving to her dripping center. She was so wet for him, she might have been embarrassed at the wet spot she'd created on his jeans except she knew he wouldn't care. And in that moment, she couldn't seem to wrap her brain around anything other than the spikes of pleasure he was forcing from her body.

"Hands over your head," he mumbled against her collar bone as he sank long, thick fingers into her pussy. She was panting so hard that she didn't register his voice at first. He reminded her, "Vee, hands over your head. Now, cariño. And leave them up there."

Vee raised her arms without question, pressing the backs of her hands against the cool hard wood of the cabinets. His nimble fingers moved down her front, sliding the buttons through the holes, until her shirt was wide open and her breasts exposed. She barely knew where she was by the time he lowered his head to take a peaked nipple into his mouth, sucking it deep into the hot recess. She moaned and dropped her hands to his head. He took her wrist and pushed her arm back up. She put the other one up herself.

Between the attention he was paying her breasts and the fingers exploring her pussy, her mind was splintered. She couldn't concentrate on any one thing. Just laid back against the counter, her arms over her head, enjoying the exquisite attention. She knew where he was headed with this hedonistic exploration, but still she held her breath as he trailed his way down her stomach, lowering himself until he was kneeling on the floor.

"Ahhh," she moaned loudly as his tongue touched her for the first time. It was explosive, it was heaven. She nearly came without any further stimulation. He spread her wide with those long, wicked fingers and licked her, sucked her, ate her the way she'd always wanted. Seconds later, he entered her with his fingers, filling her, while still torturously teasing her with his tongue. It was like he knew her body, better than she did. He tuned it like an instrument and played like an angel.

Moments later her legs started shaking and she felt the orgasm begin to rise, rushing through her, heating her limbs, her face, her everything. She bent her arms and gripped her elbows in an effort to keep her arms raised the way he wanted. She didn't dare disobey or he might take this precious treat away. She rocked her ass dangerously close to the edge. She didn't care if she fell off or if she landed on him. It was going to be so worth it, just to experience this, the best fucking orgasm ever.

His fingers pumped harder, pressing firmly against the walls of her passage, while his tongue flicked and sucked at her clit before running down the inside of her labia. Stars sparked behind her eyelids. She tossed her head back, pressing her face into her forearms as she held on for as long as she could, knowing that the higher she flew the harder and better she would fall.

"Come for me, Vee!" he demanded from between her legs.

It took a moment for his words to sink in, barely recognizable his voice was so guttural. But as soon as she recognized the command, her body obeyed, exploding with such force that it felt as though her mind shattered, a lightning bolt of pure pleasure ripping through her. She felt fluid spurt from her as he continued to pump his fingers. Again, she didn't care, she was too caught up in the intense pleasure shooting through her.

She floated down to realize his fingers were still working her and his tongue was still pressing against her clit. Only this time harder, more insistent. She shrieked as another orgasm took hold, this one even more catastrophic than the last. She reached down to shove his head away, to stop the unknown from happening. It was too much, too many feelings, too much pleasure!

He took her scrambling hands in a tight grip and held them against her stomach, forcing her to take the pleasure. Every lick, every sip, every bite. It was perfect, it was terrible, it was everything she could have hoped for but didn't know existed. Her entire body shuddered in anticipation and she shook her head back and forth, helpless against the barrage of sensations hitting her. Just as the orgasm crested she threw her head back, banging it into the cupboard.

"Isaac!" she screamed, her nails digging into the hand that held her immobile.

She soared, higher than before, felt her lungs burning from lack of breath. But she didn't have time to breathe. Her entire focus was between her legs. Then she was falling off the counter. Not by accident either, Sotza was tugging her down, his strong hands gripping her waist and controlling her fall. He cradled her as she dropped into his lap, limp and boneless.

She sat on his lap, facing him, his arm around her back, pressing her against his chest, her head falling forward against his neck. They were both slick with sweat; her from exertion, him from need. He shifted her, bringing his hand up her back to cradle her neck. He moved her so he could see her. Her eyes were half-closed and she wondered if she could fall asleep just like that when he said, "I'd intended to taste you only, bring you pleasure. But I need you now, mi amor." His voice was husky and his dark eyes burned like hot coals.

He tipped her back on the floor. She half twisted trying to catch herself, her palms striking the tile with a smack. He took advantage of her position, twisting her hips and legs until she was laying face down on the floor, her knees wide, legs sprawled across his lap. She heard the zip lower on his jeans, then he pushed her legs wider, one on either side of him.

He dragged her hips back toward him. Vee didn't have the energy to push herself up so she lay that way, with her ass up, knees curled under and arms reaching out in front of her. She didn't think she was capable of orgasming again. Her mind said no, but as soon as his hard, thick cock plowed through her slick folds, her body said yes. Yes, yes, yes! She yelled, her nails scraping the floor as ecstasy flared back into life, igniting everything she had.

He took the back of her shirt in his fist and bunched it up, using it to force her back onto his cock as he thrust forward, quickly finding a brutal, breath-stealing rhythm. She yelled each time his hips slammed into her ass. Pain and plea-sure merged, combining to create something more than just an orgasm. Something darker and intensely more pleasurable.

It didn't take long before his movements grew choppier and more demanding. His hips smashed hers in a frenzy and he yanked her shirt so hard that if the buttons were done up he'd be strangling her with it. The way in which he lost himself in her body sent her over the top, too fucking hot to resist. He shouted something guttural, unintelligible to her ears, probably Spanish as he emptied his seed into her. She felt the heat of his orgasm rush through her and pushed herself back, taking all of him until he was done pumping into her.

Vee collapsed to the floor with a groan. When he pulled

out, she didn't have the energy to close her legs. His come, her come, would just have to pool on the floor. She wasn't dealing with it. He crawled over top of her, his knees on either side of her hips, his hands pressing into the floor next to her shoulders, caging her. She felt wonderful, incredible, safe.

He bent to place a kiss between her shoulder blades, trailing his lips across her one shoulder. She shivered in response and moved her face to the side so she could see him hovering over her.

"Isaac..." she whispered.

"Si, mi amor?" he said softly, nipping her earlobe before kissing his way down her cheek toward her lips.

She moaned, both fearing and wanting his kiss. The problem with his kisses is they were like a drug. A drug she had no defense against. She wanted them desperately but wasn't sure if she could deal with the aftermath of that kind of addiction.

"Do you think we could do this in a bed next time?" she asked, her lips tilting up in a smile. "I'm getting sore from all the floor fucking."

He laughed out loud, the sound golden to her ears.

# CHAPTER THIRTY

Vee stood in the ocean, water rushing over her bare feet and ankles. She wore a simple one-piece bathing suit. Rose coloured with a splash of white flowers and green foliage low on one side. She liked it a lot. Just as she liked the sheer white wrap, tied around her waist, that went with it. And every other item of clothing that'd been chosen for her. Almost as if someone knew her tastes. Whoever was picking her clothes went that little extra mile to get Vee the things she never bothered to get herself. Items that were more expensive, more exclusive, better fabrics and nicer cuts.

She also loved Sotza's island home. It was private, spacious yet also cozy. The sand was fine and soft, the jungle-like foliage lush. The house was close enough to the beach that Vee had been going down a few times per day to swim or just sit in the sand. Sometimes Sotza joined her and sometimes he stayed up at the house. She suspected he worked when they weren't together, touched base with Mateo and whoever he set up as liaison in Miami. Regardless, he was more relaxed here on the island. He smiled easier, laughed once in awhile. When they ate together, he talked to her the way he had when she'd been locked in the bedroom, in his low quiet voice. Only Vee responded this time, listening to him and sharing her thoughts and opinions. It helped that he seemed to value the things she said, absorbing her words and turning them over in his brain before responding.

They'd been on the island for almost two days, half of their honeymoon over. Vee regretted that they had so little time, but she was eager to get back to Raina. And she knew Sotza needed to get back to the mainland, back to his empire. He'd left it for months to go sort out Miami. Vee suspected he hadn't meant to be gone so long, but after meeting her, deciding what their future would be, he stayed longer to woo his reluctant bride. She smiled at the thought. They'd virtually burned down Miami's underworld in their warring courtship. And while she missed her home, was still unsure of this new relationship, she was beginning to feel hopeful.

Maybe she shouldn't. Maybe she should still be bitter and angry. The world was changing around them, women had more power, more control over their own futures. Shouldn't she also get a say in what happens to her? Yet, the mafia world didn't change, not really. Even Vee's own bid for power, to sit as queen at the top, had lasted just a little over a year. Lasted about as long as it took for men to challenge her and another man to dethrone her.

Except the man who took her crown was the man setting her up again, at the top of a new regime. Ensuring she would maintain power, just in a different capacity. Similar, she supposed, to the way Reyes had set Casey up at his side. Allowing her control within the Bolivian organization, giving her the authority to make decisions. Vee was still sceptical. Never in her life had she experienced an equal sharing. Every one of her relationships had been an exchange of power, with Vee getting the least amount, grabbing what she could and making the best of each situation.

Frank, her first long-term lover, hadn't treated her too bad. But he'd made it clear that she was a commodity. Something easily ignored until he was ready to take what he wanted. He was generous in some capacities. Jewels, clothing, money, it had all flowed. He was also generous with his friends, occasionally passing Vee around when he needed a favour or wanted to show off. She hadn't been sad to see him go when Tony took over.

Tony had been different. Exciting at first. Exotically handsome and dangerous. His thirst for power, his reckless devil-may-care attitude, had been attractive. His pursuit had been breathtaking. He wanted her almost as bad as he wanted Frank's cut of the action. It hadn't taken Vee long to realize Tony only wanted her because she belonged to someone else. She was a beautiful, unattainable prize that Tony wanted to own. Once he had her, she became part of the scenery. Again. Just a woman, a thing to be shrugged off, pushed aside, taken out and played with when the mood struck.

Vee thought that Sotza was different, that he wouldn't do to her the things that Frank and Tony and other men had done. He seemed... different. He was definitely harsh and brutal, a product of the mafia world and the horrific things that life asked of him, but he also had a side to him that was not quite as sinister as she originally thought. He was careful, thoughtful in his actions and fair. For the most part. Vee didn't think she would ever be okay with the things he did in Miami, but she also understood that he'd had a job to do. It was just her poor luck that she happened to be his job.

Vee was a practical soul. And now that she was here, with Sotza, married and about to embark on a new path, she was ready to face the future with optimism. She would stand at his side, for a while anyway, and see how things played out. She would have to find a way to extract Raina from the organization though. Having her daughter involved in anything mafia-related was unacceptable. But once Raina was out of the picture, Vee would consider settling down and finding a way to live with the new man in her life.

She heard footsteps in the sand, the sound of rustling clothing intrusive against the stillness of the ocean backdrop. She knew whoever was approaching wasn't Sotza. He stepped lightly, carefully. He didn't want his victims to hear him coming. She tensed and turned to look, relaxing slightly when she saw John, one of the island guards.

"Señora Sotza," he said as he walked to the edge of the water and stopped. "The Señor has requested your company at the villa. Please come out of the water and accompany me up to the house."

Vee squinted at him, shading her eyes from the sun. Something was off. In the few days they'd been on the island, Sotza hadn't once sent his men to find her. Like he'd done at his mansion home, Sotza always took care of Vee himself. If he wanted her, he would come and find her. Not summon her.

She looked John over from head to foot with sharp observation. He was nervous about something, shifting a little from foot to foot, his flinty eyes restlessly scanning the area. In her time on the island she'd found the two guards to be fairly relaxed. Mindful, but part of the scenery. John was acting different, his shoulders tense, his hands held low at his sides. One of his hands was resting a little behind his thigh, as though he was holding something. She sincerely hoped it wasn't a gun. She knew they carried weapons, but they'd never openly displayed them. Vee's own gun was up at the house, packed in her suitcase.

Vee gathered the skirt of her wrap in one hand so it wouldn't tangle in her legs and walked slowly out of the water toward the guard. He relaxed a little as she approached him. She smiled benignly. About a foot away from him she pretended to stumble, reaching out to grab his arm. The one that was holding something. She used him as leverage, grabbing hold of his arms tightly and then bringing her knee up sharp and fast between his legs.

John went down into the sand with a howl. Vee whirled away from him and sprinted toward the treeline. She wanted to head for the house, but feared it wasn't safe. If she was right and John had been about to attack her then someone else was likely hitting the house, going after Sotza. The thought was gut-wrenching. She wanted to turn back and run to the house, help him if she could. But she knew better. She was next to defenseless. She had no weapon and she was wearing little more than a bathing suit. She didn't even have shoes. She would only hinder Sotza if he needed to fight. Perhaps even distract him from doing what he needed to do. No, her best bet was to hide in the trees and then circle back toward the house where she could observe it in stealth.

She didn't make it to the trees. Something hit her hard in the back, stunning her. She collapsed onto the sand face first and lay for a moment, absorbing the pain in her back. She moaned and glanced over her shoulder, John was standing over top of her, holding what looked like a gun. But she was pretty sure it wasn't, pretty sure she hadn't been shot. Before she could defend herself he shot her again and she had less than a second to realize he was using a taser on her. She was out before she could scream for help.

She didn't know how long she'd been unconscious. She suspected not long since she had flashes of being carried over John's shoulder to a vehicle, then driven somewhere. When awareness returned she found herself lying on the dirty floor of a shed. She squinted into the room. There were no lights, but she could tell it was still daytime from the dim, pale light filtering through cracks on the walls. She sat up painfully, shoving hair out of her face. She was certain she was still on the island.

She stood, swaying a little. "I'm going to fucking kill that son-of-a-bitch," she growled, reaching around to touch the spot on her back where he'd tasered her. The area was tender. She went to the door of the shed and tried it. Of course, it was locked. She threw her weight against it, hoping the wood was frail enough to give way. It didn't move and all she accomplished was to jar her shoulder.

She pressed her ear against a crack in the wood and listened. She could hear the crashing of waves and birds singing. The shed must be somewhere in the trees, but not far from the beach. She was about to start shouting when she heard a vehicle approach. She glanced frantically around for a weapon, reaching out to feel her way around. Nothing. Teeth and nails would have to do.

When the door swung open, she backed into the far corner and squared her shoulders, facing the threat bravely. She wasn't going to go down begging for her life. Light flooded the small interior, blinding her for a second. When she blinked she saw a tall, broad male figure standing in the doorway. She thought at first it must be John, come back to finish her. But when she was able to see clearly she discovered someone else entirely, someone she hadn't given a single thought to since they left Mexico.

"Nico Garza," she said coolly.

He nodded swiftly and pulled something off his belt. She stiffened thinking it was a weapon, but he brought it up to his face and began speaking in swift, angry Spanish. "Report!" he snapped. "Where is Desi? She should be here by now."

As he talked on the phone, Vee slid sideways along the wall, thinking to slip past him and run. He reached out, so suddenly, she didn't have time to duck, and gripped her throat, slamming her into the wall. They stood that way, he towering over her, pinning her against the wall, while she listened to his end of the conversation.

"You fucking find her, Diego," he snarled. "I want to know where Sotza is too, why he wasn't up at the house."

Vee's head spun with all the possibilities. Sotza wasn't at the house? That was where she'd left him, sitting on the comfy sofa, his laptop open in front of him, a mere 20 minutes before she'd been attacked. Had he found out about the intruders and gotten out of the house in time? Did he abandon Vee to the Mexicans? As soon as she had the thought she discarded it. No, Sotza wouldn't do that. He would do whatever it took to get her back and then take out the kidnappers. Knowing that he was loose on the island and not up at the house, injured or dead, was a huge relief. Once Vee extracted herself from Nico she would join her husband.

Nico clipped his phone back on his belt and turned to look at her, his cool gaze slipping over her. She regretted her outfit choice. It wasn't good for fighting and she felt nearly naked in just a bathing suit and sheer wrap. Though, thankfully, she didn't feel any lust from him.

"What are you doing?" she asked, her voice steady.

His fingers flexed threateningly around her neck before he dropped his hand away. He remained standing too close though, his big body blocking her from moving.

"I would think it's obvious."

He would be there for one of two reasons, to take out Sotza or to take out Vee. Maybe both. She didn't particularly like either option and wondered why she wasn't dead yet. Even if he was just after Sotza she should be collateral damage. It would be stupid to leave her alive as a witness and a potential enemy. She decided to play dumb. "You came all the way to Venezuela to lock me in a shed?"

He gave her a withering look. "Let's not pretend you're Sotza's bimbo blond wife. I know exactly who you are, Elvira Montana."

"Sotza," she correctly coldly. When he lifted an eyebrow

she said, "My name is Elvira Sotza, but you may call me Señora Sotza." She tried for haughty, so he would understand that she thought him an annoying worm.

He laughed, despite his obvious tension. "We were on a first name basis in Mexico, Vee." His eyes travelled over her body. "I enjoyed our time together in my home."

Vee badly wanted to cross her arms over her chest, hide her cleavage from view. But she forced herself to keep her arms loose at her side in case she needed to defend herself. "You weren't such a prick in Mexico, Mr. Garza," she said tartly. "I don't think I want to be so familiar with the man trying to take over my husband's organization."

She was fishing. Trying to draw him into divulging his reason for attacking them. He continued to look at her, assessing her. Not critically, like his compatriots had when they kept going after her in Miami, trying to take her down. No, he looked at her with respect, though he tried to hide it under the guise of lust. Though he was top of the food chain himself, dominating a large swath of Mexico, she thought perhaps he liked strong, powerful women. And though his gaze was purposefully heated, she still didn't get any sense that he actually wanted her. Something was worrying him, getting in the way of his ability to play with her properly.

"What do you want?" she finally demanded. Why beat around the bush? He was clearly on the island for a reason. And she wasn't dead, so he didn't have what he needed yet.

He continued to stare at her, his dark eyes cold. "I want what should be rightfully mine."

"And that is?" she prompted, raising an eyebrow.

"United States, East coast. Miami. I want my cut back. It belonged to me for ten years, then it fell to the Bolivians. I have spent the past year trying to get it back. But the idiotas I sent in kept failing," he said, his voice dropping a little as he searched her face.

Vee frowned as her mind whirled, trying to unravel what he was saying. "You were in partnership with Ignacio Hernandez?" Hernandez had been Casey's husband before Reyes went in and cleaned out the organization.

He nodded and moved away from her, leaning against the opposite wall, his arms crossed loosely over his broad chest. "Hernandez and Montana. I was involved in everything crossing borders." He watched for her reaction. Vee knew better than to give him one. But she was reeling with the information he was giving her.

"I don't remember ever seeing you at the house," she said of her time with Tony. "I knew who my late husband was doing business with."

His lips curled a little. "But I saw you, chica," he said. "Once only. And you made an impression. You were at your husband's side, pretending not to hear the conversation as a new drug trail into the US was negotiated. You were very high from the cocaine back then, but still sharp. I was impressed with both your beauty and the thoughts that passed across your face. You thought Montana was an idiot and you thought Juan Domingo was just as stupid. You were correct on both points. I believe if you hadn't been married I would have stolen you away."

And then she remembered. She hadn't met him, but she'd seen him. "Four years ago," she said, nodding slowly. "We were in Stage's nightclub. You asked me to dance, but I refused."

"You did," he agreed.

"But that was the only time you spoke that whole evening, to ask me for a dance," she pointed out incredulously. "Domingo did all the talking."

"He usually did. My cousin was the better businessman. I have a tendency to take what I need by force." He waved his hand between them. "Although he spent the past year fucking things up in Miami. Alienating our contact. Couldn't stand the idea of a woman in charge."

"Me," she breathed. Things began to click into place. Nico's reasons for coming to Venezuela, the vastness of his organization. "You pretended to be rivals, but you weren't. Most of us never met the leader of the Garza organization so you were able to attend meetings as one of his hired guns instead of the boss."

He was about to reply when his phone beeped. He pulled it off his belt and answered. Vee eyed the door, but she didn't think she would get far. And she wanted to find out what he had planned. He barked angrily into the phone, making her cringe inwardly. He was speaking so fast she had trouble picking out all the words, but she was fairly certain his second-in-command, Desi, the woman from their evening in Mexico, was missing. Along with another of Nico's men. And they couldn't seem to find Sotza either. Which meant Sotza probably had Nico's missing people. Whatever his plan had been, it was backfiring.

"Find them!" he snarled into the phone before hanging up.

Vee gave him a moment to compose himself before speaking. "I think I understand Miami. You laid low, let your people do the dirty work. Collected the rent, so to speak. Then things started going south when Reyes took out Hernandez and Casey took out the next guy. Everything fell to me. The Hernandez cut *and* the Montana piece of the pie. I had no idea you even existed so I kept trying to work with Domingo. But nothing I said or did could sway him to do business with a woman. When Domingo failed I turned to other sources and you lost out."

"Significantly," he said with a growl. "Do you have any idea how much money access to the East Coast is worth?"

Vee let out a small, humourless laugh. She knew exactly what it'd been worth. What she'd lost by her fight with the

Mexicans. If she'd only known that Nicolás Garza was the man at the top, she would have gone straight to him and made the necessary arrangements between their organizations. None of this would have ever happened. Not her battle with the Mexicans, not her tarnished reputation, her loss of Miami. Her meeting with Sotza. Her marriage.

"You should've come to me," she said accusingly. "When you found out what was going on, you should have come to meet with me yourself. Not hid behind your man. We could've avoided all this!" She shouldn't have been so loose with her tongue, needed to remember who she was talking to. A cartel boss. But she was too angry to heed the stiffening in his shoulders and the shadow passing across his face.

"It was too late when I found out what was happening. Sotza had already arrived in Miami."

"You could have come anyway," she snapped, recklessly pushing on. "You could have partnered with me, pushed him back, taken what you thought should have been yours to begin with. Instead of hiding in Mexico and leaving me and Domingo to battle it out. Good job there, Nico! Your cousin lost his head while you stood back."

He flinched. "It would have been suicide! No one goes head to head with The Butcher and survives." He pushed her back against the wall and shoved a finger in her face. "Domingo was reckless, stupid. Don't bother to deny it. He had a year to figure his shit out, losing his head was his payment for fucking up."

"This is suicide!" she shot back. "What do you hope to gain by attacking Sotza in his home? You were better off fighting him on foreign soil." He shoved a hand through his hair and glared at her. She continued, "You know I'm right. You've moved against Sotza. He won't allow you to walk away. He has Desi and you know it. You better just cut and run, because this is your only chance to disappear. Once he finds us you're dead."

"If he so much as touches Desiree I will cut his fucking heart out."

She saw the rage, his terrible fury over his missing second-in-command. But more importantly she saw his desperation. Desperation made people reckless. Coloured their decisions, fuelled them with emotion rather than the cold logic necessary for planning.

"She's already dead and you know it," Vee said coldly.

She was prepared for the hit. Loosened her body, watched his body language. He was right-handed, so when the hit came toward her she moved her head to the side, taking the clip in the ear and collapsing to her left to lessen the impact. But she needed him to think he'd gotten her hard so she dropped to the floor as though knocked unconscious.

He immediately bent over her. "Elvira..." he said, regret leaking into his voice.

She swung her knee up, catching him in the side. He lost balance, falling from his crouch onto his ass. Vee kicked out, aiming for his face. She got him hard on the cheek, knocking him back. The impact would've been worse if she'd been wearing shoes, but she had to work with what she had. He grabbed his face and swore. She had to scramble over top of him to reach the door. She was about to lunge out into the open when he grabbed hold of her wrap, tearing it as he dragged her back. She hit the floor hard, landing on her knees.

He was fast, faster than her. She fought, turning to aim a punch at his head. He knocked her arm aside and slapped her hard, knocking her into the wall. She collapsed onto the floor, her ears ringing and her vision fuzzy. He dragged her to the middle of the shed and straddled her. She tried to bring her hands up to defend herself, but he pinned them easily with one hand. She kicked at him, slamming her knees into his back as hard as she could. She curled her fingers and dug her nails into his hand until she felt the flesh tear and the wetness of his blood.

"Stop!" he roared and reached for his belt. He pulled a gun and pressed it against the side of her head. His eyes promised death if she kept fighting. She went limp underneath him.

"Smart chica," he growled.

Vee fought to bring her breathing back under control, not an easy thing to do with a heavy asshole Mexican on top of her. His phone rang. He didn't move the gun from her head. Instead he released her wrists and answered. Vee didn't move, kept her hands above her head so he wouldn't decide to shoot her.

"Si?" he snapped.

His entire demeanor changed as he listened. His body was rigid on top of her and fear lit his eyes. Deep, terrible fear. And not for himself. For someone else.

"I have your wife here with me. You hurt any of my people and I will – "

Even Vee heard the woman's scream that echoed through the phone, cut off by a gunshot. Vee knew her husband well enough to know that he didn't bluff. If he pulled his weapon, shot it, then he had just killed someone.

# CHAPTER THIRTY-ONE

Shock radiated through Nico's body knocking him back on his haunches. Vee still lay underneath him, but she was able to push herself up enough to watch him. Horror etched his features. He squeezed his eyes shut and breathed hard. When he opened them, Vee saw rage unlike anything she'd ever seen before. Nico put the phone on speaker and said in a surprisingly smooth voice that hinted at none of his anger, "You killed something that belongs to me, now you will hear your wife die."

Vee scrambled backwards, clawing the floor until her back hit the opposite wall. Nico got to his feet and followed her, his gun trained on her head. She wanted to say something, to try reasoning with him, but she knew it was pointless. He was past the point of reason. He moved the safety back and began pulling the trigger. Vee kept her eyes open, watched as death sped toward her.

"You would risk your woman's life like that?" Sotza said, his voice as dispassionate as Vee had ever heard it. He was not the loving husband she'd spent two days getting to know. He was the boss now. The Butcher at work.

Nico's finger eased back, though he kept the gun on Vee. "Desi is alive?" he demanded.

"For now," Sotza replied coolly.

"You will give her back… and any of my other people that you have?" Nico asked, no hint of the desperation that Vee could see in every line of his body.

"Once Vee is released into my care we will talk."

"Not good enough," Nico snarled. "You could kill them."

"There is only your woman left. The others are dead," Sotza said, his voice so disembodied, so cold, that Vee shivered, even though she knew they were on the same side.

"You killed four men?" Nico said incredulously.

"Five," Sotza corrected. "John would make six, but I'm saving him for later."

Vee could tell from Nico's complexion that he was now alone. There were no people left to help him fight. Sotza had hunted them and cut them down. All except the bodyguard that had turned on them. He would find his justice later.

"Alright," Nico growled, clearly frustrated at the loss of his people and the downfall of his grand plans. "You will release Desiree, give her back to me and we will leave you in peace."

A shot echoed through the phone and the woman began screaming, agony ripping through her voice. Vee didn't move, but Nico flinched, dropping to his knees. He couldn't speak until Desi was able to bring herself back under control, her screams dying away.

"I have now shattered her trigger hand," Sotza said calmly. "A shame, I truly don't enjoy hurting women. But she is vicious this one, went after me with my own kitchen knife. She is lucky I didn't cut her fingers off."

Nico went white at hearing his woman was now shot and bleeding somewhere on the island. Vee looked at Nico, catching his eye. She kept her face carefully controlled, though she was terrified. She knew Sotza was making the right moves, showing this man that he was willing to do whatever was necessary. But Sotza was pushing a very dangerous man toward a reckless edge. An edge that Vee stood on with him.

"He isn't bluffing you," Vee said carefully. "He will not negotiate. You're only option if you want to save your love is to release me." Vee purposely called the other woman his love, telling Sotza how much Desi meant to Nico. How far he would go to get her back. Vee suspected that Nico was seriously regretting his decision to put Desi in the path of the Venezuelan cartel boss.

Nico seemed to struggle between desperation and rage. He was having trouble controlling himself. "How do I know he'll let her go?" he asked, his voice rough. "He could take you back, my only leverage, and then kill her."

"He could," Vee acknowledged. "But he doesn't lie. If you ask him for an exchange, then he'll do it. He'll give her back, relatively unhurt." Vee thought back to the severed heads that Sotza had sent her and shuddered. She really hoped that she was telling the truth. But so far, in her experience, Sotza had never done anything other than what he said he would do. He had told her he was taking over Miami, toppling her regime, and he had done it. He'd also told her they would marry, now she was his bride.

"Sotza," Nico growled. "If I give you my word that you will get your wife back, then you will give me Desi? And you will let us leave the island alive?"

There was a pause and then Sotza said, "Agreed."

Vee slumped back against the wall as Nico made the arrangements. Right before Sotza could hang up though, Nico looked at her, his dark eyes piercing and grave. He lifted his gun and shot her.

Vee screamed, unable to hold it in as burning pain sliced through her arm. She grabbed the wound with her other hand

and doubled over as the pain slashed through her. It was like being lit on fire, like nothing she'd ever experienced before. Tears flowed down her cheeks.

"Vee!" Sotza snarled, finally losing his cool. "Answer me, right now. Tell me you're alive."

"I'm here," she yelled through her tears. "He shot my a –"

"Touch Desi one more time," Nico interrupted, "and the next bullet goes through her skull."

"You have five minutes to bring my wife to the house," Sotza snapped and hung up.

He was still at the house, Vee thought as dizziness swept through her. Nico crouched in front of her, took her wrap where it was already torn and ripped a strip off. He shoved Vee's hand away from her bleeding arm and wrapped the strip of fabric around the wound. He yanked the makeshift bandage tight and tied it off. She gasped as pain radiated through her arm and torso.

"My apologies, Señora. It must be tight enough to stop the bleeding. I was careful to hit the flesh part only. I missed artery and bone."

"Thank you," Vee said sarcastically, glaring at him through the wetness in her eyes.

He gripped her other arm and pulled her to her feet. "You will heal," he snapped and dragged her toward the door. "Unlike Desi. She will never fully recover from a bullet to the hand."

Vee cried out as he shoved her roughly into the jeep. The one that belonged to John. As he got into the driver's side, she said, "Desi wouldn't be in this position, she wouldn't be hurt, if you hadn't made the stupid decision to come here."

He slammed his fist into the dashboard and then pointed his finger at Vee. "If the fucking Butcher had never gone to Miami, none of this would be happening."

Vee took a breath as he put the jeep in gear and slammed

on the gas, jolting them forward. She reached out to steady herself. "If it wasn't Sotza, it would've been someone else. No, Nico, coming here, to Venezuela, was a bad idea."

"It wasn't supposed to be like this," he said, his voice dropping, some of the anger fading. "You were supposed to be vulnerable, both of you. I was going to take you, force him to give back my US routes and then release you as a sign of good faith. I shouldn't have sent Desi to the house as my plan B in case he wouldn't negotiate for you. That was my mistake. I underestimated him."

"I don't understand," Vee said, confused. "What did you negotiate when we were in Mexico? I thought you two were in talks for those routes."

He shook his head. "We negotiated nothing. Sotza told me I was to withdraw completely, to never step foot in the States again, or he would do his thing, cut off my body parts."

She stared at him incredulously. "But why?"

"He's an arms dealer, chica. The man hates drugs, always has."

Vee sat back in her seat, staring out the window, her good hand pressing against the wound while bracing herself on the dashboard with her injured arm as they bounced across the jungle road. Sotza hated drugs. Something triggered in her brain, a memory perhaps. She thought maybe she'd always known that The Butcher didn't tolerate drugs. But when the man himself showed up in her city, started a war, she'd been too busy fending him off to do her research. If she'd known about his plans, to dismantle instead of takeover a good portion of the organization she'd inherited, she might have asked more questions. Like, where was Reyes? Did he know of Sotza's plans? Did he approve? She didn't quite understand the relationship there. Both Reyes and Sotza were their own men. Neither worked for the other. Yet, the way she understood it, Sotza had been doing Reyes a favour by cleaning up

Miami. Did Sotza have an ulterior motive for going into the US?

When they arrived at the house Nico didn't hesitate. He pulled Vee from the jeep and strode toward the frosted glass front door. She had a vision of him shooting out the door and walking them across the broken glass. He did neither. He banged on the door with the heel of his gun. A few seconds later the door swung open. Sotza stood in the entryway, tall, strong and coldly angry. Vee had seen him angry before, but that look, especially when his eyes raked Vee from head to foot, his gaze settling on her arm, it was something else. It was feral, it was vicious. It was a death promise. Vee had always been taught that emotions made a person weak, especially expressing them to the enemy. But in this case, as she and Nico faced Sotza, she decided she was wrong. Sotza took anger to a new level. As though he promised death. Could and would deliver death. No matter what happened today with the exchange.

Sotza motioned behind him, into the kitchen. Nico dropped Vee's arm and pushed past Sotza into the other room. Vee was a little surprised he would turn his back on such a cold-hearted predator, but she supposed he'd believed her when she told him Sotza wouldn't lie. His need to get to Desi outweighed any fear he had for his own safety.

Vee straightened, walked to Sotza and stood at his side. He acknowledged her coolly, nodding at her, his sharp gaze on Nico as he bent over Desi, checked her over and then scooped her off the chair she'd been sitting in. She was far more worse for wear than Vee. She'd clearly gotten knocked around in her fight with Sotza. One side of her face was puffy, the eye nearly swollen shut and a trickle of blood made its way from her hairline down to her jaw. Her hand had been wrapped up with a kitchen towel and was now resting limply in her lap as she was pulled into Nico's chest.

Nico ignored them completely as he strode past Sotza and Vee toward the door, his head bent over his woman. Sotza's voice made him pause. "You will make it safely off this island Garza, but you won't get far. There is no place you can hide that I will not find you."

Nico stared back, clearly seething, wanting to respond in kind with his own threats. But his eyes strayed to Desi, the damage done by his decision to attack Sotza. "This is between you and me, Sotza. She has nothing more to do with this anymore."

"You attacked my wife," Sotza replied, ice dripping from his words. He stepped in front of Vee, shielding her with his body, showing the other man that she was now protected. "You laid hands on her, you shot her. There will be no pardon... for either of you."

# CHAPTER THIRTY-TWO

The moment the door closed behind Nico and Desi, Vee collapsed, her legs folding beneath her. Sotza caught her before she hit the floor. He lifted her in his arms and carried her into the kitchen, placing her on the counter. When she tried to sit up he pushed her back down.

"Looks like you've lost a fair amount of blood," he grunted examining her bandage. "I'm going to have to clean it, stitch and rewrap it. Then we need to get the fuck off this island, we have no protection. I'm certain Juan is dead. John probably killed him before taking you." His accent was stronger than usual. From the stress of Nico's attack and her injury, she guessed.

"Poor Juan... that sounds horrible," Vee said faintly, referring to the stitches and rewrapping part of his statement. "Wait, how did you know it was John that grabbed me?"

"He admitted it."

Vee could only imagine what Sotza did to the other man to induce a confession. "Still alive?" she asked as Sotza moved around the kitchen gathering what he needed to fix her arm.

"Of course," he said coldly. "He betrayed me, betrayed my wife. He doesn't get to die easily."

His deep brown eyes lifted to hers, hard and uncompromising. She looked back at him steadily. "I want to be there when you teach him the price of betrayal," she said.

"Of course."He leaned over and kissed her lips gently. "I'll be right back. I need some things from the other room." She nodded while he pulled his gun from its holster and set it on the counter, next to her good hand. Smart move. Nico could come back, though she doubted he would.

He was back within seconds, holding a needle, some thread and a bottle of peroxide. He set everything on the counter and began rolling up his sleeves, his dark eyes on her face. Though his expression remained impassive she saw the concern in those velvety depths. He approached her, ran his fingers lightly down her injured arm. Then he lifted the arm, one hand on her wrist, the other on the elbow. He made her bend it and lay it across her stomach so he would have easy access to the wound.

"Do you want a drink, cariño?" he asked in a low voice. "It's the only pain killer we have that will work quickly."

She shook her head, eyes glued to his face. "I don't drink."

His face softened a little as he moved away to roll up his sleeves and wash his hands. "You are having a very bad day. I think you can be forgiven a shot of something to ease the pain."

She held his gaze. "I don't drink, Isaac. Ever."

"Si, I hear you, cariño," he agreed. "Then never again shall I offer."

"Gracias," she said, giving him a faint smile.

He pulled one of the tall kitchen stools up next to her. He gave her a pointed look, as though to say, *This will hurt. I don't want to do it, but we don't have a choice.* Then he bent over her.

His head low, near her face. She respected him more for not actually uttering the words.

She took deep breaths as he cleansed the area, his movements quick and precise and he ran the cloth through the jagged flesh. She closed her eyes as pain hit her, followed close by dizziness. She breathed in his scent, concentrating on trying to identify the elements and why she liked them so much. He always smelled good to her and today was no different. He smelled like sweat, probably the exertion of hunting Nico's men. He also smelled spicy, like cigar smoke and woods. He must've had a quick smoke after she wandered down to the beach. He didn't like smoking around her. There was also just a hint of a cinnamon from the candies he liked to suck on while he was working.

"You smell good," she whispered, opening her eyes. His head was so close to her face that she could see the grey scattered through the dark strands of his hair. The subtle sign of age only made him that much hotter.

"You smell good too, amor," he said without looking up. "Taste good too."

Vee blushed as the memory of him going down on her only a few feet away hit her. He'd touched things in her that no one else had bothered to try. Literally and figuratively.

He set the needle against the edge of her wound. She gritted her teeth as he began sewing the flesh together, his movements sure and steady. The breath whooshed out of her in a long hiss. She slapped the palm of her other hand against the opposite side of the counter as pain engulfed her. Tears leaked slowly from her eyelids, now squeezed tightly shut. Sotza didn't pause, just continued to stab the needle through her flesh, pulling it back together, working fast and efficient.

"Talk to me, Vee," he finally said, his voice cool but strained.

"Wh-what do you want me to say?" she gasped out.

He paused for a second, thinking. "Tell me about your daughter. Did you always keep track of her?"

"Always," Vee replied immediately. She pressed her hand over her eyes to block out the lights flashing in her vision and talked to him. "From the moment she left my womb, I tracked her every move. W-wanted to make sure she had the life I'd envisioned for her. A happy, healthy family... a normal childhood. All the opportunities she deserved."

"You didn't give her money," he noted, a hint of curiosity in his voice, but no censor. "You could've paid her way through University, but you chose not to."

"She needed to learn some things herself," Vee replied. "Stand on her own two feet and all that. She did an excellent job of financing her own education without my help or the help of her adopted parents. If she'd struggled I would have stepped in."

"You parented her from afar," he said with admiration.

"I suppose you could call it that. I did the best that I could without being directly involved." Vee knew he wanted to keep her talking, keep her focused on something other than his movements. She sighed in relief when she felt the brush of his knuckles against her arm as he tied off the last stitch and leaned back.

"You gave that child everything you could," he noted quietly. "Including a part of yourself. You are the definition of sacrifice, my dear."

Vee tipped her head to the side, which took real effort given the exhaustion swamping her, and looked at him. "You know about the kidney?"

He didn't smile exactly, but the corners of his eyes and mouth crinkled. "I know everything there is to know about you, Elvira. Which means I know everything about your daughter."

She gazed up at him, trying to summon anger at the way

he'd interfered in her life, jacked her daughter's life too. But she couldn't. He was mafia, right to the marrow of his bones. He would always go his own path, ensure his success no matter how he got there. Vee understood, because she'd lived in that world her entire life. She was mafia too. The only difference between them was that she'd nurtured a person along the way, even if it was from afar. It gave her a different perspective on life. Softened her. In a way, Raina had saved Vee's life over and over again. Because as long as that child survived, Vee would do everything in her power to survive herself, to ensure the girl's future.

"Almost done," he announced. "Except this." He poured the disinfectant on her wound. Vee yelped and tried to roll away from him. He slapped a hand down on her belly and forcibly held her still holding her injured arm with his other hand so she wouldn't tear the stitches.

"You could have warned me!" she gasped angrily, settling back on the counter. She pushed a hand up into her hair, gripping the strands as the pain faded.

"Lo siento," he mumbled leaning over her.

"You aren't sorry you sadistic asshole," she growled.

He chuckled. "I just need to wrap it now, cariño. We're almost there." The warmth in his voice flowed over her like honey. Now that the pain was fading her skin felt hypersensitive to his every touch. The intimacy of the situation was getting to her.

"Just get it done."

"Si," he said and began wrapping the wound. "Is there anything you wish to know about me?"

Vee was about to demand he knock it off with all the chatter when something surfaced. Something she'd been wondering but hadn't found an opportunity to ask him. "Sure," she said in a clipped voice. "How old are you? And while we're on the topic of your age, why haven't you ever married before? Seems odd, someone in your position should want a succession plan."

She couldn't see his face, but she suspected he was amused by her questions. "I'm forty-seven, ten years older than you," he said easily. "And I never married..." he lifted his head, dark eyes pinning her where she lay, "... because I hadn't yet met you."

"Romantic," she grunted sarcastically and then yelped as he tightened her bandage and stood.

He looked down at her, his expression becoming serious. "I'm a practical man, Vee. I didn't want a woman that would merely warm my bed, grace my arm and my table, would stand behind me, ignorant of the world we live in. I wanted a woman that knew her mind. A woman with vision and the intelligence to match. I wanted you, Elvira. I've been waiting for you my entire life."

She stared at him, the breath catching in her throat. Then she reached up with her good hand and captured him around the neck, pulling him down until his face hovered over hers. He let her have her moment. "Don't call me Elvira," she whispered, but there was no heat to her tone. Inside she was melting at his words. The man was nearly impossible to resist. "Kiss me, Isaac."

He did. Leaning down to give her one of his perfect kisses. Moulding his lips to hers, exploring her lips with his. The kiss was chaste, yet passionate. It held a wealth of feeling without being a precursor to more. Sotza would never allow it. Not while she was freshly hurt. She was beginning to understand that about him. His code of ethics. He would always protect Vee. From him, from herself, from everyone.

He leaned back, still staring down at her, his dark eyes nearly black. He touched her bandage with the lightest of caresses. "I am sorry I wasn't there for you. More sorry than you can know that I wasn't there to stop this from happening."

She shook her head, trying to banish the tone of self-castigation from his tone. "You couldn't have known."

"I should have known!" he growled. "It was my responsibility to keep you safe, to ensure that my men are loyal. I failed you, Vee."

"No, you didn't," she said, lifting her hand to touch his cheek. Her fingers were still bloody from when she'd clutched her wound, but it didn't matter. Sotza had her blood smeared all over the front of his shirt. Proof that he'd been rattled while caring for her, despite his seeming calm. The Gentleman Butcher never spilled blood on himself. "We don't know why John turned, why he gave us up to the Mexicans. You have always had impeccable instincts. Don't doubt yourself now... we can't afford it."

He took her hand in his, which was also bloody, and brought it to his lips, kissing her fingers. "You will never again be harmed under my watch, Vee. This is a promise."

She smiled up at him. "And I promise to defend you as well." She held his gaze allowing the moment to flow between them, before adding, "Unless I'm the one attacking you. Then you're on your own, esposo."

He laughed. A spontaneous laugh that made her heart stutter. He helped her sit up, one hand around her back while the other still held hers. Dizziness rushed through her again and he placed a hand on her shoulder, holding her still. "Give yourself a minute to recover. You lost more blood than I am comfortable with."

"There's an amount that you would be comfortable with?" she said cheekily. Vee dipped her head and looked down at the bandage. "You did a good job," she observed. Then she felt the need to point out, "Though we both know this wound could be a lot worse. You shattered Desi's hand."

His eyes became flint and his features hardened into the mask she was becoming used to. "I slowed her down. She is a formidable enemy. Now she will need time to recover, learn to use her other hand with equal efficiency."

Vee stiffened at the casual cruelty in his words. She supposed she should thank the gods that he'd decided he wanted her, that they would be on the same side. Otherwise she might be the one with a useless hand... or worse. She was about to reply when a shout came from the front entrance. Vee twisted around to look over her shoulder while reaching for the gun. Sotza scooped it up before she could lay a finger on the weapon and then wrapped an arm around her waist, yanking her off the counter. He shoved her to the floor and crouched beside her. She was about to snap at him for leaving her weaponless when he reached down and pulled a gun from his ankle holster. Flipping the safety off he handed it to her.

Vee took the gun from him, stared at it for a moment and then looked over at him. "I think I love you," she said.

Heat flooded her face. She hadn't meant to say that! But everything about their time in the kitchen had prompted her to utter the words. He'd taken care of her, asked about Raina, apologized for not protecting her, and then given her a weapon to protect herself. It pulled something from deep within her.

He flashed a quick grin, pinched her chin between his thumb and finger and dropped a quick hard kiss on her lips. "I have loved you from the moment I set eyes on you, Vee. Every minute since has confirmed and deepened my feelings." Her mouth fell open and she stared at him incredulously as he shouted, "If you aren't Mateo, then whomever you are, you better pray."

# CHAPTER THIRTY-THREE

It was Mateo that came through the door, followed by ten of Sotza's men. Vee was shocked at how fast Sotza's second responded to their situation. It had been maybe two hours since the attack had begun, though it felt like much longer. As his men covered entrances and prepared for the couple to leave the island, he explained that when neither John or Juan made their regular hourly contact with the mainland he mobilized immediately. They were in the air and headed over probably minutes after the island was hit.

Sotza seemed to take Mateo's preparations for granted, simply nodding his head while listening. Vee was both impressed and grateful. She hugged Mateo and thanked him for showing up. It was a few minutes too late to save her from being shot, but she was still grateful. She had been nervous about leaving the house, just her and Sotza. They would've been vulnerable with Vee being injured and Sotza alone to handle any threat that came their way.

As they sped toward the mainland in two boats, Vee felt much better about their situation. She was able to relax, to succumb to the haze of pain that radiated from her arm into her shoulder and across her chest. Now that she was safe the pain didn't bother her that much. It wasn't any worse than some of the things she'd experienced in the past, and she knew she would survive the scratch to her upper arm. She would walk away with a cool scar as a trophy. She breathed in the fresh salty air, letting it centre her.

"I suppose you won't take pain meds?" Sotza murmured from behind her. He was sitting with his back against the bench while she was laying half on top of him with her back against his chest. His arms were wrapped tightly around her.

"No," she agreed, glancing up at him. "I won't."

"You would if I insisted," he said, frowning down at her, considering. "There is such thing as taking your anti-mind-altering-drug crusade too far. If I have to step in, I will."

"You won't," she said confidently. "You trust my judgement. If I couldn't cope, I would say something."

"Hmm, indeed, I do trust your judgment in most things. But not necessarily with your own health. Do not forget, cariño, I have seen you do some pretty reckless things. On more than one occasion you put the health and safety of others before yourself. That's not something I will allow you to do under my care."

She frowned, disliking the direction the conversation was going in, but settled back against him, refusing to engage further. She suspected that they would eventually clash over his dominant attitude. Probably sooner rather than later. She was a strong woman and, though sometimes stressful, she'd thoroughly enjoyed the past year of independence. She hadn't needed or wanted a man in her life. Although, now that she was married to Sotza, she was discovering a few perks.

She shifted in his lap as her body reacted to his closeness, his scent, melting a little inside. She curled up on her side, toward him, her forehead pressed against his flat belly. His arm curved over her back, holding her in place and providing comfort. Her eyes closed as she allowed herself to succumb to the exhaustion that was slowly creeping through her. The warmth of the sun seeped into her back and legs, cradling her in comfort as she drifted into sleep.

She woke up with a start as she was lifted in the air. She lurched against Sotza's chest and gripped his arms. "Go back to sleep, mi amor," he said against the top of her head, careful not to jar her arm as he stepped from the boat. "We're a few hours from being home. Relax and let me take care of you."

"Okay," she said with a yawn and, for the first time in her life, went back to sleep feeling safe in the knowledge that she wouldn't be hurt. Sotza would keep her safe.

She managed to sleep through the entire car ride back to Caracas and the transfer to the private plane. When she woke they were flying low over the mountainous jungle region that held Sotza's empire nestled within. She looked blearily at her new husband, checking to make sure he was next to her. She shouldn't have doubted it. He was watching her, his gaze a mixture of concern and possession. She glanced away, a little unnerved.

When they landed, Vee had barely disembarked when a small, blond tornado came rushing toward them. Vee watched in amusement and awe as Raina lit into Mateo.

"What the fuck was that!?" she yelled at him, poking him in the chest as she spoke. "One minute you're harassing me in the garden and the next you light out like your pants are on fire, taking half the security in this place with you. If you're going to act like the fucking country is exploding you need to tell me what's happening so I don't pace this mausoleum sick with worry!"

"Whoa, chica!" Mateo said throwing his hands up in surprise. There was a smug look about him though, like he was pleased with Raina's dramatic reaction to his withdrawal from the estate.

Raina glanced around, caught sight of Vee and flung herself toward her mother. "Mom!" she cried.

Sotza intercepted her before she could touch Vee. "No, child. She's been injured. You need to calm yourself."

Rather than calming down her eyes grew round and filled with tears. "What happened?" she demanded.

"She was shot when we were attacked," he explained.

Vee sighed and rolled her eyes as Raina's face turned stark white and she clutched at the arm Sotza held up to bar her from grabbing hold of her mother. Clearly the man did not understand children. His policy of bald truthfulness was going to send someone over the edge. Vee shoved an elbow into his side causing him to grunt and wrapped her good arm around Raina, gathering her close. Raina hugged Vee around the waist, careful not to press too tight.

"You're okay?" she asked, her voice wobbling.

"Of course," Vee assured her. They separated and walked toward the vehicles, Raina on one side of Vee and Sotza on the other. Mateo and his men fell in protectively around the family. Raina slipped her hand into Vee's, holding tight to her mother.

Vee's heart ached at the attention. They had grown steadily closer in the week moving up to the wedding, but this display of affection was new. Raina's concern was welcome, but still strange. Vee wasn't used to having so many people care about her welfare. Of course, Danny had cared, but she'd been his boss. If she fell than so did he. She wondered what'd happened to Danny, if he and his family were okay. She was hesitant to bring Sotza's attention to her former second-in-command. She didn't want him to decide to clean up that loose end. Though, in her brief time with him, it'd become clear that Sotza was meticulous when it came to planning and detail. He would not have forgotten about Danny Russo and his connection to Vee. Perhaps in a few days she would broach the subject. See if she might call Danny. For now, she would just navigate the choppy waters of her new marriage.

"I'll take care of her," Raina said coolly turning to her new stepfather when they arrived at the house. "She'll want to change and get right into bed. You can have a tray sent up with her favourite tea and a few snacks."

Vee raised an eyebrow at Raina's daring. She must be feeling brave to say such a thing to a man of Sotza's stature. Sotza merely gazed down at Raina and nodded. His voice was low but warmer than usual as he said, "I'll see to it. Take very good care of her, por favor."

Raina helped Vee up the stairs and into the bedroom, careful not to touch her arm once she saw the bandage. As they entered the room, she asked, "Were you really shot?" There was fear and awe in her voice.

"Yes, I was," Vee replied, reaching for the bed and sitting down carefully. Now that the adrenalin rushing through her system was completely gone she felt the pain of her wound. She wanted nothing more than to do as Raina suggested and take a long nap.

"Did it hurt?" Raina asked curiously.

Vee laughed. "Yes, it hurt. A lot. Can you either call a maid or help me take these clothes off? I really need to lay down and I'd rather not do it in this bathing suit."

"I'll do it," Raina said, reaching for the wrap around Vee's waist. "So the guys that shot you... Sotza will kill them right? He won't let something like this pass unchallenged."

Raina's voice held curiosity and just a bit of bloodthirsty vengeance. Vee looked at her sharply, confirming her suspicion in the girl's eyes. She was concerned for her mother, she was angry, she wanted someone to pay. In that moment something in Vee shifted. She'd spent half her life protecting this girl from the mob life. The life that had taken Vee, dirtied her, chewed her up and spit her out. Yet, she felt proud to have a child with such strength. In a short amount of time, Raina was coming to understand the gritty world that Vee lived in. And instead of feeling disgust, she was adapting with ease. Like she belonged.

"No, he won't let it go," Vee said sadly. She knew he would have to do something. That his last words to Nico had held a wealth of meaning. He would go after the Mexican boss with the deadly intent that had been directed at Vee in Miami before he decided to let her live. Only this time he had a deep-burning fury that wouldn't allow him to stop until the entire Garza cartel was decimated. Remembering the way Nico had reacted over Desi's injury made Vee feel sad that they wouldn't survive Sotza's vengeance. "He can't let it go," she said tiredly. "A challenge like the one they threw at us can't be allowed to stand. It's not how things work, Sotza would look weak."

Raina nodded, satisfied. "And he isn't weak, is he?"

"Not even a little."

Raina carefully maneuvered Vee so that she was standing and then she helped her pull her bathing suit down. Vee stopped her, feeling oddly shy around this grown-up daughter she barely knew. "I can finish," she said, turning her back and tugging the suit down with her one good hand.

Raina's gasp made her freeze. She straightened and looked over her shoulder questioningly. Raina was staring at her lower back, a look of dawning realization crossing her face. "Y-your back..." she said faintly, pointing. "Scar..."

Oh shit. Vee had completely forgotten. She so rarely saw her own scar since it was low on her back. But she knew exactly what was upsetting her daughter. Because Raina had a matching scar.

Vee gathered up her robe and wrapped it carefully around her body, not bothering to pull the sleeve over her injured arm. Once covered, she turned around to face Raina. The girl was struggling with her emotions. Everything lighting up her expressive features, from betrayal to understanding, then back to anger, then acceptance. Vee remained silent, giving Raina time to come to terms with this new knowledge, something that would shed light on one of the most painful periods in her life.

Finally, she spoke, her voice low and strained, clogged with tears. "M-my parents told me the donor was anonymous, that she'd died in an accident. I believed them, I believed that they would never lie to me."

Vee cringed at the accusation in her voice. "They told you what I wanted them to say. What you needed to know."

"You all lied to me!" she exclaimed. "You lied to a sick child. I was dying, I was miserable... so much pain."

"I know," Vee whispered. "And I couldn't stand back and let that happen if there was any chance I could give you more years."

"Do you expect me to thank you?" Raina snapped bitterly, swiping at the tears in her eyes.

Vee thought perhaps a thank you for giving up a body part wasn't too much to ask. But she also understood that Raina was working through a lot. That her anger over the donation of a kidney was about more than just a lie. Vee had been there in the shadows her entire life, watching over her, but never showing herself. And the one thing Raina had always wanted was to know where she came from. The guilt of that wish had eaten at her. She wouldn't have wanted to hurt her adoptive parents by wanting to know her birth parents, but the burning desire still remained. As shitty as Vee's own mother had been, she'd still been there during the bad times. And Vee had missed her when she died. Still missed her.

"What would you have done if you'd known about me?"

Vee asked, hardening her voice. "If you'd known that I was the one who gave you that kidney?"

"I would've found you," Raina said instantly. "I wouldn't have stopped looking until I knew where you were and then I would've gone to see you."

"Exactly. And you would have found me in a miserable marriage with a violent and unpredictable man. You would've become a pawn in the game that has held me prisoner for thirty-seven years." Vee paused, letting that sink in before adding, "And that's why I let go of you when you were born. I wanted more for you. I've always wanted more."

They stared at each other for long seconds. Raina seemed to struggle with herself, then she nodded briefly and said, "Let's get you into bed. Once you've eaten something you can take a nap." She walked around Vee and flipped the blankets back, inviting her to lay down.

Vee smiled wanly and said, "Yes, boss."

# CHAPTER THIRTY-FOUR

Something soft touched her face, brushing faintly against her cheek. It was warm, comforting. She turned her head on the pillow, burrowing her body a little deeper into the plush covers that welcomed her, beckoning her back into the deep sleep. She frowned as something moved the bed next to her, depressing the mattress. Then his scent, cigars, fresh air and cinnamon, reached out to her, wrapping her in the hazy, sexy comfort.

Sotza was here, with her.

Her frown turned to a smile as he placed his lips against hers, touching just the edge at first before settling more firmly over her mouth and pressing harder. She opened her mouth, breathing him in and allowing him access. He took her bottom lip gently in his teeth, tugging a tiny bit before leaving off to explore further, slipping his tongue first against her teeth and then further, exploring her. Her heart picked up speed, her pulse fluttered in her throat and the blood rushed beneath her skin, warming her.

He released her lips, moving back just a fraction, to say, "Hola, mi esposa. Did you sleep well?"

"Si, it was very nice," she sighed and opened her eyes to look up at him. She was surprised at the look that greeted her. She'd been expecting warmth, lust, heat. Instead she was greeted with something else. Something much darker. His face was devoid of expression, but his eyes held a sinister promise.

She pushed herself back and sat up. She didn't want to be in such an inferior position while he was looking at her like that, like he might devour her whole. She wanted some space. She shoved her blond hair back from her face, tucking it behind her ears.

"Are you up for a walk, cariño?" he asked, taking her arm. He pulled her from the bed, not giving her much choice but to stand.

"Sure," she agreed. "Where are we going?"

"The prison," he said easily walking to the closet and opening the doors.

A cold chill ran through her, obliterating the pleasant-ness of her nap. She knew where he wanted to take her. He was ready to deal with John and she had asked to be there when he did it. Suddenly, she regretted that choice. Every-thing about Sotza felt... removed, different, wrong. This was the man who had ruthlessly torn her city from her and hunted her into the ground without mercy. Not the man who had been tenderly caring for her, making love to her, showing her all the things she'd missed out on in her previous marriage.

But she couldn't refuse to go with him. Couldn't back out now. She was his wife. If she wanted to show him that she was capable of standing at his side, this was the time to do it. She would not lose his respect by chickening out, but at the same time she feared what she might see in the prison. As he helped her into a pair of black leggings, she wondered how she would react to seeing him at work.

"Lift your good arm," he instructed, his voice impersonal. "I'll help you with the other one."

She gasped in pain, nausea running through her as her arm was lifted and fitted into the sleeve of a loose silk blouse. After Sotza buttoned the front, he tipped her chin up so she was looking at him. He gave her a look that said everything. That he was going to take vengeance on her behalf and that he was going to enjoy every second.

"Which shoes?" he asked, striding back toward the closet.

"My heels," she said, trying to keep her voice strong. "The silver ones."

He returned with her steel-heeled shoes, crouched in front of her and, lifting one leg at a time, slid the shoes on. She felt better with the extra height; she needed the added confidence only a good pair of shoes could give her.

She nodded at him, indicating she was ready. He didn't take her hand, didn't touch her. He allowed her to walk on her own, showing her strength to the world. Vee was glad that Raina was nowhere in sight as they made their way down the stairs, out the back door and into the garden. Two men dropped in behind them as they walked, shadowing them as they bypassed the garden maze, walking side by side down a concrete path toward a brightly lit building. Vee hadn't noticed it before. She'd been locked inside the bedroom for most of her time in Sotza's home and she hadn't been able to see it from the angle of her windows.

It took only a few minutes for them to get to the building. Vee was relieved that her heels didn't catch in any cracks in the pavement. She really didn't want to ruin this significant moment by falling on her face, though every fibre of her being begged her to turn around and rush back to the safety of her bedroom. When they arrived at the building, the door opened for them as though they were expected, and someone had been watching for their arrival. She took a breath of fresh air before entering the foreboding place that held the stench of death. Not literally, but she knew to the very mortar of the structure that this was a building of torture, death and decay. Many who entered hadn't ever left.

The entrance was brightly lit, as was the hallway leading toward several closed doors. Vee squeezed her eyes shut for a quick second, before straitening her shoulders and looking toward Sotza for instruction. He was watching her carefully, his sharp eyes on her face, reading her. He wasn't sure of her. Didn't know if she would pass this test. Truthfully, she didn't know either. Her time as the boss of Miami had occasionally been bloody, had called for her to do some things she'd have rather not done. But she knew, deep down, that this was different. This was on another level. This was why she'd failed to hold her city. She didn't have the stomach to go to the dark places Sotza did.

"This way," Sotza said coolly, speaking for the first time since they left the house. She nodded briefly and followed him down the hall, right to the end. He stopped next to a door, gave her a pointed look, and opened it.

Mateo turned to look at them from where he was standing. He nodded and said respectfully, "Señora Sotza."

Vee stepped through, ahead of Sotza. Her eyes went right to John who was sitting in a chair, his hands cuffed behind his back. He didn't look too bad, and while Vee felt trepidation in being so deep in Sotza's lair, she also felt a bit cheated that he hadn't been more roughed up. The guys could've knocked him around a bit on their way back.

Sotza stepped up behind her, for just a moment, before he moved away, toward his victim. Vee felt bereft at the loss of his warmth. She wanted to cling to him, to keep him the way she needed him. The warm, loving husband he'd been showing glimpses of. Not the monster she knew was about to come out and play.

She swallowed hard and forced her hands to remain at her sides. John was staring grimly at the floor. He knew the price of betrayal. And yet he still chose to pay it.

"Why?" Vee demanded, taking the few steps that would close the distance between them. She stood directly in front of John and waited for him to lift his head. "Why did you betray our family?"

She purposefully used the word 'our' including not only herself and Sotza, but everyone that worked for him. For them. It made his betrayal hurt more. It made the other men who would witness this execution even angrier at John, more loyal to the Sotza cartel. She caught her husband's eye over John's head and saw a flash of warmth cross those dark soulless depths. He knew she'd chosen her words carefully.

"Speak now, John, as I run out of patience. And when my patience ends, my husband will go to work. Trust me when I say that this is something you'll wish to delay."

John lifted his head, treating her to a terrifying look. The depth of his hatred pierced her. What had she done to deserve it? She had expected desperation, fear, pleading. She hadn't expected such defiance. But then, maybe she should have. Though he betrayed them, he was still Sotza's man, one of his army of security. The job would be brutal, not for the faint of heart.

"You expect anything from me, puta?" he snarled. Sotza stiffened and Vee had to shake her head to stop him from stepping in. "You are here for two seconds and the keys to the throne are handed to you. We have heard the rumours about you. About how you open your legs to whoever will take you the highest. You disgust me!"

Vee smiled coolly. "That's a very interesting way of summing up my life, John. But my past isn't the reason for your betrayal is it? Nothing so deep as that. What was it? What did Garza promise you?" John spat at her, but she side-stepped and it landed near her feet. She sighed in annoyance and held her hand out to Mateo. "Gun please."

Mateo looked toward Sotza with a raised brow. Sotza gave him a nod and Mateo passed his weapon over to her, butt first. She took the gun, looked it over, cocked it, putting a bullet in the chamber and then holding it to John's head.

"You need to speak to me John, make me understand. Because if you don't talk then there's no reason to keep you alive. You see, as much as my husband likes to play with his food, I prefer a quick death. Perhaps you need to decide which you would prefer?" She put the gun against his arm and shot, aiming toward the bone so the bullet wouldn't go through and ricochet. Mateo looked toward his boss again, but Sotza merely looked amused as blood sprayed across her white blouse and John started screaming. She gave him a moment to compose himself. She knew exactly how much a gunshot wound to the arm hurt, he was going to need a few minutes. When his screams died away and he began swearing at her, she slapped him in the side of the head with the gun and put it back to his ear. "That was just to prove that I'm a woman of my word. I don't fuck around, John. The next bullet will end you. Start talking if you want a few more minutes of life."

"You fucking puta cunt!" he yelled, glaring up at her. "Do your worst, I give you nothing."

"Nothing?" she said conversationally. "That's really too bad. I was hoping you might tell us exactly what it takes to become Garza's second." A flash of surprise crossed his features, quickly smothered, but not before both she and Mateo caught it. "Yes, that's it, isn't it? You do Garza's bidding and he sets you up in the position you always wanted here, with Sotza. But that dream went further out of reach with my arrival didn't it? I owned Miami, I negotiated alliances. Sotza doesn't need any more in his inner circle now that I've arrived. What did Garza want, eh Johnny? He wanted me separated from Sotza, that was clear. We all know Sotza was to be the main victim. But what about me, was I to die as well?"

"Both," he snarled. "And good riddance. You will weaken his hold on this country, on his trade. And he is allowing you to do this to him. He deserves to go as much as you do. Venezuela needs new leadership."

"Your leadership?" she asked smoothly.

"Yes!"

"And who are you to think you deserve such an elevated position?" she said coldly stepping away from him. "You are nothing. Garza isn't stupid. He would have killed you the moment he took over. He doesn't like treasonous assholes any better than we do."

John spewed his hatred and anger at them, giving them everything he had to give. Vee didn't need to ask more questions. Sotza watched the proceedings calmly for several minutes, then he asked Vee, raising his voice above John's angry outbursts, "Are you done?"

She nodded and waved her hand toward their captive, giving her husband permission to go to work. A light flared in Sotza's eyes. Happiness. She shivered and took a few more steps back. Had she done enough? Could she gracefully exit the room without incurring her husband's wrath? She glanced toward the door and then caught Mateo's eye. He shook his head slightly, subtly telling her that she must remain.

Sotza turned his back to the room and took his jacket off. She watched the play of muscles beneath his shirt as he moved, rolling first one sleeve up his strong, corded arm, and then the other. When this was done, he opened a drawer in the desk tucked into the corner. He pulled a knife from the depths, unsheathed it and held it up to the light so he could look it over. Then he turned.

Vee nearly cried out at the look on his face. It was ecstasy. Pure and complete sadistic ecstasy. He was enjoying himself, looking forward to what he was about to do. The look of death that she'd learned to associate with men like him had disappeared, leaving in its place a warped pleasure. Her gut clenched and nausea gripped her. She knew she had to leave before she disgraced herself. Maybe she could've stayed if his face had stayed emotionless, if she could imagine that he regretted what he was about to do. But he didn't, he wouldn't. He would enjoy every second of the blood he spilled.

Before she could run from the room, he attacked, so fast that she stumbled back a few steps as though he were coming after her. He gripped john's chin in one hand, yanked his tongue from between his lips with the other and sliced it off. Blood spilled down John's chin and chest like a gory waterfall. His screams stopped abruptly and only a watery garbled sound remained. Vee had to bite her lips to keep from crying out. Dizziness washed over her. She locked her knees so she would remain standing.

"This is how I usually begin," Sotza explained, lifting his eyes to hers. They were bright, manic, like he had a fever. "The screaming is distracting. I prefer music."

Vee felt like she was swimming, like she was watching him through water or glass. Almost slow motion as he turned to the table he'd pulled the knife from, dropped John's severed tongue on top and tapped a button on a black box. Music filled the room. Some kind of classical music. Vee didn't know what it was. She didn't listen to classical music. She usually preferred silence so she could hear her thoughts.

Sotza stepped back to John, standing at his side, staring down, his face a terrifying mask. "You tasered my wife, John. Look at her." He gripped John by the back of the head and forced his face up toward Vee. "She is small, she is delicate. She should never be harmed, let alone hit with 100,000 volts.

That's about how much it was, right John? You shot her twice with a weapon I provided in case you needed to subdue someone without killing them. Except you messed up, John. You shot my beautiful wife then you handed her over to my enemy. Bad. Fucking. Move. John."

Vee closed her eyes as Sotza attacked the man again, his knife flashing. She didn't want to know what was happening, but from the horrific sounds coming from john she suspected it was awful. When she opened her eyes again she saw blood trickling down razor thin cuts across his cheeks, upper lip and chin. Sotza was slicing him open one piece at a time. Her gaze strayed to the blood making a path down the side of John's head then shifted to the floor where she saw a strip of flesh she suspected was an ear. Her stomach lurched and she didn't have time to close her eyes again when Sotza bent behind John. She heard something hit the floor, saw the agony twisting John's face, suspected he'd just lost a finger or two.

This was The Butcher. The man she never wanted to meet, the man she'd married. Gone to bed with. Hoped for a future with. It was like watching the devil dance with his prey. Macabre, graceful, twisted. She couldn't watch but she wouldn't turn away either. She was caught, helpless in his spell.

"You've seen me do this before," Sotza said quietly from behind his victim, leaning over to speak in John's good ear. "You know exactly how long this can go on for. You know how good I am at keeping my prisoners alive, squeezing out every last drop of pain. You know this is my favourite part, don't you John?"

He rounded the chair to stand in front of John, staring down at him. He bent to one knee, lifted the hem of John's pant leg and made a quick slice. John lurched in the chair, his face twisting harder than she'd seen yet.

"Achilles tendon," Sotza said. She didn't know who he was talking to. He was still bent in front of John. "Supposed to be one of the most painful cuts a person can experience. A particular favourite of mine." He sliced through the other one and stood, staring down at John as he writhed and screamed as best he could without a tongue.

Vee couldn't see Sotza's face from where they were standing, but she knew exactly what she would see. The maniacal ecstasy. The gratification he was receiving from this gruesome display.

"Stop," she whispered, her voice shaky. She didn't think he would hear her, but then he looked over at her, a frown marring the perfection of his happiness. "Just stop," she said in a stronger voice. "You've played l-long enough. Put him down, Sotza. Right now."

She wasn't asking. She was demanding. Drawing her line in the sand and telling him where she wasn't willing to go with him. This was it, the moment she feared would come all too fast. Their reckoning as a couple. Would he step back over the line toward her? Salvage the few good moments she'd managed to find in their war. Or would he forcibly drag her over to his side, be like every other man in her life, prove his dominance, his superior strength over her.

"Leave." His voice was so cold, so devoid of any hint of affection that Vee knew she was in trouble. Knew she'd gone too far. "Now. Wait for me up at the house."

"You leave with me," she whispered pleadingly, refusing to back down.

"Get out!" he roared, shouting at her for the first time. She was so shocked it took her a few seconds to register the depth of his anger.

She lifted her chin and made to walk past him, but before she reached the door she spun around. She was between Sotza and Mateo. Neither man had time to react as she lifted

Mateo's gun and emptied it into John. One bullet to the head, one to the heart, three in his torso. His head flew back, his body shuddered with each impact and then he went limp. Dead.

Vee handed the gun to Mateo who was quick to take it from her. She turned back to Sotza, facing what she knew could be her execution.

## CHAPTER THIRTY-FIVE

Vee paced the bedroom, trying everything she could to get her mind off those horrifying images. She'd killed before. Twice to be exact... well three times now. But the other times had been in self-defence, mostly. Tony didn't count, she was ending her marriage, not conducting business. Every time she'd had to kill she'd used a gun. She hadn't tortured anyone... mostly. Hadn't taken pleasure in slicing off little pieces of them. Not the way Sotza had. He'd enjoyed every moment of his victim's pain.

She shuddered in disgust, reliving the bloody scene. She would never forget the image, it was burned into her memory. After she killed John, Sotza sent her back up to the house with one of his men, instructing him to lock Vee in the bedroom. She'd gone quietly. What else could she do? She wasn't the type to fight a losing battle. And she had felt the anger rolling off Sotza, knew he probably sent her away so he wouldn't do something irreparable to her.

She wrapped her arms around herself as she continued to pace, trying to swallow the rising panic. She made the wrong move in every way. She'd interrupted Sotza at work, she undermined him, she forced her will on the situation. In short, she'd acted without thinking. Not something Vee usually did. Like Sotza, she was a planner, she made decisions with cool, careful thought. Sotza had every right to be angry with her.

Knowing that didn't help her anxiety. She had crossed The Butcher. She would have to pay the price of betrayal, as John had. She was probably going to die. Thinking about what he'd done to John hit her again and she nearly ran for the toilet.

"Nice work, Vee," she mumbled to herself. "You finally find a husband you can possibly live with and in less than a week you manage to royally fuck that up."

The door opened. Vee froze as Sotza strode into the room. He looked the same. Sleeves rolled up his arms, tie missing. There was no blood on him, not a single drop. There should be blood on him considering what she'd witnessed. Yet he looked immaculate. He looked at her as she assessed him. He watched without emotion, his gaze cold and dead, eyes flat. He gave her a minute as she struggled to come to terms with him as a man, a murderer and a husband.

"Sotza," she said trying for a conciliatory tone. "I'm sorry. I didn't expect - "

"You will not defy me like that in front of my second, or any of my men. Ever," he said quietly, menacingly. He took a step toward her, his dark eyes blazing to life with fury.

"Sotza, let's talk about this. I know I fucked up, but the way you were acting - "

"You will not defy me again, Elvira," he interrupted sharply, repeating himself.

An answering anger flared to life within her. He wouldn't accept either apology or explanation. She had suspected, no, she *knew*, that they would clash over something like this. The dominant mafia boss who talked lip service about giving her freedom and setting her up at his side only to strip it away the moment they disagreed. He was reliving her last marriage.

"Or what?" she cried. If he wouldn't accept her apology then she would fight him, try to make her point. "You'll do to me what you did to John? Isn't that what you were going to do to me in Miami? Before you met me?"

"I was working," he said icily. "You know the difference."

"You fucking enjoyed every minute out there in that disgusting prison. Don't bother to deny it. I was there, I saw your face as you cut him to pieces while he was still alive."

"Vee," he said warningly, stepping toward her. She backed up, her legs bumping the bed. "I won't deny I enjoyed torturing the man that handed my wife over to the Mexican cartel. I would have done just as much damage for less."

"No," she snapped. "There's a difference between revenge killing and what you did. You like it, you like hurting people. You're a fucking psychopath!"

"Enough!" he yelled, reaching for her.

Vee jumped back, swiping her good arm at him. "Don't you fucking touch me!"

The look that crossed his face was utterly terrifying. She'd seen it in her nightmares, before Sotza captured her and showed her his loving side. She'd seen it out in his prison building when he was cutting John to pieces. She wondered if she was about to die. He grabbed her, so suddenly that she was standing next to him one moment, then on her back a second later, trapped beneath him. His hands gripped her arms tightly. She yelped in pain as his hand squeezed her injured arm.

"You will never again refuse my touch," he said to her, his voice chilling.

"Fuck you!" she hissed, struggling to heave him off, roll out from underneath him.

He ripped her blouse, right down the middle, popping the

buttons. She cried out and slapped at him, but he held her arms while ripping the rest of her clothes from her body. What the fuck was he doing? She was naked beneath him now, only her bra still on and he'd yanked it so her small breasts were pushed over the top. She didn't understand until he shifted his body, placing his hips between her legs and reaching for his zipper. His movements were quick, efficient.

His intent became obvious and Vee started to really freak out. "Stop, Sotza!" she begged, her voice rising. "Isaac, what are you doing?"

"Don't fight me, Vee. You'll injure you're arm," he said, his voice impassionate, though anger poured off him in spades. He gripped her face in one hand, shoving her chin up and to the side. His elbow rested on her sternum, pinning her to the bed. She tried to slap at him, but she couldn't see what she was doing, couldn't properly reach him. She kept hitting his arms and it was like hitting a brick wall – it didn't move him.

"If you do this I'll find a way to kill you!" Tears sparking in her eyes.

She gasped as his fingers touched her, entered her. Anger sizzled through her veins sparking an erotic charge. The air practically snapped with the tension between them. She brought her knee up, trying to slam it into his side. He was right, she couldn't keep slapping him without hurting her shoulder. But her legs worked just fine. He grunted when her sharp knee connected with his ribs. Unfortunately, the move gave him better access to her vulnerable pussy. He pushed his fingers further into her, harder, more firmly against her g-spot. He flicked a thumb over her clit and she cried out. He wasn't just going to brutally take her body, he was going to force a response.

He kept her pinned with an elbow on her chest and grabbed her leg, gripping it just above her knee and forcing it higher, opening her wider. She growled as he pumped his fingers in her, applying pressure to all the right spots and sliding his thumb over her clit. Her hips picked up the rhythm though her brain splintered in every direction; caught between the need to greedily sponge all the pleasure he was offering and horrified by his actions.

"Fuck!" she yelled as her orgasm built. She squirmed and fought, but he was much heavier and stronger. And she was fighting with an injury.

He took her chin and moved her head to face him. "Look at me," he demanded, his voice a deep growl. "Am I The Butcher now, Elvira?"

"Fuck... you!" she snarled.

His eyes darkened at her defiance and he thrust himself harder between her legs. Unable to pull him away from him she wound her fingers in the cuff of his shirt and held on. He pulled his fingers from her and she cried out at the loss. She thought he would enter her then, push his long, thick cock against her and fill her up. The way she needed. Instead his fingers, saturated in her wet, sticky response, moved lower. She cried out and tensed up when his fingers sought her back entrance, touching her, exploring, then shoving past the barrier of her anal ring in one thrust. She cried out and dug her fingernails into his arm.

Pain shot through her body as she tried to adjust to his rough entry. She panted, trying to breathe through the new and strange feelings flooding through her. She tried to close her legs, deny him further entry, but he effortlessly kept her positioned, spread wide for his assault. She wanted to yell, to swear at him but she was too swamped by sensations. She couldn't catch her breath enough to form the words. He began moving his fingers in her tight passage, raking them across sensitive erogenous zones she didn't know she had, lighting her lower body up with a heady combination of pain and pleasure.

He was mastering her, showing her that he could do anything he wanted to her, whether it was to cause pain or pleasure. He could give her the world and he could take it away just as easily. While he wreaked havoc on her body, he devastated her mind. As long as she knew he was capable of doing this to her, attacking her, forcing her pleasure against her will, she would never be his equal partner. She would always be just a woman.

He twisted his fingers inside her. She cried out as his knuckles dug into her sending sparks of pain radiating through her ass. But as quick as the pain came, it receded and was replaced by an equally unbearable pleasure. He pressed his thumb into her pussy, until he was hooking her in both holes. The pressure was so intense she didn't know which way was up. She was so far past fighting him, she was now just trying to survive what he was doing to her. She covered her face with her hand, trying to at least visually block him out.

"Look at me," he demanded. She moved her hand without thinking. She wouldn't defy him now, not while he had complete control over her. His fingers picked up a rhythm that made everything within her focus on that precious orgasmic point. Her salvation. To fly into oblivion, away from him. "You will not take your eyes off me when you come."

She stared up at him, watching his hard, implacable face while he forced the forbidden on her. Drove her higher and higher. She tipped her head back, but kept her eyes glued to him as her orgasm screamed towards her.

"Who is your master?" His voice was harsh.

She bit her lip and shook her head, refusing to give him what he wanted. Suddenly the pressure in her anal passage increased. She didn't know what he did, was beyond being able to follow his movements, but the shift sent her soaring higher. Higher than she thought possible. She thought she would shatter, that her heart would stop from this sexual torture he was playing out on her. He was going to kill her with sex.

"Who do you obey?" he asked, his voice a guttural snarl.

She couldn't take any more. "You!" she screamed as she hurtled over the edge of her orgasm. He didn't let her enjoy it though, he kept pumping his fingers, demanding more from her.

"Say my name!"

"Sotza!" she yelled, tears leaking.

He moved his hand to her throat and squeezed, just shy of choking her. "Again," he demanded, pulling his fingers from her ass and lining his cock up.

"Please," she begged him, sobbing, not even knowing what she was begging for. She was terrified that he was going to enter her anally and tear her to shreds. But a dark part of her wanted him to. Wanted that magnificent pressure to come back.

"My name!" he shouted from above her.

"Isaac Sotza!" she yelled back. He thrust into, taking her vaginally. Relief and pleasure shot through her sending her soaring.

"Again," he growled hovering over her. A bead of sweat fell from his forehead onto her cheek.

"Isaac Sotza!" she screamed, digging her fingernails into whatever piece of flesh she could reach.

"Who owns you, Elvira Sotza?"

"Isaac Sotza..." She sobbed. She would have promised him the world in that moment.

His fingers tightened around her throat, cutting off her ability to breathe. She didn't care. In fact, she was so caught up in the moment, drugged with endorphins that her lack of breath pushed her higher toward the intense peak she was desperately seeking. Her mouth opened in a wordless cry of ecstasy, she pressed her knees into his sides, cradling him, taking each brutal thrust and silently begging for more.

He lowered his face until it was inches from her own and watched her, his wild dark eyes holding hers captive as he fucked her with a brutality that was exciting, erotic, terrifying. She didn't know if she would survive, blackness dotted her vision and she felt helpless to do anything but take the savagery he was forcing on her. She felt his cock grow bigger inside her as he neared his own release, as he drove her toward another exhilarating peak. She tried to gasp for breath, but nothing came out.

Just as he slammed into her one last time, releasing his tight grip on her neck and forcing a shattering orgasm from her, he lowered his lips and growled into her ear, "Mi esposa. Hasta la muerte."

My wife. Until death.

# CHAPTER THIRTY-SIX

"She's planning something."

Mateo had asked for this meeting. Was giving Sotza a complete picture of Vee's movements for the week. Since meeting Vee in person, getting to know her intelligence and cunning, Mateo had more respect for her. Was more willing to babysit a woman. It certainly didn't hurt that her daughter was a stunning, younger version. And the two women spent a lot of time together.

"Explain," Sotza said, sitting back in his chair and watching the younger man coldly.

Mateo didn't sit. He rarely sat down unless invited to dinner at the main house. He was energetic, athletic and driven. Sotza suspected he also wasn't conformable enough to settle easily around his boss. Sotza didn't have a problem with his subordinates feeling ill at ease around him. It indicated healthy respect.

"She's watching the security rotations with more than passing interest and asking questions."

"That is her right as my wife and mistress of my property. If she were to see a fault in my security I would expect corrective action to be taken immediately." Sotza placed a hand on the desk. The one with his wedding band.

Mateo's eyes flickered to the plain gold band. He pushed forward, despite the subtle warning. "No, she's not complaining about security. She's filing the information away in that sharp brain of hers. She's definitely planning something, and I don't like it."

Sotza watched the other man, silently thinking over his words. "You want me to put a leash on my wife?" His tone was quiet, pleasant almost. Deadly.

To Mateo's credit he didn't flinch. Though he'd heard that tone many times. Usually as Sotza was explaining something to the person sitting under his knife. "No, Señor Sotza. I would not suggest such a thing."

"I didn't think so," Sotza said, satisfied. "You may go back to work now." Mateo nodded sharply, turned on his heel and strode to the door. Sotza's voice stopped him. "And Mateo?"

"Si, Señor?"

"You will continue to attend to my wife. Catalogue her movements, but do not interfere. No matter what. Am I understood?"

"Of course, Señor." Mateo left the office. Likely more confused and annoyed about the situation than he had been. It amused Sotza to fuck with his second-in-command a little. The man was arrogant, cocky, sure of his skills. While his attitude had been well earned under Sotza's regime, it still wouldn't hurt the man to get knocked down a peg. And Sotza needed to play this situation carefully.

Sotza was in love with his wife. It was unexpected. It was uncomfortable, inconvenient, aggravating, exhilarating. He had sensed from their very first meeting that they would be compatible, both physically and practically. Vee was a sharp woman and brutal in her own right. She didn't realize it, but she was the eye of the storm. Everything whirled around her, chaotic and elemental, eventually crashing down to land at her feet. She demanded the chaos bow to her, and it did.

She was beautiful in a way she didn't perceive. Yes, she understood her physical allure, her sexiness, and she used it to draw people in like flies to honey. But she couldn't possibly understand how intoxicating her idealistic innocence was to the dark world she inhabited, to Sotza. For a thirty-seven-year old woman with several lifetimes worth of experience, she was innocent to so many things. She was intelligent, she operated in the underworld with relative ease, could hold her own, yet she still held onto that purity. Whether she realized it or not, she wanted the world to be a better place and she took action to push it in that direction. As his wife, he wanted to preserve this characteristic, nurture it, bask in the essence of something he'd been forced to lose as a child, maybe never had.

Vee pardoned people that shouldn't be pardoned, giving them free passes when they fucked up. She was protective of the people that drifted into her circle. She wasn't just mother to Raina, she was mother to all that she deemed worthy. She loved and protected. She listened with her ears and her heart.

It was gratifying that she tried to step up with him, bold that she wanted to watch him at work. But also, it made him a little happy that she wasn't as bloodthirsty as he. It made her softer, more feminine. Alluring. Made him want her even more. His mistake, letting her come with him to deal with John. A mistake he wouldn't repeat.

Now it was up to Sotza to protect the things he loved about his wife. She thought he was trying to force her into the shadows, to force her obedience with his heavy handedness. And, in a way he was. He needed her to listen and obey no matter the situation. It was the only way to protect the precious woman she'd somehow managed to preserve through decades of abuse. She couldn't shine until she was free to do it without obstacles. And one of those obstacles was Vee herself. If she couldn't settle into the structured, brutal and demanding lifestyle that came with standing at Sotza's side, then he would have to keep her locked up, away from the world. A pity. Someone like Vee should always stand in the sun.

During the days she coldly ignored him. She would attend meals with him, speak when spoken to, but she refused to extend to him the warmth she showed others. Her attitude amused him and assured him that his rough handling hadn't broken the part of her he wished to protect, that fiery independence, the softness that allowed her feelings to be hurt by his actions. Sotza was nothing if not patient. He'd learned over his years of leadership that quiet patience would lure his prey to him, rather than send them running into hiding. Not that he minded chasing Vee back in Miami, but now was the time to let her find her way to him.

She still had free reign of the house and grounds so she spent her time exploring, spending time with Raina and getting to know his staff. He was aware she had the ulterior motive of trying to find out his security rotations. Sotza trusted his people. They were flawless when it came to security.

Sotza spent the next week waging a campaign of dominance over her body, proving to her that he was her master. At first, she tried to resist, tried to push him away, but the more he pushed back, the more he loved her body with erotic violence, the more she fell victim to his advances. He would purposely disconcert her, cornering her in some part of the house, sometimes a room that was more public than she was comfortable with. He would shove her against a wall, bend her over a table, whatever his imagination decided, and he would fuck her. Sometimes hard, when she resisted, and other times leisurely, teasing her, bringing her senses alive before fulfilling them both.

Each evening, as she was getting ready for sleep, Sotza would come to their bed. After the first night, she stopped trying to deny him. There was no point. He always won the fight, by sheer physical strength and by mental fortitude. He wanted to own her, show her that every part of her belonged to him, even the heart she tried so hard to shield from him. He'd proved it the first night after John's death, and every night since, ruthlessly bringing her body alive under his touch. Forcing the words he wanted to hear past her lips.

Some might say his coercive methods wouldn't work. That what his wife said in the throes of passion meant nothing. Sotza considered what he was doing to Vee in the same light as torture. Sure, what the victim said while under duress could mean anything. Any person would lie under extreme circumstances. But Sotza looked beyond the words. He looked into the eyes and hearts of his victims and pulled the truth from them. More importantly, they saw the truth for themselves. Eventually, when left to linger on the matter long enough. Vee had shortened John's life considerably more than Sotza had intended. He would have kept the man alive long enough to allow him to recognize his errors in life. Long enough to make peace with his God. But she was soft. And kind. She didn't understand the necessity of pain as truth.

It was his intention to show her the way to truth between them. He would break her down until he conquered her, owned her. Mind, body and soul.

## CHAPTER THIRTY-SEVEN

"Vee." His deep voice disturbed her thoughts and stopped her in midstride. She turned slowly on the spot, mentally preparing herself for the coming confrontation.

She was walking through the gardens, searching for Raina who seemed to love the hedge maze. Vee didn't see the appeal, she kept hitting dead ends which frustrated her almost to the point of wanting to burn the damn thing down. Vee was too no-nonsense for something as whimsical as a garden maze. While she could understand the visual appeal, she hated wasting her time. Which she did every time she went into the damn thing. A part of this garden, especially the maze, called to Raina. She spent hours sitting among the shrubbery, thinking and writing. Sometimes Vee sat with her, quietly observing while Raina did her thing. Sometimes they would walk and talk.

Her heels clicked on the paving stones as she wandered through, lost for the most part, searching for her daughter. Somehow she'd either stumbled on Sotza or he'd known exactly where to find her. She suspected it was the latter. The man was incredibly good at always knowing precisely where to find her and sneaking up on her. She gave him a pointed look, refusing to speak.

As she much as she thrilled at his touch, the truth of their relationship was hammered home, again and again. Each time he cornered her, fucked her, brought her body alive against her will. She was not his equal, and she never would be.

"Walk with me," he said. His eyes took on a warm glow as they slipped over her body, taking in her neat white blouse, buttoned right up her neck with a little ruffle around the top, her grey satin pencil skirt and high heels.

Sotza was more casual at home. Dress pants, button up shirt with the top few buttons undone and sleeves rolled up. He wore a vest too. And though it was a little old-fashioned, it looked mouth-wateringly good on him. It highlighted his lean frame. He looked good to her. He always looked good though.

"Do I have a choice?" she asked coldly.

"You always have a choice, Vee." He stepped up toward her. "But, as you have learned, your choice will inform my subsequent action."

"You're a bastard." But she allowed him to take her arm.

He ignored her provocativeness. "I want to show you something."

"Is it a severed head?" she asked sarcastically. "Because I'd rather wait until lunch has settled."

As if she hadn't spoken, he led her leisurely through the maze, like they were simply a couple, out for a simple stroll in the estate gardens. Vee forced some of the tension from her shoulders and relaxed, at least as much as she could while in Sotza's presence. She inhaled the fragrant scent of the greenery, intermingled with the perfume of the flowers. It was impossible to resist the allure of his garden, to remain angry while she was in the presence of such beauty.

"Why did you have this garden built?" A bit of warmth infused her words. "It doesn't serve a purpose. Unless you force your victims to try to get through the damn maze as a form of torture."

He chuckled and shifted his hand from her arm to slide it across her back, resting his palm just above the curve of her ass. He reached for her with his other hand, holding her hand in a light grip. The move was almost romantic or would have been had she trusted him.

"I didn't build the garden, my father did. But I maintained it and expanded. I had the maze added to the grounds about twenty years ago. It's relaxing to come to such a place when my thoughts are chaotic. I feel more at peace here than most places." He led them toward what she thought must be the center of the maze.

"It's magnificent," she admitted hesitantly.

"But?" he prodded.

She sighed and shrugged a shoulder. "I keep getting lost."

He smiled down at her as they took the last turn. They were in the middle of the maze. There was a bench and the hedges had been allowed to grow as tall as trees. Vee thought it looked ominous and didn't enjoy spending time in that section, even with Raina.

"I've been here before," Vee pointed out.

Sotza didn't respond and she began to wonder if he brought her to the middle of the maze so they might have a secluded moment for him to continue his campaign of dominance over her. She stopped walking, eyeing the bench with trepidation. There was no chance she wanted to fuck around out there, in the cool mountain air where anyone could stumble upon them. If that was his intention then he was about to be sorely disabused, via a heel stabbed into the centre of his foot.

"Sotza..." she said warningly. He didn't say a word, just

held her hand and led her toward the far corner of the section they were standing in. She shivered and squinted as shadows embraced them. "What are you doing? It looks like spiders might live back there. I don't like spiders."

His chuckle of amusement ran through her like warm spicy rum. It felt good, comforting and incredibly sexy. Though it'd been well over a year since she had a drink, the memory felt right. Sotza was an addiction. He was intoxicating. Even when she wanted to hate him she still craved him.

"No spiders," he said in his deep soft voice. "I promise."

He dropped her hand and took several steps forward, further into the shadows, then, even though she was looking right at the shady spot he'd been striding toward, he disappeared. "Sotza!" she gasped.

"Come to me, Vee," he said. His voice clear and crisp. "Step toward my voice."

She blinked several times and tried to figure out where he'd gone, why she could hear him as though he was standing next to her, but she couldn't see any part of him. She held an arm out and walked forward. The darkness settled around her and she swore she was about to walk directly into a hedge filled with spiders.

She jumped when a hand came out of the shadows and landed on her arm. He wrapped his long fingers around her forearm and pulled her gently forward. Vee took small hesitant steps not wanting to trip over a paving stone. It was so dark she couldn't even see her own feet. She could sort of see Sotza's outline as he walked in front of her pulling her forward. Then he was taking steps to the side, pulling her along. She twisted to look behind her. Her mouth dropped open when she realized she was completely engulfed by the shadowy hedges.

"A hidden passage?" she murmured. She didn't want to

speak too loudly. It felt inappropriate in a space where the only sound was the tapping of her heels.

"An optical challenge," he said. "The hedges have been allowed to grow taller here, reaching a certain length and particularly shadowing that back corner, creating the illusion of a wall. It's impossible to see the true passage unless you walk right through it."

Vee was both stunned and a little creeped out by the hidden passage Sotza was leading her down. If he wanted to kill her without witnesses, this would be the place to do it. Although, if Sotza really wanted to kill her, he could do it easily. And he wouldn't give two fucks who saw.

Sotza stopped, his hand tightened a little on her arm before falling away. She heard rustling as he touched the brush. Then she heard a soft scrape. "This," Sotza said, "is the true center of the maze."

He pushed open a door, flooding the passage around them with light. Vee slid past him, her mouth open in awe as she walked through the door. It was an area the size of a large room. Somehow, the hedges had been trimmed in such a way that the area was brightly lit, the sun shining in every corner. In the middle was a sundial. Ivy wrapped up the marble base, twining through the dial. The entire area was filled with pink, red and white roses. In one corner, surrounded by roses, was a bench.

Vee walked to the sundial. Looking down at it she traced her fingers across the roman numerals. Warmth from the sun shining on it touched her fingertips. She turned to look at Sotza, studying him.

"This is yours?" she asked.

He nodded, staring at her, a small smile playing around his lips. "Yes, I built this. It's where I come when I need an escape. No one knows about it, except the gardener who helped me design and install it. He still maintains it for me, though he's well past retirement age."

"It's... beautiful," she said softly.

She wandered to the bench and sat down. Again, the warmth that'd seeped into the wood was now caressing Vee. Sotza sat next to her, close enough that his knee brushed hers. But he didn't touch her beyond that. He leaned forward and rested his elbows on his knees, his hands clasped together in front of him.

"You're the first person I've brought here."

Her breath caught and she watched him, watched his profile, the beauty of the garden in her peripheral, the sensual perfume of the roses wrapping her in a cocoon. The moment held significance. She thought she understood. Sotza was a killer. Out of necessity he killed. But just because he was cold and efficient at his job didn't mean that he couldn't perceive beauty. That the monster, The Butcher, wasn't able to understand the personal cost of being an underworld boss. And he brought Vee to his private sanctuary. Was he trying to tell her that she gave him peace too? Or perhaps it was that she was the beauty that tamed his inner monster? It didn't matter. She was happy to be here with him in this place.

"My father was a cold man," Sotza said unexpectedly.

Vee smiled and lifted a brow, "I figured that you got it from somewhere. My best guess would've been your dad."

Sotza turned his head to look at her, his expression serious. "You think I'm a cold man?"

She considered him. "I think you can be cold, yes," she said softly. "But you have those moments where I know you're anything but cold."

The corner of his lip lifted in a smile and his dark eyes lingered over her curves, stopping on her bare knees where her legs were crossed. "I can assure you, Vee, when it comes to you, I am an inferno of heat."

Her face warmed. She was actually blushing, and from an almost poetic statement. He hadn't even said anything crude. But the erotic undertone to his words charged the atmosphere around them and she was unprepared for his next words. "I was nine the first time I killed someone."

Vee's heart lurched. She tried picturing him as a child. "What happened?" she asked.

"My father wanted me to learn the family business, to understand my duty. He forced me to participate in something..." His voice trailed off. Vee felt devastated for him. For the child forced to do something so awful. He looked over at her, pinning her with that dark gaze. "Don't pity the child, Vee. Even at that young age I was not innocent. I'd done things that would shock you. Murder was just the next step in an evolution."

"An unnatural one," she said. "You were only a child. And you'd been forced to live a life without choices. Even if you'd done terrible things, it wasn't your fault. What happened to your parents?"

He paused for a moment, then, "My father died of pancreatic cancer fifteen years ago. My mother lives in Bogotá, Columbia. She spends her days travelling, shopping and visiting friends. I'm sure you'll meet eventually, though she doesn't often make her way up here."

The explanation of his family was so normal it was unexpected. Vee had expected something more dramatic, like an enemy taking them out or something, Sotza becoming The Gentleman Butcher in bloody revenge. Despite the normal, something had shaped him, changed him to the man he'd become. "You should never have been forced into the family business. Your father was wrong to do that to you."

He studied her, his face impassive. "Are you defending me, Vee?" he asked.

She frowned and thought about it. "Yes, I suppose I am."

"Good," he said, satisfaction leaking into his tone. "This is the woman I saw when we were in Miami. This is the woman I want by my side. I want your loyalty. The loyalty you so easily give to others."

Vee jumped to her feet and would've moved away from him except he grabbed her wrist.

"The people who have my loyalty earned it," she snapped twisting her wrist.

"And I demand your loyalty," Sotza said standing. When he stood that close to her, he towered over her.

She tipped her head back and glared at him. "You tricked me into this garden... to prey on my sympathies!"

He held her locked against him. "I brought you here so you could experience my sanctuary."

"You played me," she accused.

"I spoke the truth, Elvira." He hunched his shoulders and lowered his head to press his face into the curve of her neck. His breath tickled just below her ear as he breathed her in. "You are my peace. You belong in this place with me."

"I belong where I choose..." Her voice came out more breathless than she intended as he kissed her behind the ear, right next to her hairline, his nose nuzzled against her.

"You belong to me," he said gruffly, his arms tightening. "Say it, tell me who you belong to."

"Isaac..." she said warningly.

"Yes," he agreed. "You belong to Isaac Sotza. Now say it again."

A smile quirked her lips and she tilted her head back, closing her eyes and soaking up the sun. She wouldn't win against his brand of persuasion and his touch was too heavenly to resist. "Why don't you make me..."

# CHAPTER THIRTY-EIGHT

It was pouring rain as they ran behind the garden hedges, ducking the security that Vee knew had passed less than thirty seconds before. It hadn't rained since her arrival in Venezuela, but it sure as hell was raining like some kind of vengeance water apocalypse now. Vee wasn't sure if it was a good thing because the rain would provide cover, or if they were likely to drown before she accomplished her mission. She also worried about the helicopter being able to land.

"I don't think I could possibly be any wetter," Raina complained from beside her, swiping at her glasses in an attempt to clear the water.

Vee agreed. They were both dressed in dark clothes, hats pulled low over pale faces. They weren't wearing any kind of rain gear. Vee's shoes sent up a shower of water from the grass with every footfall.

"We don't have a choice," Vee said to her daughter as she hustled them around the backside of the garden. She had intended to use the shadows cast by the bushes to hide from the moonlight, but the rain eliminated the need.

"I thought you said we were going to brazen this out,"

Raina yelled as loud as she dared so Vee would hear her over the pounding rain. "This feels a lot like covert sneakiness."

Vee ignored her daughter and reached out to grip her wrist dragging her across a dip in the lawn. Raina tripped and nearly landed face down in a puddle. Their timing was definitely bad. Especially if they went through all this and rescue wasn't able to land in the deluge. She just had to hope that they were coming no matter what.

The trek out to the small airfield took much longer than usual since they were on foot. Her getaway plan was going to go down in a fizzle if they both caught pneumonia and died. She gripped Raina harder as they sloshed across the soggy lawn under the cover of darkness. They stopped at certain points while Vee looked down at the timer on her phone counting down the seconds until she knew security had either passed or not arrived yet, then she would hustle her daughter to the next stopping point.

She had decided to leave the mansion directly after their evening meal. Sotza always closeted himself in his office after supper, attending to oversea markets as they opened. He rarely paid Vee any attention once he disappeared, leaving her alone for three to four hours until he was finished and ready to come to their bed. His predictable pattern was a benefit to Vee, though if she'd been a good wife she would have pointed it out, insisted he change his routine so he wouldn't be caught by surprise by an enemy. Instead, she was taking advantage. She shoved a sliver of guilt aside. She had no choice, she needed this to work. After spending two decades protecting her child she wouldn't just roll over and allow the mafia to have her.

As they approached the airstrip, Vee looked around, her sharp eyes attempting to see through the haze of rain. It was difficult to tell but she was pretty sure that there was no security beyond one man, who was currently hiding out inside the control booth. She gritted her teeth, hoping she was right about both her observations and instincts. She watched her phone intently. It was turned off to any signal, but the timer and clock still worked. She hoped Sotza wasn't tracking them by any other method, that her careful planning would be enough to enable an escape.

She stared down, hunching to protect the device from getting wet, counting down with the clock until it ran out. 19:10. Time to go.

"Now," she said to Raina.

Raina glanced back toward the estate, almost longingly, before she nodded decisively and followed her mother onto the tarmac. They didn't run, they didn't hide. They strode confidently toward the shack, two soaking wet blonds with matching attitudes that blazed bright despite the rain.

Vee flung the door to the control room open, surprising the man who huddled within. He leapt to his feet, gun in hand, facing the two women. He gaped for a moment before lowering his weapon.

"Señora Sotza," he said, surprise in his voice.

"Rodrigo," she acknowledged, nodding toward the instrument panel in front of him. "Someone will be landing here in two minutes. You need to give them clearance."

He eyed her sceptically. "Do they have permission to land?"

"I'm giving them permission, Rodrigo. They're my friends." She stared him down until his dark eyes darted away. "Tell me, what has my husband told you and the other men about my needs?"

"That any and all requests are to be met immediately," he said without hesitation.

"And I am requesting that my friends be allowed to land," she said sharply. "Without difficulty from you or anyone else on the Señor's security team."

He frowned as though contemplating her words. She glanced out the window and was gratified to see a shadow against the mountainous backdrop moving rapidly toward their positon, all but obscured by the rain. It didn't matter what conclusion he came to at this point, the helicopter was about to land. Apparently Rodrigo decided that he didn't entirely trust her. He began reaching toward the phone on the desk. "I think I'd better..."

Vee pulled her gun from the holster hidden beneath her dark jacket and pointed it at him. "I was a little worried you would think something like that," she said coldly. "Drop your weapon. Hands up and away from that phone, Rodrigo."

"Si, Señora," he said, his eyes darting around nervously. He carefully placed his gun on the desk and raised his hands slowly. They twitched a little as though he wanted to go for the phone anyway, despite her threat.

She sighed and tapped the gun against her thigh. "I think you better step over here so you won't be tempted to interfere. I don't want to have to kill you Rodrigo. Up now, please stand and walk toward us, slowly. Hands behind your head, fingers locked."

He did as he was told, perhaps correctly reading the deadly glint in Vee's eyes. Her gaze snapped rapidly from him to the incoming helicopter, still barely visible through the rain. He took two steps toward them, away from the panel, away from the phone. Vee shot him and barely paused to let him fall as she stepped over him and reached toward the phone. She lifted the receiver and pressed it against her ear and then glared down at Rodrigo.

"You need to shut up so they can hear me," she snapped impatiently over his shouts of pain.

"But you shot him!" Raina said loudly crouching at his side. "Why did you do that?"

Vee ignored her horrified daughter and called the cell

number her friend had provided. "We're here," she said, then listened for a moment. "Yes, both of us. You're safe to land."

She dropped the phone back into the cradle. Although most people used cell phones, land lines were better for security. Sotza was smart in his choice to keep parts of his organization old-fashioned. She dropped to her knees next to Rodrigo and pressed her gun against his side so he wouldn't do something stupid like grab her or Raina. She checked his injury and nodded to herself. "You'll be fine. I didn't hit either arteries or bone."

He glared at her and didn't respond.

"But why did you do it?" Raina asked angrily, her hand on his shoulder. "You promised no one would get hurt, yet you shot the first person we came across."

Vee frowned a little. Clearly Raina didn't understand. "He's not hurt."

"He has a gaping hole in him that you put there!" Raina snapped. "Obviously he's hurt."

Vee thought 'gaping' was a little melodramatic. She raised an eyebrow considering, trying to see things from her daughter's perspective. Was this what Sotza experienced when he tried to understand her objection to the way he cold-bloodedly tortured his victims? She tried to calm her annoyance and said, "He isn't dead, child. He'll survive. Trust me, it needed to be this way. If your dear step-daddy thought that Rodrigo had let us land a helicopter here he would do a lot worse to the man. I'm saving him from Sotza's wrath and making sure he doesn't get in our way. You know, killing two birds with one stone."

Rodrigo's complaints suddenly died away as he saw the truth of her words. He pressed his hands against his wound and watched her silently, new respect lighting his brown eyes. Raina frowned down at him unsure. Vee wanted to hold her daughter. She was caught between worlds. Between the brutality of mob life and the kind, loving family she'd grown up in. This was why Vee wanted her out. She wanted Raina to have the choices she didn't have.

"We need to tie him up," Vee said, her voice hardening. "So he can't come after us or call for help while we're boarding the helicopter."

Raina nodded hesitantly, clearly uncomfortable. She helped her mother tie Rodrigo with his hands behind his back. Vee was efficient in knot work and was able to tie him quickly and tightly.

"Let's go, they're waiting for us," she said pulling Raina to her feet.

After securing Rodrigo, they pushed the door to the shack open and ran back out into the rain. Vee gripped Raina's arm and made a beeline for the helicopter which was just finishing its landing. She didn't want it to have to wait. She wanted it to take off immediately. She rushed toward it, grateful when she saw the side door open and a person crouch in the doorway, beckoning them.

When they were within feet of the chopper a female voice shouted, "Raina!" Vee grinned as Diane Duncan hurled herself out of the door, into the rain and on top of her daughter. "Oh god, Raina, I was so worried!"

The older woman sobbed as she gripped her adopted daughter.

"Mom?" Raina asked, completely shocked and mystified at how her sweet old mom was standing on the tarmac of a notorious mob boss. "What are you doing here?"

Diane looked up, her eyes meeting Vee's. "Elvira," she said softly, reaching out to pull Vee in for a strong hug. Vee wrapped her arms around the other woman, hugging her back, tears forming in her eyes.

"I'm so sorry, Diane," she said, her voice catching with

emotion. "I thought I did a good enough job of protecting her…"

"Don't blame yourself," Joe's gruff voice reached them through the rain as he stepped from the helicopter, enveloping Raina in a tight hug, holding her close to his chest. "We always knew there was a possibility she could get pulled in, one way or the other. You did everything you could to make sure she lived happily."

Vee nodded, unable to speak, tears mingling with the rain. She reached out blindly, gripping Raina, who was sobbing in the arms of her dad. Vee needed the connection. Needed to experience the wonder of touching the child she created, the child she'd given up to these people who loved her just as much as Vee ever could.

"You… you know each other?" Raina asked pulling away from her dad and swiping at the tears leaking from beneath her glasses with the back of her arm. It was a useless gesture as she was immediately soaked.

"Yes," Diane said, beckoning them toward the helicopter. "We've known Elvira almost since she was a child. In fact, we consider her as much a daughter as you are."

"Diane…" Vee said softly, climbing in behind the others, into the dry warmth of the helicopter. She glanced worriedly behind her and turned to Raina gripping her arms. "We helped each other when we were at our most desperate. Diane and Joe wanted out of the mob life and I needed to hide a baby. They were low level enough that they could disappear with a little help."

"She gave us everything she had," Diane said fondly. "Enough money to start over in a part of the country that no one would think to look for us."

"I had access to records, things that might make them traceable. So I was able to destroy anything that would make them a target. No one thought I was smart enough to understand or care about such things." She looked out the window squinting into the darkness again. "But your parents can explain all that, you need to go."

"What?" Raina asked, her voice high-pitched. "No, you need to tell me more! I don't understand."

Vee shook her head and tried to step out the door. Raina tackled her in a surprisingly tight hug. "No!" she yelled, her arms tight around Vee's neck. She could feel the girl's hot tears against her skin. Her own forlorn tears made paths down her cheeks. "You're my parent too, I can't let you go, not after I've just found you."

Vee allowed the hug for as long as she could, a few precious seconds, and then she pushed her daughter away. She took Raina's face in her hands, memorizing it, the features that matched hers so exactly but also had a life of their own. "He will never stop looking for me, Raina," she explained, hardening her words so she could push them past the lump in her throat. "I need you to go so I can breathe easy again. I need to know that you're free. And I need to be with my husband. One day our needs will meet and so will we. Until then, go, and be happy... for me."

"But mom..." Raina sobbed unabashedly. Diane reached out and held Raina's shoulders.

"I love you, Raina."

# CHAPTER THIRTY-NINE

Almost as soon as the helicopter took off Vee was surrounded by Sotza's men. Mateo strode toward her, his anger almost a living thing. He took her gun and threw it at one of his men. He snatched her neck and dragged her toward him, nearly lifting her off her feet. Rain streaked his face, dripping off his clenched jaw.

"Where is she?" he snarled.

She stared at him, willing her heart to slow. She wasn't in danger. Mateo wouldn't hurt her. Not only because she was the wife to his boss, but because she was the mother of his love. She knew he cared deeply about her daughter. It didn't matter though. Mateo was mafia and Raina was not.

Instead of answering his question, she said softly, for his ears only, "You need to let me go, Mateo. Before Sotza sees. We both know he won't react well to anyone else touching me. I don't want to be responsible for what happens to you."

He surprised her by tightening his fingers just a fraction, threateningly. Then he shoved her away. "If you don't wanna tell me where she went then you'll tell him. I guarantee it."

He ordered two of his men to take her up to the house

while he turned and strode to the control shack. She hoped Rodrigo would be ok. Not from the shot she gave him, he would definitely survive that tiny nick. No, she worried he wouldn't survive Mateo if the man decided to take his frustrations out on the guard who had failed in his job.

Vee walked through the rain, setting the pace between the two men. She wanted out of the rain, but she certainly wasn't going to rush toward her own reckoning. They took a car this time, which she was grateful for. She didn't particulalry want to walk back through the deluge.

She had no idea what she would find when she entered Sotza's office. She remembered the last time she'd angered him, the way he attacked her after, asserted his dominance. Since their time in his flower garden he'd been treating her with more respect, giving her the tools she needed to stand at his side without fear. Now, she worried that this action, helping Raina escape, would set their relationship back.

The front door opened and she stepped through into the estate foyer. Heat rushed at her and she basked in the warmth as it penetrated the dripping layers she wore. Adriana, the evening maid, rushed toward her with a towel clutched in her hands. She wrapped it around Vee's shoulders and walked swiftly toward the stairs, her arm firmly around the Señora. Vee raised a brow at Adriana's almost affectionate behaviour. While Vee had been polite to the staff, she hadn't taken any pains to get to know them. She was first and foremost a businesswoman. She didn't really care about cooking or cleaning and left house tasks to the housekeeper and her staff.

"Where are you taking her?" One of Vee's guards asked sharply. "She is to go immediately to the Señor."

Adriana sent the man a bold stare over her shoulder and snapped, "And how will the Señor react if she falls ill from remaining in these wet clothes?"

When he hesitated, she wrapped her arm around Vee's and pulled her up the stairs. Vee was grateful for the intervention. They didn't talk as they walked side by side to the master bedroom. Adriana hustled Vee inside and closed the door behind them.

"I thought you could use a few minutes to gather yourself," she explained walking toward Vee's closet and opening the double doors. Her muffled voce reached out to Vee. "You better hurry and get those clothes off. The Señor won't wait long. Especially not for you. You seem to make him very impatient."

She emerged from the closet with a slinky dark blue silk night dress. It dipped deep in the front between her breasts, flowed to the floor with slits up both sides showing a healthy amount of leg every time she moved. The nightdress was blatantly sexual. She pursed her lips and raised an eyebrow.

"That one seems... inappropriate for an interview with my husband, who will most likely be quite angry with me." Still, she began removing her wet clothes, peeling them off with gratitude. Her skin was chilled through and pimpled in goosebumps.

Adriana grinned. "Si, a little inappropriate for wandering through the house but feminine and irresistible. The Señor already has difficulty resisting his new esposa. In this dress, he will not remain angry for long."

Vee raised an eyebrow, hesitated for a fraction of a second and then reached for the sapphire nightdress. At least she wouldn't have to wear a bra with it. There wasn't much worse than putting a bra on over diamond hard nipples and damp skin. She pulled it over her head and stood still as Adriana took over, tugging it down Vee's lithe frame.

"Why are you helping me?" she asked pointedly once the material was in place.

"You are the Señora," she said simply. "We must take care

of you, no?"

Vee laughed in disbelief. "Sure, now why are you really helping me?"

Adriana rolled her eyes toward the door and then grinned secretively. "The Señor, he has never married before, right? We have not had a mistress around the estate until now. You are special."

Vee snorted. "I'm not much of a mistress. I've barely talked to most of the staff and to be honest I only know your name because you're the only night maid around here. I was told to ask you if I needed anything before bed."

Adriana went back to the closet and emerged seconds later with a pair of sandaled high heels, cream satin, that would strap in place around her ankles. This was definitely going to be overkill, but she allowed it. Perhaps the girl knew what she was talking about. If it saved Vee a beating she would even wear the ass half of a horse costume.

Adriana bent in front of Vee and helped her put the shoes on. Finally, she answered. "The Señor... he was lonely for many years. With the demands of his work, he has become harsh and brutal. Though not cruel to us by any means he was a cold master. He rarely spoke and when he did it was to demand this or that. For all these years he has not changed, just gotten gruffer." She stood and faced Vee, her eyes serious. "Then you existed. A Señora, yes, but not just any Señora. One that is rumoured to be powerful. And when you arrived it became clear that you had power over the Señor. If you need something, he demands it immediately. If you are hurt, he is hurt too. If you are happy... then so is he."

Vee was beginning to see Adriana's point.

"He is in love with you. And his love has changed things around here for the better." She sighed happily, stars in her young eyes. "If keeping you happy means we keep this newer master, then we will do what we must."

Vee smiled back. "Well, whatever the reason. I appreciate your help. I'm much more comfortable in these clothes, though maybe a little cold with the lack of fabric."

Adriana giggled and ran to grab the matching peignoir. Vee pulled it on gratefully. It wasn't a cable knit sweater, but it would do. And she knew what she must look like. Walking sex. While she no longer believed in trading sex for favours, she wasn't at all opposed to playing up her sexuality if it meant Sotza might go a little easier on her.

The pit of her stomach churned as Adriana ran a brush through her damp locks and handed Vee some lip gloss. Was he going to be furious? She didn't know how he could not be. She had done something he had expressly forbidden. He'd wanted Raina here, in his territory, where he could control and protect her. He'd been unwilling to negotiate with Vee on the matter.

Well, she was unwilling to negotiate on it either. She wanted Raina as far from the mob as the child could get. Vee wanted her to grow up, escape her roots, discover a world that women could inhabit without fear. Raina was headstrong, stubborn and determined. She would make her new life a success.

"Time to go," Adriana whispered, her eyes wide in trepidation. "I do not think the Señor will wait much longer. Best to go to him on his terms than have him come looking for you."

Vee thought Adriana was being a little dramatic. Though she did remember their last violent confrontation in the bedroom, after Vee had been shot. Though explosive and passionate, she would rather not be handled so roughly. Which meant, for the coming battle, she needed to keep her temper in check. Act contrite. Don't piss off The Butcher.

"Yes," Vee said decisively, striding toward the door with confidence. "Time to see my husband."

## CHAPTER FORTY

Sotza sat behind his desk, appearing to be completely at ease when she knocked briefly and let herself in. He was reading something on his laptop, leaning slightly forward, one arm resting on the desk. He'd discarded his jacket and vest and opened the collar of his shirt showing his strong masculine throat. A few hairs curled toward the top of his shirt. His serious, rugged face was expressionless except for a deeper than usual groove between his brows. As though he was slightly disturbed by whatever he was reading.

She knew better. He was pissed off at her. Trying to decide how to play this situation. Would he attack her, like he did the last time she fucked up? Or would he treat her with the cold indifference he treated the rest of the world? Or maybe he would come up with some new way to throw her off balance.

Well, two could play that game. Vee was not a woman used to being ignored. Nor was she used to waiting on someone's leisure. She liked to control her environment and the situations she found herself in. Which meant she wasn't going to wait for Mr. Sotza to finally give her the time of day.

She strode purposefully toward his wet bar. A small, sturdy cabinet with a neat top that held high ball and small sherry glasses. She picked up one of the tumblers and crouched in front of the cabinet. She scanned the labels. Most were Spanish, but a few were imported. All very top shelf, which meant she shouldn't have a problem drinking it straight up. She chose the brandy bottle, pulling it toward her. She stood gracefully and poured a healthy measure, her gaze greedily devouring the liquor as it hit the glass.

Her heart pounded as she made the decision to break her abstinence. Her nerves were completely shot, between having to say a heartbreaking good-bye to her daughter and then face her husband, not knowing how he would react to her disobedience. If ever there was a time for a drink, this was it. And Vee knew her strength, knew that one drink wouldn't break her. She was stronger than her addiction.

She capped the bottle and set it on top of the bar. She picked up the glass and turned. As she expected, Sotza's eyes were on her. All over her to be completely accurate. He looked at her the way she was looking at the brandy, taking in her skimpy outfit. His eyes glowed with feral heat, though his face gave nothing of his thoughts or intentions.

"You disobeyed me, Vee," his deep voice rumbled.

She lifted her chin and moved to the seat in front of his desk, sliding into it and crossing her legs. The slit in her dress revealed her leg to the top of her thigh. His eyes lingered on her skin, but his gaze was cold when it lifted to hers.

"You have an explanation, I trust?"

Vee wanted to snort but swallowed the impulse. *Be good, Vee*, she silently begged herself, *don't prod the man and maybe you'll get through this*. "I get to make the decisions in my daughter's life and I decided that she needed to go. I made arrangements."

"Indeed," he agreed, ice dripping from his tone. "However, you are aware, that I had other wishes for the child's welfare. You went against a direct order when you spirited her into the night."

"She is not your child," Vee said, struggling to keep the anger from her voice. "She's mine and I alone make the decisions regarding her welfare. You are the man who abducted her."

A chill passed over her and she knew she was dangerously pushing the line. He would already be angry with her, she shouldn't be arguing. But this was about her daughter, it was one of the most important discussions she could have. She needed to argue until she won.

"You belong to me, Elvira," he said, his voice dangerously quiet, his stern eyes never leaving her. "You are mine to love and to hold, to keep until one or both of us dies. What belongs to you, belongs to me as well. To maintain and to cherish, the same as I would do for you."

A sharp pain struck her chest as she absorbed his words. He loved her. And her heart was telling her that she loved him too, completely. This man was willing to love her grown-up daughter simply because she was a part of Vee. Women the world over searched for such a man to have in their lives. But Sotza was still mafia, and he always would be. Which meant that Vee would always be mafia too. Neither of them were good enough to be in Raina's life. She couldn't allow him to keep Raina in their organization, even if he believed he was protecting her.

"You can't have her," she said defiantly, standing and stepping right up to his desk. She dropped her untouched glass on the desk and spread her hands wide as she emphasized her words. "The further from your reach she goes, the safer she'll be."

His gaze wandered down her chest, dipping to her cleavage, now even more exposed as she leaned on his desk. She resisted the urge to cross her arms. He looked down at her hands, contemplating his next words.

"I knew the moment you left the mansion this evening," he finally said. "I could have stopped you at any time. Could have kept Raina here."

She suspected as much. His security had small holes in it, holes that she happily took advantage of, holes that she would be fixing when or if they got over this intense clashing of wills. But despite the small deficiencies in his security, Sotza was by no means stupid. During the entire escape she'd had the niggling thought that her powerful husband knew what she was up to and either laid a trap or... now confirmed, had sanctioned the action.

"Why didn't you have us picked up then?" She hoped it was because he finally saw things her way. Or maybe decided that he loved her enough to let her have her way.

"I wanted to know if you would go with her," he admitted, looking directly at her as he questioned her loyalty. "Wanted to see if you would get on the helicopter."

Anger surged through her, heating her pale skin. She took in a sharp breath and let it out in a huff. "And what exactly would you have done if I'd gotten on that helicopter?"

He didn't hesitate. "I would have stopped you and killed them, then brought you home and chained you to my side for the rest of your life."

"Raina?" she gasped, a wave of dizziness hitting her as she lost the ability to breathe. Would he truly kill her only child?

"Not her," he relented. "Through you she is now part of me. No harm with ever fall on the girl from my quarter."

Vee's hand shook as she picked up her glass, gazing at the amber liquid. If ever she needed a drink it was right fucking now. She lifted it to her lips.

"Stop," he commanded her, standing from behind his desk and glaring at her. "Do not drink it, Vee."

She glared right back and slammed the liquor to the back of her throat. Though the brandy was top shelf and mostly smooth going down she had to fight the need to cough, it'd been so long since her last drink. She thudded the glass on his desk and wiped her mouth with the back of her hand.

"Fuck you," she said, her voice huskier than usual from the drink.

He struck out at her, fast like lightening. She flinched and tried to step back, expecting his fist to collide with the side of her face. He didn't hit her though, he wrapped his hand around the back of her neck, tangling his long fingers in her hair and forcing her forward until she was half on his desk.

"You want to fuck, Vee?" he said in a guttural voice, eyes blazing with the emotion. "Is that what you're saying to me right now?"

The savage look on his face, coupled with the way he'd been playing her body all week, called to her. Sent her libido soaring. She wanted to accept his challenge.

"Yes." The words rushed out of her in an angry hiss. "That's what I want."

Pure lust sizzled between them as they stared each other down. She didn't know who made the next move. If she crawled onto the desk or if he pulled her over top, but suddenly she was in his arms and he was kissing her with a passion that hurt, singeing her lips with the heat that constantly flowed between them until a single spark ignited the inferno. His arms banded around her, locking her against him until she was opening her mouth to gasp for the breath he was squeezing out of her only to be denied by his invading tongue. She could do nothing but hold on and take his onslaught of passion, sinking her nails into whatever she could reach.

She thought she would pass out from lack of oxygen, black dots swarming her vision, when he finally tore his lips from hers. He shoved her back on the desk, his hand cradling her head so it wouldn't thump against the wood. Still, she cried out as something dug into her back. He lifted her just enough to sweep a broad hand beneath her, shoving everything to the side. She reached for him as his head was descending to take a nipple into his mouth. He soaked the silk fabric of her gown as he nipped at her and then sucked it into his devouring mouth. He squeezed her other breast at the same time, taking her to the edge of pain before backing off. She yelped in protest, but she was squirming under his handling of her body, need crashing through her veins like a tidal wave.

She thought she might come from the stimulation to her breasts alone, he backed off, flipped her over and laid her face-down across his desk. She heard the skirt of her dress tear as he yanked it up her legs and settled it on her hips. She knew what he was seeing, her lace thong, soaked through with her own juices.

She tried to twist around to look at him, but his hand landed on her back, shoving her forward. Then his other hand landed on her bare ass cheek, hard. Pain shot through her bottom and she yelped, attempting to claw her way back over the desk. He held her firm and continued spanking her, alternating cheeks until she was hot and panting... aroused.

He leaned over her back, his lips next to her ear. She felt his fingers against her ass as he unbuckled his belt and unzipped his pants. "You were a bad girl today, Vee. What do bad girls get?"

She gritted her teeth and pushed herself back against his cock as he was freeing, helpless against the need flooding through her. "Bad women get fucked!" she said, tensing against the next onslaught.

Sure enough, his hand fell firmly against her ass again,

meting out the discipline he thought she deserved. "Bad girls get spanked," he growled.

Vee had reached the point that she didn't care. She wanted his hand striking her ass, she wanted his hands all over her body any way she could get them. If this agonizing, glorious feeling was the result, she would start purposely trying to earn these spankings. She would smuggle every damn person she could get her hands on off his estate.

Finally, the spanking stopped, leaving her ass hot and swollen, her pussy wet and needy. She didn't have long to wait for relief though. He yanked the crotch of her thong to the side and sank his delicious cock deep. She yelled her pleasure for everyone to hear as he filled her aching pussy.

He slammed into her, rocking her hips against the desk. She brought her hands down to her sides and bent her elbows, lifting a little, trying to relieve the pressure. He took her hair in a fist and yanked her head back and to the side just enough that she could see his face hovering over her back. See his chest as he moved over her, slamming again and again, burying himself balls deep in each punishing thrust.

"What do bad girls get, Vee?" he asked, his accent strong, his voice guttural.

She let out a breathless laugh and said, "Bad women get the kingdom!"

He slammed into her so hard she would have been pushed forward across the desk if he wasn't holding her hair, pulling it back toward him, forcing her to arch her chest, thrusting out her breasts.

"Bad girls get punished," he snarled and continued to slam into her. His thrusts increased in tempo until she thought she really might break from his rough handling. Her pussy told her otherwise. It clenched him tight, pulling him deep, welcoming him. The orgasm ripped through her before she was ready. The crushing impact of her clit against the desk, coupled with the incredible way he was hammering into it sent her careening into the path of a beautiful orgasm. As she hurtled over her own peak he reached his, grunting his pleasure as he fucked into her, bathing her in his come. He pushed his elbow into the middle of her back while pulling her hair back toward him. He twisted her head until he could reach her lips, claiming them in a surprisingly soft kiss.

He released her almost as soon as he finished, laying her across the desk and pulling out of her. She heard the zip of his pants as he tucked himself back inside. She rolled to her side, gathering the tattered remnants of her nightgown around her bare legs and gazed up at him. Sotza, her husband. He was cold when he wanted to be, but hotly passionate around her, especially when she challenged his authority. He was brutal in his regime, but kind to her. Despite the provocation, despite the punishing sex, he hadn't harmed a hair on her head, even when he was using it to yank her back toward him. He was incredible, and he belonged to her.

Instead of letting her bask in the post-orgasm glory he leaned over her, took her jaw in hand and forced her to look at him. "I let you get away with one drink, don't do it again."

"But you drink," she pointed out, her voice husky from screaming.

"You don't," he said, his voice hard. "I'll do what it takes to preserve who you are, Vee. Even if it means protecting you against yourself."

"People change," she whispered.

"Are you going to argue with me about this?" he asked with a raised eyebrow.

She bit her lip and stared at him for a few seconds thinking about pushing it. Then she grinned. "Depends, are you going to fuck me on your desk again if I do?"

He growled and reached for her, proving that he would indeed fuck her on his desk again, taking her on another, more leisurely, but no less satisfying, orgasmic trip. After, he gathered the shreds of her gown around her and pulled her into his arms, tucking the fabric so that she wasn't showing anything indecent to the staff. He carried her through the house to their bedroom where he undressed her and tucked her naked into bed.

She propped an arm up, hand under her ear as she watched him undress, devouring his long, lean frame, roped in heavy muscles. Despite the multiple orgasms he'd just treated her to, her body heated once more, melting for her husband.

"Are you going to fuck me again, esposo?" she asked mischievously as he bent over and she got a nice view of his perfectly formed ass.

He straightened and gave her a stern look. "Mercy, Señora, this old man needs some rest first. If you keep this up I will think you are better at torture than me."

She snorted. Then, completely by-passing his comment about torture, as she still wasn't ready to go there yet, said, "If this is you as an old man then I'd hate to have experienced sex with the younger version."

He crawled into the bed beside her and turned her over, pulling her against him so her ass was nestled against the cradle of his thighs. She settled down with a sigh.

"Only you can do this to me, Vee. I was never this way with other women."

She reached back to smack him on the hip. "Now I get why you want me around. Sex on tap."

He laughed and kissed her shoulder. "Peace, Vee. You are too perfect for me to think that about you."

They fell silent for a few minutes. Vee's thoughts turned to Raina and she desperately hoped she was safe. She'd decided that no communication was best, so no one could trace the girl. But now, Vee thought she might contact Diane in a few days. Just to make sure they landed safely and Raina was able to continue on her journey unmolested.

As if reading the direction of her thoughts, Sotza said quietly, "Mateo wants her, you know. He even asked if he could keep her. Weeks ago, before I brought you here. He's going to be angry that she's disappeared." Vee glanced back at him over her shoulder, her expression pleading. He sighed, his lips tilting a little at the corner. "I suppose we can give her a head start. Slow him down. Perhaps I'll give him the task of hunting and disposing of Garza. Dismantling the Garza empire should keep him busy for a while."

"Thank you," she said hoping he heard the wealth of sincerity in her tone.

"He will find her eventually."

She smiled. "I know. He reminds me a little of you. That dogged determination to get what he wants. But I want Raina to experience life and all it has to offer before she gets pulled back into this."

"I understand, cariño, you want her to have the things you missed out on."

"Maybe," she said softly. "I don't feel like I'm missing anything anymore though."

He ran his fingers lightly over the scar on her back, low down toward her waist. "You are a brave woman. Generous too."

Vee shrugged her shoulder and continued to lay on her side, her face turned away from him. She enjoyed the way his fingers tickled down her back, it made her want to curl against him and purr. This kind of intimacy was new to her but definitely addicting.

"Giving my daughter life the first time was a difficult decision to make," she said, her voice quiet. "Giving her life the second time was as easy as breathing. I didn't have a choice.

She would've died otherwise and I didn't want to live in a world without her."

He kissed between her shoulder blades and then rolled her over. Vee brought her hands up to cover her naked chest. He let her though he placed a hand possessively over the slight rise of her stomach.

"These are the things I want from you, my wife. The same devotion and loyalty you show a child that doesn't know enough to be grateful of the sacrifices you've made."

"You have it, Isaac," she said without hesitation. "My loyalty, my life, everything. By letting my daughter go you've proved that I can be loyal to you without losing the things I want most."

"Te amo, Elvira," he whispered against the back of her neck.

She smiled. "I love you too, Issac. But you really need to never call me Elvira again. I know exactly where to shoot a person to give them maximum pain without much damage."

He chuckled and leaned down to press his lips against hers, giving her one of his kisses that she knew she would crave forever.

## EPILOGUE

### Two years later

"Anny Pee!"

Vee looked up, startled as Sally hurtled toward her, chubby legs pumping faster than Vee thought a toddler should go. She reached out and scooped the baby up, settling her on her lap. She gave Sally a stern look and said, "I'm sorry, but did you just call me Aunty Pee? As in urine? Do you have any idea who you're talking to, child? I could have you executed for such disrespect."

Sally just giggled and grabbed at Vee's long straight hair, burying her fingers in the fine strands. "That's it, off with her head!" Vee yelped, laughing as she was forced to twist her head to ease the pressure on her scalp.

"I'm sorry, Vee!" Casey cried. She'd been following close behind her daughter and helped Vee extricate the tiny, but torturously effective hands. Vee sighed in relief as Sally was lifted from her lap and set free to terrorize the garden.

"Seriously though, did she just call me Pee? What are you teaching this child?"

Casey laughed and settled on the bench next to Vee, her

sharp eyes following the trail of flower destruction as Sally did her best to tear up every one she could get her hands on. "She's having a little difficulty with names, so she tends to rename people after her favourite things."

Vee wrinkled her nose. "And she likes pee? That's weird Casey. You know that's weird, right?"

"She likes to go pee because she gets treats for going on the potty. She probably sees you as being just as awesome as those treats."

"Nice save," Vee said sarcastically. Then she pointed out, "You're training your daughter like a dog, you know."

Casey shrugged. "Whatever works."

Vee felt a small pang. She'd missed these years with Raina. The good, the bad, the fun and funny. She watched over Raina from a distance, but she didn't get to experience these moments. Maybe one day she would become a grandmother and get the chance to live the memories she missed with her own daughter.

"She calls Sotza, Uncle Toaster, only it sounds more like Untle Toata."

Vee burst out laughing as she imagined the tiny human naming her stern, unyielding husband after a toaster. "It really is a miracle she's survived this long."

"Reyes would destroy the world if anything happens to her," Casey pointed out. They both sobered as they imagined the far-reaching damage Reyes could cause if any harm came to the women in his life.

Vee understood. Sotza was exactly the same. In the two years that they'd been married he had become more over-bearing in his desire to keep Vee from harm. She would have balked except he also treated her with respect. He kept her apprised of all the business he conducted, and after she'd learned the ropes, brought her on as an equal partner. It hadn't been an easy transition moving from drugs to arms dealing, but she was a fast learner. It helped that Sotza was a patient and loving instructor. He listened to her opinions and, after he deemed her ready, allowed her to take on several negotiations. They found that the men they worked with often preferred her softer touch to his harsh, uncompromising way of doing business. The organization had benefitted twofold by her presence.

Married life suited them both. They rarely left Venezuela, spending most of their time either on the estate or the island. They preferred their home turf. When they did have to travel for business they always went together. They'd become inseparable. They worked side-by-side and lived as a unit. This marriage was nothing like any of her previous relationships. Sotza had even accompanied her on a shopping trip to Caracas, insisting they go together or not at all. She thought he would be bored out of his mind. Of course, he wasn't. Somehow the man found pleasure in anything and everything that had to do with his wife. He gave her that small tilt of the lips as she tried on clothes and showed them to him. He offered his opinion, which of course matched hers, when she was looking at purses and shoes. He had been the perfect shopping companion.

After their trip into the capital Vee had approached him about the ridiculous high prices for food and basic necessities. Money had no meaning to them, it was endless. But it had meaning to the people of Venezuela, many of whom were starving. From talking with the staff, she knew that most of them saved every penny of their paychecks and sent the money home to their families. Sotza already had a bead on local politicians, engaging them in talks about funding for social programs. But at Vee's insistence they started a charity that would make sure more people in more regions were fed.

And if that didn't work, they would use other parts of their organization to make sure people had the necessary paperwork to immigrate to neighboring countries if that was their wish.

Not every part of married life was perfect. Vee missed Raina terribly, but refused to have any contact in case it could be used to trace her. It was like having her heart stabbed for a second time, having to give her up at birth and then again just when they were developing a relationship. Raina's absence caused tension between Vee and Mateo. He refused to forgive her for helping his woman escape. And she refused to regret that decision. Not for a single second. Every time her heart ached she would imagine what Raina was doing, what kind of experiences she was having. Knowing that Raina was free to make her own choices and that she had a good head on her was enough for Vee.

Her absent gaze fell on Sally who was crawling after a caterpillar. "Have you ever thought about having another one?" she asked Casey.

Casey seemed to think about it for a few seconds and then said, "Yes. I want one, and so does Reyes. But he's terrified that I could have a stroke or something since I'm higher risk for those things. I think we probably will one day, but for now, we're happy indulging our baby Llama."

"Llama!" Vee burst out laughing.

Casey laughed too. "I wanted her pet name to be something native to Bolivia and there are llamas everywhere. We even have a herd that lives wild in our area." Casey watched Vee for a moment and then said softly. "Have you thought of having another? It's not too late, plenty of women have babies in their forties."

"No," she said quietly. "I'll never have another child. I won't bring another life into the mafia."

"I understand," Casey said, reaching out to grab Sally as she was about to squish the caterpillar. "It's a bit hypocritical isn't it? How we'll take advantage of all the riches the mafia has to offer but despise the parts we don't find appetizing."

Vee thought about it. About her beautiful garden, even nicer house filled with all the staff she could ever want. Her private jet, her private island. The clothes, the jewels, everything. Was it worth it?

"We're the women of the mafia, Casey, we were born to this. We didn't have a choice. We may as well take advantage of the privileges, they help us get through the awful parts." She looked down at Casey's scarred hand, which was splayed across Sally's back, holding her in place. The raised 'H' would be with her forever, a reminder of her dead husband's cruelty. "We are the children of mobsters. You were born to the mob, I was born to it. Gina and her unborn child are mafia." She named Casey's cousin, currently in Bolivia with her husband, Alejandro. He wouldn't allow his young wife to travel while pregnant or she would have been right there on the bench with them. Vee continued, "Sally was born to it and so was Raina. She'll have to come home eventually, to face her roots. I've made my peace with that."

"That sounds so bleak," Casey said, her voice catching a little. "True, but bleak." She stared at her daughter, allowing the horror of Vee's words to sink in. Sally would always be mafia, she would never be free.

"Maybe," Vee agreed, turning to look fully at her best friend. She reached out to trace a finger over the brand on Casey's neck, the tiny feminine crown. A matching masculine one adorned Reyes' throat. "But we're the Queens. Bad or good, right or wrong, we rule our Kings and everything around them."

"Amen," Casey breathed.

Deciding it was best to lighten the mood, they changed topics and played with Sally a little longer in the garden. The weather was warmer than usual, heating the paving stones, so the women sat on the ground, Sally tottering around them giggling, carefree in her childish innocence.

"Vee," Sotza's voice reached out to her and she turned to look as he strode toward them, Reyes at his side. The two men together were utterly breathtaking. Handsome, hard and dominant. Sotza was taller and more regal than Reyes, but Reyes was broader, more muscular. Both men exuded that casual confidence that came with their positions in the world. The top of their respective regimes.

"You know... it was my husband that decided to send Sotza to Miami, to go after you," Casey murmured.

"And who suggested he might be a good fit for my particular situation?" Vee replied, turning back to eye her friend.

Casey grinned unabashedly. "It worked out, right? You seem happy to me."

"That is a pretty deadly game of match-making you played there, Señora Reyes. You couldn't have known he would fall in love with me."

"I never had a single doubt," Casey whispered as the men approached.

Although Reyes and Casey had come to Venezuela for a visit, they were there first and foremost for business. The four of them were in the process of creating a strong alliance that would consolidate power throughout South America. Both Vee and Casey joined in most of the negotiations. The major debate among the group, once the alliance was set in stone, was what to do about Mexico, now that Nicolas Garza was dead. Hunted down and taken out by Mateo, under Sotza's orders. Without Domingo or Garza heading operations, Mexico was becoming even more desperately violent as men fought to take over the shreds of the Garza cartel.

The next order of business was Miami. The hub for all underworld traffic on the East coast of the United States was in chaos. The region needed strong leadership and they needed to find someone they trusted for the job.

Vee stood, brushing her skirt off. She cringed inside, side-eyeing the serious damage Sally had done to Sotza's precious garden. She was definitely going to hear about it later. How she'd allowed a toddler to storm the shrubbery without once lifting a finger to stop the destruction. She opened her mouth to speak, to pardon the small creature, when Sotza took her arm in a tight grip.

"Isaac —" she started to say, but he interrupted her, directing his words toward Casey. Reyes had stopped beside his wife and crouched down to retrieve his daughter, holding her delighted squirming body against his chest.

"Please excuse us, Señora Reyes, I must speak to my wife. It is urgent."

"Of course," Casey said, her voice holding some confusion and worry.

Sotza nodded toward Reyes and turned on his heel, striding toward the house. He by-passed the cobbled paths and walked straight across the grass, something she'd never seen him do. Even when he was in a hurry to go down to his prison and interrogate someone. He always respected his immaculate lawns and gardens.

"Isaac!" Vee gasped, trying to keep up with his long strides and failing. "My shoes!"

Her steel-spiked heels were sinking into the grass with each step. When she tried to walk on the ball of her foot instead of the heel she started to pitch forward as he dragged her. He glanced back at her, seeing her struggle and stopped. She was about to bend over and remove the shoes, leaving her to walk barefoot through the grass when he scooped her up into his arms and continued walking, his pace even faster now.

"What's going on? Is it something to do with Reyes?" she asked worriedly. The two men got along well enough, but there was still some tension. They were both leaders, both loners. It was always a possibility that they could clash. But the past few days seemed to dispel some of that tension. They were far from friends, but for their wives sakes, they had become friendly. Vee didn't know what she would do if they went to war.

Sotza stopped walking. He looked down at her. His expression was grim. Her heart thumped hard in her chest and she knew without words that something terrible had happened.

"Raina?" she asked, a chill crawling across her, leaving goosebumps in its wake.

He nodded.

Vee let out a desperate sound. She couldn't help it. Raina was her only vulnerability. The one thing that could destroy her. She clutched Sotza tight, burying her head against his chest and gasping hard to swallow the tears. "J-just tell me."

"She's alive," he said, his voice quiet. "But she's been shot. Mateo is with her."

Vee struggled to bring herself under control. Sotza kneeled with her, holding her cradled against him until she managed to leash her emotions. She leaned back in his arms. Eyes glittering like blue diamonds. "Do you remember when you told me if you loved me I should ask for the world and see what happened?"

"Si, mi amor, I forget nothing we have said to each other."

"I want it," she said, her voice husky. "I want my daughter to come home and I want the people responsible. I want the world to burn until I get those things."

He watched her, dark eyes glowing with love and vengeance. "Consider it done."

**THE END**

# THANK YOU FOR READING!

If you enjoyed Queen's Move, or any of my other novels, please consider leaving a review. Reviews are like food, they help authors survive. Thank you to all of my fabulous reviewers!

**Review pages:**

AMAZON

GOODREADS

BOOKBUB

## ACKNOWLEDGMENTS

Thank you so much dear readers for taking the time to read Queen's Move. Scarred Queen was a tough act to follow, but I absolutely loved writing this book. Vee was the same age as me when I started writing and I really enjoyed stepping into her character. The subject of adoption is close to my heart as my son is adopted. Many of the scenes between Vee and her daughter were emotional to write. I can't wait to explore Raina's character further in her book, Born a Queen.

I want to say a special thank you to my mom. She's been a rock in my life when I most needed one. She never judges and she supports me in everything. She checks on me, we talk, we laugh. She reads my books and loves them. She is an empowering person and I love her for it.

Thank you to Jen for being the woman that talks me on and off ledges. For teaching me that kidnapping isn't a crime unless you get caught. This is the woman you need if ever you find yourself in a bar fight, she has a girl's back no matter what (side note: she probably caused the fight).

Thank you to everyone in my circle that helps me create the magic: my wonderful editor, my cover artist, my author friends (special thank you to DD Prince for taking on the majority of my crazy), Sansa, Kimberly, Barbie, Kristi, and many more. Thank you to my rocking PA, Alicia. She always has my back even when she's threatening to spank me for forgetting to tell her about my promos and releases (I plead artist brain!).

Again, thank you for reading! It's always a pleasure to hear from my readers so please check out my social media links and drop in for a chat.

Love,

Nikita

## SNEAK PEEK: EXCERPT FROM BORN A QUEEN: THE QUEENS SERIES

It was Raina's twenty-first birthday. She wanted to go out and party, dance all night, make friends, flirt, maybe take a guy home if she really felt like it. She'd never done that. Never taken a guy home before. In fact, she'd never even had sex. It wasn't that she didn't want to. She really, really did. But life had thrown a major curveball at her two years ago and she'd been running ever since. This time, it appeared she was running into a dead end.

Raina didn't think she was going to get to party for her birthday. No, she was pretty sure she was going to die. She peered out into the dark night from the window of her rented room. She was on the fourth floor of a very old building. One that was sinking. But then, all the buildings were sinking in Venice.

Italy was her ninth country in two years. When she left Venezuela, leaving the mother she just met behind, she went on the run. She had to assume there were people after her, or watching. And she knew she was right. Sometimes she would come home from an evening out and she would have that eerie feeling that someone had been in her apartment. She suspected dear old stepdad, Sotza, the Venezuelan mafia boss, had people keeping an eye on her. He probably knew from the moment she left his estate where to find her.

But did his second-in-command? Her mind flashed back to her time in Venezuela. The brief month before her mother ushered her out of the country in a daring escape. Mateo Gutierrez. Cartel to the marrow of his bones. Sotza's right hand man. And her constant shadow while she was in Sotza's care. Mateo was everything she hated in a man, arrogant, dangerous, rude. But he was also indecently attractive. And for some reason he'd wanted her. She wondered if the two years since she last saw him had dimmed his regard. Somehow she doubted it. Even in her brief time observing the mafia, guys like them didn't just let things go. They held on to their grudges, their obsessions. Those qualities were what made the men of the mafia so hard, and so successful.

Raina flitted around her apartment, shoving her possessions into a small suitcase. She didn't have much. She travelled light because she never knew when she'd have to pick up and run. She had done it before, but never in this much of a hurry. That was because she'd done something stupid. She crossed the wrong people. And it was only a matter of time before they found out and came after her. She suspected sooner rather than later.

And she was right. Seconds after that thought entered her head, as she was reaching for her purse preparing to leave her tiny apartment for good, the door crashed open. The only thing that saved her from being shot in the heart as she stood gaping at the man that kicked the door in, was the fact that he kicked the door so hard it rebounded off the wall and slammed shut again. The bullet meant for her thudded into the heavy wooden door.

Raina dropped her purse and ran for the only place in her apartment with a door that would close and lock. Her bathroom. As she ran, reaching for the frame, her front door was flung open again and the room sprayed in bullets. She felt a tearing, hot pain hit her in the back. The force of the bullet flung her into the bathroom. She landed hard on her knees. She didn't have time to assess herself. She rolled onto her back and kicked the door shut, reaching up to lock it. Thank god these old Italian buildings had thick doors. Bullets thunked into the wood as she crawled toward the bathtub and dragged herself inside.

"Fuck!" she snarled, reaching behind her to touch the spot on her back. Her hand came away covered in blood. She really hoped they hadn't taken out her only good kidney. Even if they hadn't, the blood loss for someone like her could be catastrophic.

She had to get out before they got in. She'd picked this place because it had a window in the washroom with a fire escape. She was going to have to get out of the bathtub though, since the window was over the toilet. She took a deep breath, eyed the bathroom door, which was still in one piece and flung herself out of the tub. As she was kneeling on the toilet reaching for the latch she realized there was no more sounds hitting the door. Had they given up on coming after her?

That didn't make sense. The front door was thicker than the bathroom door and they'd had no problem breaking through that one. She stopped, her hands hovering against the window, and listened. At first there was nothing, and then she heard muffled thumping sounds. A man shouted, but it was cut off. What were they doing out there, killing each other?

Raina wasn't going to wait around to find out. Whatever was happening it couldn't be good. And she needed medical attention right away.

She turned back to the window. A scream leapt from her

throat and she fell off the toilet as bullets crashed through the window. A man had come up the fire escape to cover the window and she'd come face to face with him. She huddled on the floor as small as she could get and covered her arms with her head.

She knew she was dead when she finally heard the sound she'd been expecting. The bathroom door crashed open, smashing against the bath tub. She tensed, waiting for that awful hot tearing sensation to rip through her again as she was shot full of holes. Instead, she heard two muffled shots and a shout from the balcony.

When three seconds passed and she was still alive she chanced a peek through her arms. Mateo Guiterrez was standing over top of her, tall, scowling, eyes and gun trained on the window.

"Mateo!" she gasped.

"Raina," he acknowledged grimly and looked down at her, satisfied that he'd gotten the guy on the fire escape. He reached for her, dragging her off the floor.

She groaned in pain but was forced to follow as he pulled her out of the bathroom and into the main room. She gaped at the two dead men decorating her place. They probably hadn't stood a chance. Probably thought they were going to kill a helpless woman. They would have no idea that she had an entire cartel at her back and, apparently, at her disposal.

"Jacket, shoes, purse. Hurry up," he barked at her.

Raina didn't pause. Her only chance of survival was with this man. She dragged a leather coat on, flinching in pain as it stuck to her back. She bent over to tie up her running shoes, but as she straightened, dizziness engulfed her. Mateo caught her before she hit the floor, grabbing the part of her back that had been shot. She cried out, clutching his arm to shove him away.

"What's wrong?" he demanded.

"Shot," she muttered.

He turned her around and lifted her jacket and shirt. He muttered something she suspected was a nasty swear word in Spanish.

"Is it bad?" she asked, peeking at him over her shoulder.

"No," he growled, and then picked her up in his arms.

This was the second time he'd done this. The first time he'd been kidnapping her from her University campus. This time? She didn't know. He was definitely saving her life, but she suspected there was more to him being here. The timing was too convenient.

"Mateo?" she whispered as he glanced into the hallway before striding out her door.

"Si, Raina?" He took the stairs down two at a time, careful to hold her tight against his chest so he wouldn't jar her wound.

"Thanks for coming for me." She had to say the words just in case she didn't get another chance.

He paused for a moment on the second-floor landing and looked down at her, his dark eyes hot with anger, possession and longing. "I will follow you into hell, chica."

"Let's hope not," she sighed right before passing out.

---

*Release date for Born a Queen TBA*

BONUS: EXCERPT FROM SCARRED QUEEN: THE QUEENS SERIES

Ignacio Hernandez had never before brought a woman to a meet. Then, they'd never met at a club before. The entire scene was unprecedented. Reyes didn't do unprecedented, but he was willing to make an exception because he was curious. He could sever the Miami connection if he had to. It would cause some shockwaves, but it wasn't out of the question. Ignacio was beginning to annoy him anyway. His poor decisions were beginning to affect the Bolivian. Such as bringing a woman like *her* to a meet with a man like *him*. Something that was meant to show off Ignacio's power and wealth would become a big mistake.

His gaze flickered over the woman, calmly drinking her champagne and orange juice as though she weren't sitting at a table with four of the most dangerous men on the continental East coast. Two kingpins and their right hands. Only Reyes didn't think she was as calm as she appeared. Her wrist trembled slightly, giving her away. She had enough presence to make sure that tiny shake ceased by the time it got to her slim fingers where they clenched the crystal of her glass. It wasn't the fingers or her ability to remain coolly poised while the men around her talked business that captured his curiosity. It was the mark on the back of her delicate hand, permanent slash lines, viciously marring her porcelain skin.

Anger burned deep in his gut, surprising him. Reyes rarely felt anything. Ever. Certainly not for a woman. This was how he made effective decisions. How he moved trade across borders with ease and cool logic. Emotion had been removed from him. First by a ruthless father, then by a vicious military stint in his home country and finally by an unrelenting, merciless prison sentence that had systematically broken him before he had, in turn, broken down the prison itself and owned it from the inside out. By the time he was released it was into a world of his own making; a world shaped by him on the inside and ruled by him on the outside.

Yet the sight of this cool, blond beauty, so broken yet utterly resilient was doing something to him, forcing him to *feel*. He shifted in his seat, sliding his arm across the back of the leather, his eyes never leaving her while he listened to the other men speak. Negotiate terms. He didn't need to add his voice. Alejandro, his right hand, knew the terms. Knew not to fuck up while in pursuit of new deals for the boss.

Reyes wanted her. The electrifying anger he felt when his eyes caressed that mark assured him he would take the woman and make her his. Not because it infuriated him that she had been abused. No, he was not a good enough man to care about that. He was under no illusions he would treat her any better than Ignacio. Hell, he'd probably treat her much worse. Because Ignacio undoubtedly set her up like a trophy in his great mausoleum of a house and then ignored the unapproachable beauty.

Reyes had no intention of ignoring her. He was going to take her and fuck every inch of her, just the way he wanted. Hard, brutal, mean. Exactly how he was. Exactly how this world had shaped him. Because he could. She was about to become spoils of war.

No, he wasn't angry about the mark on her hand at all. He was pissed that the mark was twisted into the shape of an "H" and not an "R." He wanted her to belong to him, to the King. When he got his hands on the woman, that would be the first thing he changed.

Finally, after nearly an hour of sitting in the booth together, his eyes rarely leaving her face, she lifted hers to meet his uncompromising gaze. And for the first time in his life, he felt his heart stop in his chest. He was unprepared for the impact. Her eyes – one startling green and the other amber brown – were vivid, stunning and unrelenting. Though her expression didn't flicker once from the blank mask of icy beauty, he saw the burning disdain, the heated fury buried deep within those fiery orbs for the men that surrounded her. She despised all of them.

His lip lifted in an answering sneer. She refused to drop her eyes from his challenge, despite her husband sitting at the same table. He wanted nothing more, in that moment, than to take this scarred Queen from her throne and tame her. He vowed, then and there, that he would eventually have her.

---

*Keep reading today on Amazon.com*

"I had so much fun!" Gina exclaimed, pulling her headset off and grinning at Miguel who was doing the same on the other side of her. "It was so refreshing getting out of the valley for a few hours."

He nodded and smiled back, his eyes warm and his expression kind. "I agree. I had a wonderful time, Gina. Hopefully we can do it again soon."

She averted her face feeling slightly guilty, knowing he felt more for her than she did for him. In a way, she'd used him and his feelings for her to get out of the damn mountains for the day. But she'd needed to get out from under a certain dictator's thumb. And she wasn't talking about the boss, Reyes. She meant his oppressive second-in-command. The man that stalked her every step, watching and waiting as though readying himself to pounce... but then nothing. The tension was driving her crazy.

And his insane rules! What was wrong with the man?

Alejandro made it his business to get in *her* business everywhere she went, tossing out arbitrary rules that made no sense to her. She couldn't eat or spend time alone with anyone except the immediate family unless he was present. If one of his men so much as spoke to her, even to ask about her day, he'd be lucky if scrubbing toilets for a month was his only punishment. She wasn't allowed to communicate with the outside world unless Alejandro approved her phone calls and emails. He even opened and read her incoming and outgoing mail, and not discreetly!

When she balked at his many edicts he simply added more rules and enforced them either physically, by locking her in her bedroom or by cutting off her communication to the outside world altogether. And though she'd wanted to throw a temper tantrum worthy of her dear cousin, Casey, she was terrified of the big man and his psychotic boss. So she'd quietly acquiesced, occasionally finding ways to break the rules with Casey's help. Thankfully Alejandro never seemed to find out about her small rebellions.

"Me too," she said enthusiastically. "But I don't know when we'll get the helicopter again. I think Casey had to pull some strings with Reyes to get us this trip. I'm surprised he even said yes."

Miguel got out of the helicopter first and reached a hand in to help her out. She never got a chance to take it. He was wrenched away from the opening with such force that she was left stunned. She rushed to the door when she heard flesh hitting flesh and saw Miguel on the ground with a bloody face, Alejandro standing over top of him. Gina shrieked and scrambled from the helicopter.

Alejandro turned dark, coldly furious eyes on her, stopping her in her tracks. She glanced helplessly toward Miguel. She wanted to rush to his aid, but she didn't want to get anywhere near the terrifying mob enforcer.

"What did I tell you about being alone with anyone

except family, Gina," Alejandro snapped at her as though she were one of his soldiers.

She swallowed and dropped her eyes to the ground. "Y-you told me not to," she said, barely above a whisper. "Except he's practically family!"

"This scum is not family," Alejandro snarled and kicked Miguel in the side.

Setting her terror of the big man's fury aside, Gina hurled herself toward the men, intent on putting herself between them. She was hoping Alejandro wouldn't actually harm her since he hadn't physically done so yet. He grabbed her arm in an iron grip before she could fling herself on top of the doctor. She cried out as he brought her around to face him.

Alejandro stood much taller than her, around 6'4", which would have made her almost a foot shorter if she hadn't been wearing three-inch heels. He was nearly twice as wide as her with broad, muscular shoulders and huge biceps. She knew exactly how conditioned and honed to perfection his body was, having seen him work out many times with his men. She shivered at the look in his eyes. Cold, terrifying and utterly without mercy. Had she really just courted the attention of such a man by going out with another? Was she insane?

"Get back on the helicopter, Gina," he said in a chillingly quiet voice as though giving an everyday command instead of telling her to do something she knew she shouldn't.

The breath caught in her throat and she watched him through wary grey eyes. She understood that if she got on the helicopter he would get on with her and then he would take her somewhere where they would be alone. *Finally, alone.* The invisible sand had run out. Whatever timeline he'd given her when she'd first moved to the valley was over; he was done waiting.

But was she done running from him? When she'd set this day up she'd done it with the full comprehension that she would be provoking a reaction from a very dangerous man. Unfortunately, she thought she would be back in the safety of her home, under her cousin's wing when Alejandro's wrath fell. Holding his terrifying gaze, she slowly shook her head and held her ground. She would rather deal with his temper within the safety of the compound.

"Are you refusing to go away with me?" he asked, almost pleasantly.

"Y-yes," she whispered. The wind caught her honey-blond, layered locks and flung them across her face. He reached to move them away for her, tucking them behind her ear, his touch gentle. Still, she flinched.

He moved her to his side, retaining his hold on her arm. He pulled his sidearm and pointed it at Miguel, aiming for the doctor's head. Miguel groaned and covered his head with his arms, as though his flesh could stop a bullet.

"You still refuse to get on the helicopter?" Alejandro asked, eyebrow raised.

She stared back at him and then said as defiantly as she could, "You're a bastard, Alejandro, but I'll go with you. Just please leave him alone."

He released her arm and gave her a shove toward the helicopter. When she turned and walked slowly back the way she'd come Alejandro made eye contact with the pilot and gave him a twirling motion with his finger. The pilot nodded back and started the helicopter up again, setting the blades in motion. Gina looked back over her shoulder as she climbed on board. Trepidation clutched at her heart. Alejandro was crouched over Miguel, the gun pressed against the other man's skull. He was speaking to him with a look of feral rage plastered across his face, a look she'd never seen before. She'd known him to be angry, but his anger was always coldly efficient, never this heated fury.

Alejandro stood and turned to where Gina was crouched

in the doorway of the helicopter. His eyes devoured her for a second, taking in the way her skirt and hair lifted slightly from the breeze created by the blades as they picked up speed. Then he was striding toward her, intent glittering through his narrowed gaze. Gina quickly backed away from the door and took the seat she'd been in only minutes before. Alejandro swung through the door, closed and locked it as he settled in beside her.

When he reached for her seatbelt she tried to slap his hand away, mumbling that she could do it herself. He took her hands firmly in his. "You do not want to test my patience right now, Gina. It's thin at best. Now be a good girl and shut up."

Her mouth fell open and she sat in helpless silence as he latched her seatbelt, tugged on it to make sure it was snug against her body and then pulled her headset back on. Satisfied, he did the same for himself. Moments later they were airborne. Gina watched him through black-tinted lashes, cataloguing every move he made. Alejandro was beautiful, like a large, lethal cat when he moved. Maybe a panther. One moment lazy, the next he would strike with such quick efficiency, his victim was on the ground before he knew what was happening. For the moment though, he appeared relaxed in the seat next to hers, his elbows resting on the arms of the chair, his hands loose against his long legs.

It occurred to Gina that this was almost the first time she was left alone with Alejandro with a handful of exceptions. Absently she lifted her fingers against the pulse beat in her throat as it accelerated. After they had been flying for about fifteen minutes in complete silence she finally turned to him and asked, attempting to keep her voice steady, "Where are we going?"

He flashed her a grin. "Ah, so the little mouse finally gets brave enough to speak."

"Alejandro," she pleaded with him. "Please just tell me. Where are we going?"

The playful grin slid from his face, but the predatory look remained firmly in place as his eyes slid over her possessively. "We have a date with a priest, *mi amor*."

---

*Keep reading today on Amazon.com*

# ALSO BY NIKITA SLATER

If you enjoyed this book, check out some other works by bestselling author, Nikita Slater. More titles are always in progress, so check back often to see what's new!

## ANGELS & ASSASSINS SERIES

Book One – The Assassin's Wife

## THE QUEENS SERIES

Book One – Scarred Queen

Book Two - Queen's Move

Alejandro's Prey (a novella)

## FIRE & VICE SERIES

Book One – Prisoner of Fortune

Book Two – Fight or Flight

Book Three – King's Command

Book Four – Savage Vendetta

Book Five – Fear in Her Eyes

Book Six – Bound by Blood

Book Seven – In His Sights

Book Eight - Burning Beauty (Coming 2019)

## THE DRIVEN HEARTS SERIES

Book One - Driven by Desire

Book Two - Thieving Hearts

Book Three - Capturing Victory

## OTHER BOOKS

Because You're Mine

Mine to Keep (a novella)

Stalked

Visit *nikitaslater.com* for more information

and the latest updates!

# NIKITA'S UNDERWORLD!

Join the conversation in Nikita's Underworld, a private Facebook group, for access to exclusive giveaways, WIP, games, book talks and more!

- **Become part of Nikita's Underworld today!**

www.ingramcontent.com/pod-product-compliance
Lightning Source LLC
Chambersburg PA
CBHW071208210726
48293CB00002B/331

9 781990 355165